ONE SAD DAY

By
Brendan Maguire

©2025 Kintyre Publishing
ISBN No: 978-1-0369-1507-0

- Cover design by Gillian Baines

Also by Brendan Maguire

Whatever it Takes

'A person often meets his destiny
on the road he took to avoid it'
Jean de La Fontaine

ACKNOWLEDGEMENTS

This is my opportunity to express my personal thanks to a few important people who have provided invaluable assistance during the course of my writing journey.

Firstly to my wife, Gill for her forbearance, patience and unstinting support during the last few months, during which time my mind has been submerged in Glasgow's criminal underworld.

A debt of gratitude is also owed to long-term friend and Principal Procurator Fiscal Depute, Liz Ross, for kindly updating me in relation to current practices within Scotland's prosecution services.

I am, of course, extremely grateful to my posse of indispensable beta readers. This includes my daughter, Laura McArthur, and my sister, Joan Calvert. Also, my good friends, Carol Evans, Julia Weedon, Sue Gartrell and Fiona Henderson. I am also indebted to our very valued friends and neighbours, Line and John Uppard, for their general encouragement and practical support in relation to my book launch event in Spain.

Perhaps it would be remiss of me not to mention our two giant pooches, Hank and Skyler, who have been deprived of the enjoyment of some walks, while I have been striving to meet my publishing deadline.

And finally, a grateful nod to Nespresso for helping to keep me awake during all those bleary-eyed, early morning hours.

PROLOGUE

Cleo Jackson has subconsciously abandoned herself to the sublime state of "hypnopompia". This is the transitional stage of consciousness between sleep and wakefulness. That dreamy, sometimes euphoric state we often experience when we are prone to hallucinations, but when we can also enjoy extremely imaginative ideas. The mirror of this state is referred to as 'hypnagogia'. It is the transitional state from wakefulness to sleep. Many an inspirational, creative and even life-changing idea has been borne out of one of these two transient stages in our consciousness.

While entering the wakefulness stage, Cleo feels empowered, inspired, even visionary. She wearily glances at her bedside clock to check the time. It has just gone 7.00am. In times gone by, she would have had her mobile phone on her bedside table. However, having recently immersed herself in a Panorama TV programme around the dangers, both physical and mental, of over-reliance on mobile phones, Cleo has very significantly restricted her usage. She has also made the conscious decision to ban it from ever again sharing her bedroom, like a discarded lover.

The very morning after the programme aired, she had promptly popped down to the little charity shop at the end of her road. There, she purchased for a mere twelve pounds a small, vintage travel alarm clock, one which fits very conveniently inside its glossy red ceramic casing while not in use. Cleo felt quite pleased about her new acquisition.

Also on her bedside table is a flip-over calendar. This was gifted to her by one of her girlfriends several months earlier.

It was by way of a less-than-subtle hint after she had completely overlooked a social get-together they had planned. The calendar has proved to be particularly useful, given that she no longer has her mobile as a bedside companion.

She regards these two acquisitions, her calendar and alarm clock, as her own little personal weapons in the war against the ever-advancing onslaught of technology. A war that she knows she can never win, but then again, she is keen to not go down without a fight. She also very much cherishes the touchy-feely, old-fashioned charm of these outdated items, soon-to-be fossils.

In any event, this is not just any old calendar - not at all. No, this one is quite unique in that below each day of the month it highlights the significance of that particular day. This "alternative calendar" does not include the usual noteworthy dates such as Mayday, Easter Sunday, Thanksgiving and Boxing Day. Rather, and much more significantly from Cleo's perspective, are the listings of much lesser-known awareness days, events, celebrations and cultural milestones, each one with its own individual acronym.

In her state of hypnopompia, she dreamily imagines the total embracement of these "awareness days". Little does she know that this passing embryonic thought is going to become something of an obsession for her, one which is to preoccupy her mind. Like so many obsessions, it starts in a very modest way, before eventually taking up permanent residency in the brain.

Since first receiving the calendar, Cleo has tried, wherever practical, to wholeheartedly immerse herself in the sentiment of each particular day. The list is pretty exhaustive, but by way of example, includes:

a. On World Blood Donor Day (WBDD), she donated blood.

b. On National Doughnut Day (NDD), she purchased and ate copious amounts of doughnuts.

c. On Polar Bear Plunge Day (PBPD), which perhaps not surprisingly fell on 01 January, she took a dip in the freezing waters of a nearby lake with a few friends.

d. On National Puzzle Day (NPD), she tackled, unsuccessfully, a Rubik's Cube.

e. On Festival of Sleep Day (FOSD), she did not get out of bed for twenty-four hours. (Fortunately for her employers, the date conveniently fell on a weekend.)

f. On Take a Dog to Work Day (TADTWD), Cleo felt obliged to borrow a friend's pooch to accompany her to work.

g. On National Penguin Day (NPD), she visited and fed the penguins in her local zoo.

h. On National Redhead Day (NRD), she dyed her hair red. Later, she considered that she was perhaps being a little disingenuous on the basis that true redheads should be entitled to their own special day, devoid of any interlopers.

Significantly, Cleo also actively encouraged her friends to follow in her footsteps. The "movement" then grew exponentially, and with the ever-increasing power of social media, created a community which bordered on being cult-like. From a simple, hypnopompia-induced germ of an idea, Cleo now enjoyed quite a following. Locally, 'The Calendar Girls' were becoming quite a sensation on Facebook, which was very much on the rise in 2008.

ONE SAD DAY

Cleo, her friends and newly acquired "disciples" would regularly meet up for a couple of drinks to plan for future calendar events. There was no official membership as such, but her followers, for the most part, were required to be multi-talented if they were truly going to embrace the concept. These talents would include, for example:

...having a charitable disposition

...having a sense of humour

...having the ability to laugh at oneself

...and sometimes simply having sheer effrontery.

Yes, paying due homage to "awareness days" is not for the shy, the retiring or the introverted.

It is now some several months later. This particular morning, Cleo gradually emerges from a deep sleep. As she slowly comes to her senses, she rejoices in the sure knowledge that it is a Friday, the start of her weekend, with no work on Saturday - happy days! She instinctively glances towards her trusty calendar and flips it over to reveal today's page. It reads as follows:

Friday 15 February 2008
Single Awareness Day
(SAD)

She is instantly reminded of the significance of the day. Single Awareness Day is celebrated on February 15 each year, an unofficial holiday celebrated by single people. It serves as a complement to Valentine's Day for those people who are not married or in a romantic relationship. Unsurprisingly, there are plans afoot to commemorate and celebrate the day.

Cleo had been in a relatively long-term relationship, but is now more than happy to rejoice in her single status. She is enjoying the independence and freedom that comes with being single. However, if truth be told, she would probably be just as happy to have the comfort, security and reassurance that a relationship tends to provide. Like most things in life, every situation has its advantages and disadvantages, its pros and cons.

To mark the occasion, Cleo, aided by some of her faithful followers, has arranged to hire a club known as The Serpent for a SAD party. Although the evening is entirely Cleo's initiative, the event is also available to members of the general public.

Cleo views it as an ideal opportunity to meet up with a number of her friends and work colleagues, at least those who are single and proud to be so. In her mind she fast-forwards to them all being in a bar later laughing, drinking and generally having a good time. She makes a mental note to herself to remember to raise a toast to SAD. Her mind then drifts as she ponders on how it is such a totally unfortunate, inappropriate and inaccurate acronym. There should be nothing sad about Singles Awareness Day, rather it is a cause for celebration. A celebration of the love of family, love between friends, and most importantly love of oneself.

Alas, sadly fate is to dictate otherwise. This will prove to be the very last awareness day celebrated by Cleo Jackson.

CHAPTER 1

Early February 2008

By any standard, Matt has enjoyed a privileged upbringing. Matthew Adam Goldstein is the product of a union between Adam Goldstein and Sarah Goldstein, their only child.

His parents had been trying for a family for some considerable time and were just about to throw in the parental towel when little Matt appeared on the scene, a cute little bundle of loveliness.

The Goldsteins have lived in Whitecraigs for many years, a very opulent and predominantly Jewish southern suburb of Glasgow. They own and run a substantial chain of retail clothing outlets throughout the West of Scotland and beyond. It is fair to say that the plucky, steadfast and resilient Glaswegians have long been known for their sardonic wit. In times gone by, before the advent of central heating they would have said of such privileged classes: 'so posh that they would carry their ashes out to the rubbish bin in a suitcase!'

Matt is eighteen and very recently left his local private school armed with a plethora of qualifications. While extremely bright, his outstanding academic achievements were further enhanced due to the appointment by his parents of personal tutors for a number of his subjects. It is fair to say that Matthew Adam Goldstein will prove to be a major achiever if Adam and Sarah are to have any say in the matter.

Matt has the twin assets of brain and brawn. A tad over six feet, his muscular frame belies his relatively tender age and in no small way contributes to his prowess and notoriety as a key member of his school rugby team.

Moreover, with his sharp facial features and sweeping jet-black hair, allied with a slightly coyish grin, he has plenty of admirers. This is a fact that has clearly not escaped him.

While Matt may appear to have the world at his feet, he is a young man not without his demons. As has become increasingly common within his generation, he suffers from periodic bouts of severe depression. These have occasionally been so intense that he would often not leave his house for a number of days on end. Of course, no amount of material possessions or family wealth offers a defence against this invisible illness. His condition is a transient one, as his GP continually experiments with anti-depressant drugs in an attempt to keep his depression at bay - with varying and sporadic degrees of success.

Matt has decided to pursue a career in the legal profession and has applied to Glasgow, Strathclyde, Edinburgh and Aberdeen Universities. It is no great surprise that, in the event of Matt not electing to study in Glasgow, Adam and Sarah have offered to buy him a flat in his preferred location. Once again, they are able to justify this extravagance, quoting the premise that property is always a sound investment, especially in a university town.

CHAPTER 2

January 2023

It is 7.30am on a cold, frosty morning in Glasgow, and a mist has descended, creating a somewhat eerie atmosphere. A small group have assembled, standing in a close circle, akin to a colony of penguins struggling to keep severe arctic conditions at bay. Their hands are as cold as a polar bear's nose as they rub them together furiously, seeking some warmth from the friction. Each of them walks on the spot in an attempt to aid their blood circulation.

There is an expectancy in the air as all eyes are on the large, imposing gates of HM Prison Barlinnie as they eagerly await the appearance of the patriarch of the renowned Watson family. Sidney Archibald Watson, known to most as "Sid", is a much revered and feared member of the Glasgow criminal fraternity. Aged in his mid-sixties, Sid is a mountain of a man with chiselled, battle-hardened features, a prominent scar running down his left cheek and a confident gait and presence that has made many a lesser man shake in his boots.

Most significantly, among the assembled group is his long-suffering wife, Nancy. She might well have been considered in the past to have been somewhat of a "trophy wife", but sadly, the stresses and strains of being married to a lifelong serial criminal are now cruelly etched in her tired, drained and lined face. Mother Nature is not always kind! Her rather long unkempt hair picture-frames her face which today, for one day only, is caked with make-up, to herald the long-awaited return of her spouse.

Also among the awaiting throng are their three sons, Archie, Billy and Jimmy, Archie being the oldest and Jimmy, the youngest. Each one has been adopted into the family's illegitimate business, which includes the selling of drugs, loan sharking, protection, prostitution and general racketeering.

Thankfully, they do not have to wait too long before Sid exits the gates of Barlinnie, having just served three years for the assault of a police officer. His smile is as wide as the River Clyde. Life has obviously not treated him too badly while inside, as he has certainly not lost any weight. Being high up the prison pecking order obviously comes with certain fringe benefits.

While it is perhaps too early, and cold, to open champagne and celebrate wildly, very warm and heartfelt embraces are exchanged as the Watson family reunite. Then, minutes later, Sid is whisked off in a black Range Rover Sport, seemingly the preferred go-to vehicle these days for those who benefit substantially from their ill-gotten gains. Also present are a handful of Sid's "lieutenants" who have made the effort to be there to show their allegiance. During his period "inside" the Watson criminal enterprise has been run relatively successfully by the heir apparent and eldest sibling, Archie. Sid's period of incarceration has served as a valuable probationary period for Archie for the day ahead when he will eventually take over the reins of their criminal enterprise.

The Watson family originally hail from the north side of the city, in Ruchill, a very working class, depressed area with high unemployment, few amenities and an endemic drug culture. While they still have business interests there and prominence in the streets, none of the immediate family reside there any longer. Sid and Nancy own a substantial detached home in a leafy suburb of Glasgow known as Lenzie. The house itself is immediately identifiable. At either side of the large, imposing, electric steel gates is a life-size stone sculpture of a growling lion, perhaps serving as some kind of warning to those outwith their criminal fraternity. Through the gates is a long sweeping drive, leading to their distinctive, leaded-windowed, period home.

By contrast, each of the three sons have bungalows in neighbouring Bishopbriggs, a relatively affluent commuter suburb on the northern fringe of Greater Glasgow. The two elder sons are both married with children. There is then quite an age gap between them and young Jimmy. In his early twenties, he is still enjoying the single life. To some extent, Jimmy revels in the notoriety of being an integral part of the feared Watson criminal clan, but his involvement is much less than that of his elder brothers. Nevertheless, he does enjoy the trappings that come his way.

CHAPTER 3

Early February 2008

Darren Alexander is pretty much a law unto himself - a twenty-four-year-old loose cannon who lives every day as if it is his last. From a relatively stable, lower middle-class background, he is the youngest of four children, all boys. In chronological order, there is Brian, Robert (known as Bobby), Paul, and, of course, Darren. All four share the same physical characteristics, but not necessarily similar temperaments. They are relatively tall and slim, giving them an almost willowy appearance. Equally, one could not dispute the fact that they are all also follicly challenged. Their facial characteristics are extremely similar all having a strong jawline, bordering on being prominent. Furthermore, they all possess the same trademark 'Alexander' glint in their eye.

For their mum and dad, Mia and Henry, bringing up their first two children had been relatively plain sailing - the next two, absolutely not so. By the time Paul and Darren came along, they thought they had nailed their parenting skills, but sadly not. This is when they were truly tested and struggled as a consequence.

Perhaps not surprisingly, given the age gap, Brian and Bobby were always quite close and had similar personalities. The same could also be said for the younger two, Paul and Darren.

Brian, perhaps by virtue of being the eldest, has always been very much of a 'steady-eddie', utterly dependable, never giving his parents a day's trouble throughout his life.

Above average at school, he went on to train as a surveyor, operating in the residential sector. He has been happily married to Jean since they both met at the tender age of eighteen.

Child number two, Bobby, was also a very biddable child but, upon growing up, was infinitely more flamboyant and artistic than his elder brother. After leaving school, he made good use of his creative flair by pursuing a career in graphic design. At the age of fourteen, his parents had an inkling that he was perhaps gay, and not so long afterwards, this was confirmed. He is now happily married to Simon, whom he had been with for quite a few years. They are currently looking to adopt a child and are fairly far down that laborious and painstaking process.

As mentioned, there was then quite a gap until out popped number three, a quite beautiful baby with dazzling blue eyes and a wide smile that would break any heart. At that point, his parents must have thought that they could do no wrong. Little did they know then the trouble and heartache Paul Alexander would cause them growing up. As a very young teenager, the early warning signs were there. Always the tearaway, it soon became blatantly obvious to his parents that further trouble would lie ahead.

Sadly, they are now at a stage in life where they are not capable of coping with him, either on a physical or mental level. He is continually up to no good and can run rings around them. They feel useless and defenceless.

By his late teens he had gone entirely off the rails with drink, drugs and gambling. He was an archetypal miscreant. Before long, he left the family home and shared a run-down flat with a couple of undesirables. By this point, his parents only ever heard from him whenever he was looking for money, which in turn usually indicated that he was in some kind of trouble. Sadly, Henry and Mia had always blamed themselves for his behaviour. Yet, in their hearts, they understood that it was simply in his genes and that they would always have been rendered impotent and helpless.

Darren was the fourth Alexander child to enter this world. While he could be described as a bit of a tearaway, or a proverbial 'jack-the-lad', he was not a waster like his elder brother Paul. In fact, he had never had a single brush with the law. Generally speaking, most folk who know him would tend to view him as a bit of a likeable rogue, perhaps even a man slightly more sinned against than sinning. Also, being relatively close in age to Paul, they had always enjoyed a very close bond, one that was to transcend time. To his credit, Darren often tried to persuade Paul to mend his ways, somewhat like trying to push water uphill.

Since leaving school, Darren has had a transient work history, never settling anywhere for any great length of time, always assuming that the grass on the other side was somewhat greener. Throughout his short working career, his position had always been sales-related - a job very well aligned with his talents. The expression "having the gift of the gab" was almost written for him and allied to the "Alexander" glint in his eye, had proved to be a powerfully persuasive cocktail.

He would very often secure employment with a salary package heavily weighted on the commission side. Indeed, so confident was he of his own sales ability that, on occasion, he had even taken up positions on a commission-only basis. Almost everywhere he has been employed he has proved to be one of their top sellers. A number of jobs have, in fact, been telesales positions, in which he has developed his own very successful and quite unique style. While always being allocated his own desk and chair, Darren invariably prefers to pace up and down, often wearing out the carpet in the process. The nearer he comes to closing a sale, the faster he walks and talks. He thrives on the adrenaline of the potential sale and becomes totally oblivious to the sights and sounds around him. Instead, he is intently focused on the call and upon hooking whichever fish happens to be on the other end of the line. Very rarely do any of them get off the hook. Over his few years of working, he has applied his talents to various industries, including mobile phones, travel and job recruitment, as well as double glazing.

Sadly, however, he never remains in any one job for any appreciable period of time. Sometimes, this is of his own volition, and occasionally the decision is taken out of his hands. In terms of the former, quite simply he has a very low boredom threshold, and itchy feet tend to get the better of him. As regards the latter, there could be a myriad of reasons as to why he might be relieved of his duties. Relatively high on the list would tend to be absenteeism and poor timekeeping. Having said that, having the attention span of a gnat does not do him any favours!

Despite his undoubted skills as a salesperson, Darren's personal make-up is such that he is never capable of accumulating funds or savings. Rather, Darren simply lives for today and "spend, spend, spend" tends to be his mantra. Tomorrow is simply left to take care of itself. His expenditure is primarily on clothes and socialising. His car of choice is a beaten-up Ford Escort of indeterminate age and, somewhat distinctively, a driver's door that is a contrasting colour from the other three. Inside, it is littered with empty juice cans, sweet wrappings and the like. In essence, it is a mobile dustbin that adequately serves its principal purpose, transporting him from A to B.

Darren lacks any genuine long-term goals in life. Of an evening, he is likely to be found, glass in hand, in a bar or nightclub, more often than not with female company. His history with girlfriends, as per his work history, tends to be very much on a stop/start basis.

Darren would never be considered classically good-looking. Moreover, he dresses in a style bordering on the bohemian rather than following any current trends. He is anything but a lemming. He is very much his own man in so many ways. However, he does exude a kind of rustic, slightly rough around the edges, almost old-fashioned innate charm that holds a certain appeal for many.

CHAPTER 4

January 2023

Glasgow has long suffered from a deep-rooted religious divide between Protestants and Catholics. It is a malaise that is a major blot on the city's landscape, and a source of acute embarrassment to all fair-minded citizens. To say it is a 'religious' divide is a bit of a misnomer, as religion plays very little part. In reality, it is highly unlikely that the protagonists on either side could be described as regular churchgoers, more likely they will never have seen the inside of one. Nor would I imagine would they have any appreciation of the nuances of the religious and historical background to this divide.

It is often argued that this religious bigotry is on the decline, and perhaps, just perhaps, this is so. However, in families on both sides of the divide the bigotry, often allied to vitriolic bile, is passed down from parent to child, generation to generation.

It is often suggested that there are two particular reasons for this prejudice continuing to flourish (if that is the right word) in the West of Scotland.

Firstly, there is secular education. There exists in Scotland both Catholic schools and non-Catholic schools. This unnecessary division at a very young age creates an 'us and them' attitude which can become intrinsic to one's very thinking.

Secondly, Rangers and Celtic football teams are sadly vehicles for the continuance of bigotry throughout Scotland.

Support for Rangers Football Club has traditionally been drawn from the Protestant population, whereas those of the Catholic persuasion generally follow Celtic Football Club.

While the Watsons play a significant role in the Glasgow criminal underground, they do not enjoy a monopoly. There are, of course, other gangs operating in the city, their nemesis is undoubtedly the Byrne family with roots in the east of the city. While the Watsons are of the Protestant persuasion, the Byrne family are from the other side of the divide. Speaking very euphemistically, there is absolutely no love lost between the two factions. Indeed, the hatred and ill-feeling between the rival families could only be described as being rancorous and caustic in the extreme.

The Byrne family, in many ways, mirror the Watsons in that there is a very powerful and dominant patriarch, in this case, John Byrne. He and his wife, Rosie, have just two sons, Kevin and Aidan, with their youngest offspring being a girl called Cara. Both the boys are as bitter, angry and battle-hardened as their counterparts in the north of the city. Think "Peaky Blinders" and you might not be too far off the mark! However, Cara has successfully managed to extract herself from the criminal side of the business and is consumed in carving out a career for herself as a local journalist.

In recent years, there have been a number of tit-for-tat assaults involving the two families, the most recent one culminating in Aidan Byrne being hospitalised following a knife attack. His chest was punctured, and had the knife entered a couple of centimetres to the left, it could well have proved to have been a fatal blow. This latest attack has merely ratcheted up the stakes by a couple more notches. Perhaps not surprisingly, the Byrne family are intent upon revenge, and so the vortex of violence is most likely to continue.

CHAPTER 5

15 February 2008

It is Friday night. Then again, almost every night is a Friday or Saturday night for Darren, the only real difference being that there are more people congregating in the bars, restaurants and surrounding streets. He lives just south of Glasgow city centre in an area popular among the younger generation, known as Shawlands. Those from north of the River Clyde would tend to look down their noses a little at this area and refer to it as a "poor man's West End." However, Shawlands proved to be a far more affordable option for Darren when purchasing his modestly sized studio flat.

Nevertheless, it constitutes a very reasonable price to pay for his independence. It will probably come as no surprise that his flat is kept as tidy as his car. However, it does serve as an ideal base and is a mere stroll away from a plethora of bars and restaurants, as well as a couple of late-night clubs. In essence, it is perfect for his purposes.

His bar of choice in Shawlands is called The Lair, which generally attracts a mixed crowd, both in terms of age and gender. During the week, it tends to attract the "tea-time drinkers" who like to call in for a drink or two and a chat on their way home from work. By contrast, on Friday and Saturday evenings, the background music constitutes more than just background, the clientele tends to be younger, and there is generally more of a buzz. Also, at the weekend there is far more chance of him meeting friends.

Darren has been in the bar for about an hour or so. In that time, he has eagerly consumed three long-awaited and gratefully received perfectly chilled pints of lager. Suddenly, his attention turns to the main door as a dozen or so girls of various ages enter the bar. Going by their excitable, loud voices, he deduces that this is not the first bar they have frequented this particular evening. Upon overhearing their chat, he is aware that they work in various capacities at the relatively nearby Victoria Hospital. They all appear in pretty good spirits. Their arrival coincides with the noise level in The Lair rising by a fair few decibels as they enthusiastically discuss their preferred choice of cocktail.

Fast forward a couple of hours, and Darren is firmly nestled in the corner of the bar, engrossed in conversation with two of these new arrivals. His eyes appear to be fixated on one of them. Cleo is tall and slender, and he subsequently learns that her parents are both African American. Darren imagines that she is in her early thirties, a little older than himself. It transpires that she has a senior administrative role within the hospital. She is wearing a very figure-hugging blue woollen dress, which highlights her shapely figure. Her smooth olive skin, jet black curly hair, deep penetrating hazel eyes, long eyelashes and slender cheekbones complement the ensemble and do not go unnoticed by Darren. Nor does the occasional, albeit very light, touching of his arm during conversation. Shortly after the group had entered the bar, Darren had noticed her enthusiastically raising a toast to all the girls in her company, which met with raucous applause. He was not quite able to make out the justification for the toast, but admired her apparent free spirit. He also found her to be instantly appealing.

The other girl in his company, Ava, is the exception in the group in that she does not actually work in the hospital, but has been invited along as an acquaintance of one of the other girls. By contrast, she owns and runs a modest but extremely select and upmarket estate agency and property rental business located close to the city centre. She is slightly smaller in height than Cleo, with an endearing smile, short blonde bobbed hair, large olive green eyes and is dressed in a very business-like black trouser suit over a crisp white shirt, which has the appearance of having just come out of the wrapper. All three appear to be totally engrossed in conversation, although it transpires that Cleo and Ava have never actually met before. Darren is secretly enjoying the attention in stereo.

'And what line of work are you in?' asks Cleo of Darren.

'Sales' responds Darren, being deliberately vague in the hope of adding just a dash of intrigue.

'Currently in the recruitment field,' adds Darren when further prompted. 'I specialise in recruitment at executive level.'

'I've always had an ambition to be head-hunted!' responds Cleo, laughing loudly and this time again allowing her hand to rest momentarily on Darren's arm, but just a fraction longer than before. There is now the slightest suggestion of sexual frisson between the pair. This "electricity" does not go unnoticed by Ava who again consciously participates more actively in the conversation, clearly not wishing to adopt the role of a gooseberry:

'And how long have you worked for this recruitment company?'

'Only six months,' responds Darren before charting his transitory employment history, since having left school. It then occurs to him that he is talking too much about himself, which he appreciates is not the most admirable of qualities.

He recalls one of the very few times his father had seen fit to give him some words of worldly advice:

'Son, people love talking about themselves. If you want to be popular in life, ask questions of others rather than talk about yourself.' He then adds: 'If the Lord had intended you to speak more than you listen, he would not have given you two ears and only one mouth!' Advice from Darren's Dad might well have been scarcer than hen's teeth, but when he did take the trouble, it was worth heeding.

As the evening wears on, the three of them become more and more engrossed in conversation and, as a consequence, also become more detached from the rest of the group. Each of them in turn have now bought a round of drinks, and Darren is conscious of the fact that he is beginning to feel a tad inebriated. Notwithstanding, he has enough of his wits about him to appreciate that he definitely feels a genuine attraction and fondness for Cleo. As the evening progresses, the volume of the music is turned up a few more notches, but it still struggles to compete with the cacophony of noise emanating from the ever-growing number of revellers. Darren simply does not want the evening to end and suspects, and certainly hopes, that Cleo is of a similar mind. There then follows "one drink for the road", then another and then one final one! Cleo once again proposes a toast. 'Cheers, here's to SAD day' and encourages the other two to knock them back. Darren does not have the slightest clue as to what she actually means but simply attributes this to his level of alcohol intake. Nevertheless, he heartily participates in the toast.

As always, time moves faster when one is enjoying oneself and closing time soon beckons. This is heralded by that extremely irritating, quintessentially British custom which has prevailed in drinking establishments up and down the country for decades. The management elects to suddenly open the main doors, allowing access to the Scottish elements. Allied to this is the switching on of the brightest lights available, thereby exposing every individual's personal and physical insecurities. In an instant, any prior feelings of self-confidence are eroded.

In her eagerness to prolong the evening with Darren, she invites him to accompany them to The Serpent, a popular local nightclub where the "Sad Party" is taking place. All three decide upon going, given that none of them have work the following day. All seems good with the world! In normal circumstances, it would take merely five or six minutes to walk to the club. However, the three, linking arms with Darren in the middle, unwittingly adopt a somewhat circuitous route, eventually arriving at The Serpent some twenty minutes later.

CHAPTER 6

January 2023

Cara Byrne is a youthful 22-year-old, extremely attractive in a very natural way with a warm, welcoming smile, wide captivating eyes and petite figure. Her most striking feature is her quite stunning, long, almost copper-coloured hair, complemented by some very cute freckles. When growing up, she resented their very existence, predominantly because they were the source of some ridicule by her school friends. However, nowadays, she has taken full ownership and is secretly rather proud of them. Add to this cocktail a magnetic personality, cheery disposition and her almost universal popularity is far from being a surprise. It is said that redheads are extremely emotional, passionate, intense and possess a fiery temperament. Cara fits this stereotype like a perfectly sized glove.

Yet Cara's love life of late has been anything but straightforward. Having had the occasional dalliance, some eighteen months ago she fell head-over-heels in love with Ronnie Carson, a fellow student at the college where she was studying journalism. It was almost a case of love at first sight and no real surprise to anyone when, three months later, they decided to get engaged. Cara's mind was in the clouds as she dreamt of the perfect wedding day, followed by a honeymoon on a sun-kissed beach. She even envisaged a couple of redheaded toddlers running around their exquisitely kept garden lawn. Perfect matrimonial bliss! However, some months later, her dream was well and truly shattered. It was one Saturday afternoon whilst shopping in

Glasgow city centre. She could hardly believe her eyes when walking towards her she noticed her smiling fiancé hand in hand with a young brunette. Not surprisingly, she felt completely devastated and betrayed, and since that day, her self-confidence has been at a low ebb. Also, perhaps understandably, she thereafter blocked all his calls and decided to move on.

Eventually, just a few months ago, following continual encouragement from her closest friends she, (albeit reluctantly), chose to dip her toe into the shark-infested waters of online dating.

Her first few experiences were relatively soul-destroying as she encountered all the flotsam and jetsam that the Glasgow online dating world had to throw at her. She had the worst of introductions in the shape of Thomas, a bald, overweight fifty-year-old who had understated his age just a tad - and had obviously used a fake photo.

This was followed by John, a relatively good-looking young man in his thirties with truly atrocious bad breath.

Next was "Hands Harry", whose hands wandered over her body with such alacrity that she could have sworn that she was dating an octopus.

Following Harry was Norman. Now Norman was a reasonably handsome twenty-six-year-old - so far so good. That is except for the fact that his conversation did not extend beyond discussing his apparently extensive collection of killer spiders and snakes. Suffice to say that none of these candidates made it beyond the first date.

Cara was beginning to lose the will to live, when along comes James Gibson:

Young - tick

Good looking - tick

Nice eyes - tick

Interesting - tick

Sense of humour - tick

Sporty - tick

Apparently normal - massive tick.

This could be the one she thinks to herself. He is almost too good to be true! As pumped up as a balloon, and without the slightest delay, she enthusiastically and purposefully swipes right. She then stares at her mobile with such intent as if she imagines that James is actually going to jump out of her screen. In fact, it takes a painstakingly long twenty-four hours before he actually responds - and positively. There then follows some online communication between them - the "getting to know one another" phase. It transpires that James Gibson works with his family business and without him saying anything specific, she forms the distinct impression that he is relatively monied - one extra tick! He is also apparently a keen and able footballer. Good looking, fit and wealthy! "What an intoxicating combination." thinks Cara to herself. "What's not to like?"

They arrange to meet up for a drink in the city centre just a few days later. For Cara, she just knows that these days will pass agonisingly slowly. In the meantime, with a noticeable spring in her step, she goes into the kitchen to pour herself a celebratory glass of white wine. Oozing with contentment, she then records her forthcoming rendezvous in her phone calendar - as if she is ever likely to forget it!

CHAPTER 7

15 February 2008

It is after 11.00pm, and the constant beat, beat, beat of the music within The Serpent can be heard a couple of streets away. Inside, Darren, Cleo and Ava are dancing feverishly in the crowd. Any inhibitions they may have had have long since vanished as the alcohol really starts to take its toll. It is Ava's turn to buy a round, and she ventures up to the bar. Very soon she is cursing the intense competition to get served, or even catch the eye of a bar person. Eventually, after what seems like an eternity, she reaches the bar counter, having managed to squeeze her slight frame in between two strapping young men. The next challenge is getting noticed by one of the overworked and probably underpaid bar staff. One of the guys standing next to her catches her eye and smiles warmly before pointing out that he had been queuing for some ten minutes and was next in line. He then offers to get her drinks as well, an offer she kindly accepts whilst looking out her purse to reimburse him. However, being a true gent, he refuses to accept payment, and, flashing a smile, he retorts:

'No such thing as a free drink! But all I ask in return is one dance.' Ava laughed and replied: 'I think we've got ourselves a deal! Let me just give my friends their drinks and I'll be right back.'

'Cleo, I've just been chatting to this lovely guy at the bar and he even paid for our drinks. He's just asked me to dance and he's pretty fit!'

Cleo felt really pleased for her. She had another reason to be pleased, as she will now have Darren all to herself!

Ava then enthusiastically introduces Matt to the other two, and they all start chatting as best they can given the intrusive background noise. A short time later, they funnel out of the club. Matt is aware that his parents are away, and he has an "empty", and invites Cleo, Ava and Darren to go to his place. The response is a resounding and unanimous "yes", everyone being in good spirits and happy to extend the party into the "wee small hours".

Although Matt had arrived in Shawlands in his shiny, light blue, metallic car, his intention had always been to leave it there overnight with a view to picking it up the following day. So, the two now entwined couples make their way to the local taxi rank only to discover a tortuously long queue snaking along the pavement and around the corner. They duly fall in line behind a number of equally drunken revellers, all secretly wishing they had left the Serpent a little earlier in order to avoid this bottleneck. Some half an hour later, they have only made minimal progress in the queue and the gloss of the evening is beginning to vanish. Eventually, Matt duly announces that he now feels relatively sober, having been out in the open air for a while and that he has decided to drive. The other three voice only token resistance but are all secretly pleased to be able to vacate the taxi queue. It is now late into the night. The streets in the suburbs are virtually deserted as their car, with its four incumbents, makes its way southwards, towards Whitecraigs. Matt has Ava for company in the front passenger seat while Darren and Cleo cuddle in the back seat, totally engrossed in one another, and by this point, quite oblivious to their surroundings.

CHAPTER 8

March 2023

Cara and James have now been going out together for a couple of months, usually about twice a week, sometimes to the cinema, occasionally for a meal or just meeting up in town for a couple of drinks. It is clear that they have a very genuine fondness for one another, and their relationship seems to be slowly intensifying. Most certainly, there is a very real mutual, physical attraction. Cara has not felt this way since her time with Ronnie Carson, a relationship which had caused her considerable mental scarring and from which she might never completely recover. With that unfortunate episode always lurking at the back of her mind, she is understandably somewhat cautious and a little afraid to commit to someone new. Yet, she is becoming increasingly keen on James.

Certainly, when they are out together, she feels a really deep bond between them. There are always laughs aplenty and never any shortage of good conversation. And yet, she still feels a sense of foreboding. She senses that there is something not quite right and she just cannot put her finger on it. This "something" has been niggling away at her for quite some time and is causing her to feel uneasy. While she talks freely to him regarding her own family background, he is a completely closed book when it comes to his own. Also, while she has on occasion asked him back to her house, he has always come up with an excuse of some kind or another, usually a pretty feeble one. In addition, he has never invited her to meet with his family. Whenever she does enquire about his family, he inevitably tries to change the subject. Apart from these concerns, albeit very genuine ones, he is otherwise extremely loving and considerate towards her and treats her like a princess.

One stunningly beautiful and untypically mild spring evening, Cara is struck by a bombshell. James and Cara have gone for a drive towards Loch Lomond and decide to stop for a drink in a very established and well-known hotel, the Duck Bay Marina. James returns to their table in the beer garden armed with an inviting-looking pint of lager shandy in a frosted, globe-shaped glass, together with a perfectly chilled glass of wine for Cara. The evening sun is shining brightly as they clink glasses and say "cheers" in unison. All seems well with the world, but little does Cara know that her bubble of happiness is just about to be well and truly burst.

CHAPTER 9

Early hours of 16 February 2008

Matt switches on the exquisite Bosch sound system in his Audi. The rhythmic beat of Duffy's "Mercy" fills the car, blending with the laughter and lively conversation of his passengers. The night is still, the roads eerily quiet, when suddenly—a dark shape appears in the headlights. A deafening thud shatters the atmosphere as the body strikes the hood, ricochets against the windscreen, and collapses limply onto the roadside.

"Fuck, fuck, fuck!" Matt yells, his fists pounding the steering wheel. His heart thumps against his ribs, his breath coming in rapid gasps. The car is now motionless, but inside, panic spreads like wildfire. Cleo sobs uncontrollably in the backseat, Ava stares blankly out of the window, and Darren sits frozen, a deer caught in the headlights.

Matt is the first to move. His steps are heavy, as if wading through thick mud. The figure on the ground is frail, dressed in ragged, unkempt clothes. In the pale glow of the streetlights, a glint of crimson catches his eye—blood, trickling from the man's mouth, pooling onto the pavement. "I think he's dead," Matt whispers, his voice hollow and unrecognizable.

"We have to call the police," Cleo insists, her voice trembling but resolute. Matt spins around, his eyes wild with fear. "No! No one saw us. No one knows we were here. If we leave now, it's like it never happened."

A tense silence hangs between them, thick with fear and indecision. Then, as if bound by an unspoken agreement, they climb back into the car. The engine roars to life, the wheels spin, and the darkness swallows them whole.

In deadly silence they set off for the haven of Matt's parents' house, each one harbouring their own deep, dark thoughts - and regrets. Before long, Matt slows down and stops outside a very impressive and substantial-looking white detached house, hesitating for a minute or two before the large, black and imposing electric gates usher them in. Although Darren, Ava and Cleo are almost paralysed with fear, the sheer ostentatiousness of the property does not go unnoticed. Matt then presses another electric gadget, and the car and its occupants are swallowed up into a large, triple, integral garage where it has a white convertible Bentley as company for the evening. Matt then ushers the three of them into one of the public rooms, where they all sit for a few minutes without saying a word - in a state of complete shock.

Eventually, Cleo breaks the silence. 'It's never too late to contact the police. We can just say that following the accident we panicked, were traumatised, and therefore did not act rationally. Surely, they would understand?'

'It's OK for you' responded Matt, 'you're not the one who could be facing a long prison sentence.'

For the first time, Ava, who was sitting on a couch next to Matt, then contributes to the discussion:

We should've contacted the police at the time of the accident - and I so wish we had. It will now look so much worse for us.'

'Look,' said Matt, we're all in this together, we all left the scene of the accident.' He was about to say, 'the scene of the crime' and managed to just stop himself. He continued: 'We need to stick together and not break ranks. There's nothing at all to link us with the accident, so let's keep it that way. I checked the car, and the damage is fairly minimal. Where it's parked in the garage, with the bonnet facing the back wall, even my parents won't notice anything.'

Again, there is a period of complete hush as the others consider what has been said and the severity of their own situation. At one point, Ava has to run to the bathroom to be physically sick. Upon returning Matt again takes the initiative, trying to do his best to influence the others. Ava then interjects by stating a very obvious point, the very one that Matt did not want to hear:

'Matt, you talk about us all being in this together, but we aren't really. Your situation is much more serious than ours because you were driving the car.'

'But we all left the dead man lying at the side of the road. If I go down, we all go down and we're all screwed.' A very random and somewhat frivolous thought enters her head, given the circumstances. She ponders that at least she is finding out at a very early stage in their potential relationship that Matt is a totally selfish, egotistical and uncaring type of person.

It is now approaching daylight. They are all feeling very distressed and weary as Matt once again takes control.

'What is done is done, we cannot undo it. It is in all our interests that we show a united front for the sake of our futures. I suggest we make a secret pact among the four of us. Basically, we all agree that, for the rest of our lives, we will never utter a single word to anyone about tonight's events. We take the memory of this terrible accident to our graves. All in favour?' With a degree of reluctance, Darren raises his hand in support of this proposal, shortly followed by Ava. On the basis of majority rule, Cleo then also raises her hand, albeit very hesitantly. Matt, trying to disguise his intense relief at having achieved some sort of consensus, then leans forward to put out his hand, inviting the others to place their hand on top. This gesture seems somewhat frivolous and perhaps more befitting of a Famous Five or Secret Seven novel. Nevertheless, they all comply, as if partaking in some kind of formal medieval ritual that will morally bind them together.

Having achieved his intended goal, Matt then volunteers to arrange a taxi for the three of them, and very soon they are making their way towards Glasgow. Not one word passes among them in the taxi. En route, their attention is drawn to a lengthy queue of traffic crawling very slowly in the opposite direction. They also notice the flashing lights of stationary police cars, together with an ambulance. A tent has been erected around the crime scene and errant strands of yellow crime scene tape dance merrily in the morning breeze, clearly oblivious to the serenity of the occasion. This vision is to haunt them for the rest of their lives. They are all secretly relieved that the taxi driver is not of a talkative disposition, and they are able to maintain their silence.

As long as they live, the three of them will never again set eyes on one another.

CHAPTER 10

March 2023

The Tavern is a typical Scottish 'drinking man's', spit and sawdust-type pub which has graced the same corner location in the Springburn area of Glasgow since the late nineteenth century. The gantry is still in its virgin state, built of sturdy mahogany and well worthy of preservation, almost qualifying as something of architectural interest. It also has the appearance of not having been dusted since the nineteenth century, perhaps for fear of it disintegrating. This particular watering hole has another relatively unique feature. As well as being able to sit or stand at the substantial, wooden, curved bar counter, customers can also avail themselves of one of eight small private booths, each one accommodating up to six. These booths are numbered one to eight, with number one being nearest the door and number eight being in the furthest away corner of the bar, adjacent to the toilets. These prove to be very popular with the locals for a myriad of reasons. Some simply enjoy the intimacy and cosiness of the booth. Some younger locals, and maybe even the not-so-young, like meeting there as they can then enjoy a furtive fondle or even a gratuitous grope. Others opt for the privacy of the booth as it serves as the perfect spot for indulging in gossip and frivolous tittle-tattle.

Such activities go on in booth numbers two to seven. However, it is an unwritten rule that booth number one is reserved for the dubious practice of resetting - the selling or passing on of illicit or stolen goods. This booth will have been selected for this nefarious activity as it provides the best opportunity of a quick getaway, in the event of a chance visit from the police (referred to as the 'polis' in this part of the world).

And what of booth number eight? Well, this is the domain of and reserved exclusively for use by Sid Watson and his criminal family. The location of booth number eight is pretty crucial. When the door to the booth is ajar the occupants are able to see the bar almost in its entirety and, more significantly, they have a view of anyone entering. In theory, this could either be the "polis", or indeed members of a rival gang. There is a parallel with the gunslinger from a Western scene, who always chooses to sit facing the swinging saloon doors, in order to give himself every possible advantage in the not unlikely event of a shoot-out.

Nobody else would dare attempt to occupy booth number eight for fear of repercussions or reprisals. Also, it is certainly not the type of "boozer" where a non-local or visitor would be inclined to casually pop in for a refreshment. No, in The Tavern everybody knows everybody else and their business. Equally, everybody knows to be respectful to, and fearful of, the criminal hierarchy in booth number eight.

It is also considered to be a "Rangers pub". On match days in particular, red, white and blue scarfs are in evidence and at all times a couple of Union Jack flags fly from the gantry. On 12 July, it also serves as a meeting point for those venturing on the Orange Walk, a parade by members of the Orange Order to commemorate King William III (King Billy) and the Battle of the Boyne, which took place in the year 1690.

On this particular evening, Sid Watson, becoming accustomed to his new-found freedom, has called a meeting of the family in their usual locale. In attendance, in addition to Sid himself, are Archie and Billy. Their youngest son,

Jimmy, has made his excuses, and not for the first time. His enthusiasm for working in the business on a day-to-day basis is questionable. He has a variety of other interests and, in this respect, is somewhat of a disappointment to his older brothers. Sid Watson, by any standards, is a very hard man, both stubborn and resolute. Yet, for whatever reason, he appears to have a soft spot for his youngest born, and sometimes, much to the chagrin of the rest of the family, often chooses to cut him some slack.

The remaining members of the Watson family are duly assembled. The barman brings a tray of pre-ordered drinks - not surprisingly, not a level of service made available to ordinary "punters". The door to booth number eight is duly closed and they get down to villainous business.

CHAPTER 11

17 February 2008

In the Glasgow Division Police Headquarters, an incident room has been set up to investigate the death by hit and run of a certain Samuel Geddes, of no fixed abode. The Major Investigation Team (MIT) has discovered that he was a vagrant, in fact a well-known face around the streets of Glasgow. Normally he would be spotted nursing a bottle of cheap wine or else sitting in his "home", which consists of a large, well-worn, three-sided cardboard box which has moulded over time to the shape of his body. He would inevitably have by his side his trusted little black, mongrel pooch, Scamp, his sympathy-invoking companion. Yes, Scamp and the tramp would be well-nigh inseparable and, by their side, would be a dirty old saucer containing, on a good day, a few coins.

While it transpires that he was known to a few of the local officers, he was initially identified by way of a blood donor card discovered on his person.

As a matter of routine, any suspicious, accidental or unexplained death has to be reported by Police Scotland to the Crown Office & Procurator Fiscal Service (COPFS) where investigations are carried out on behalf of the Lord Advocate. In this case, a post-mortem examination will also be carried out as part of the death investigation, as is the case with all suspicious deaths.

A member of MIT has been carrying out background checks to try to determine the whereabouts of any next-of-kin of the deceased - so far without any success. It seems that Samuel Geddes was very much a loner who had been living on the streets for quite a number of years, scraping to survive. Why he would have been wandering around that quiet, residential part of southern Glasgow on that fateful night is anybody's guess.

In charge of the investigation is Detective Inspector Hilary Simpson, who addresses her team:

'At the moment, the investigation is going absolutely nowhere. We have invited information from the general public regarding the incident, but so far, we are facing a brick wall. It would appear that nobody saw the accident, or indeed, any vehicle departing the scene of the crime. In hit-and-run cases, there is often vehicle debris recovered, from which it is possible to identify the make or model of the offending vehicle - but there is very little on this occasion. There were, however, very tiny fragments of blue, metallic paint located at the location, and these are being examined for identification purposes. That aside, the forensic team working at the scene has not managed to come up with anything which would assist in tracing the offender. To add to our woes, there are no CCTV cameras on that particular stretch of road. Nor does it appear there are any houses in the vicinity that have personal security cameras, which would be likely to be of any assistance.'

In the meantime, an appeal has gone out on the local TV channel calling for potential witnesses, or indeed for any information that might lead to the ultimate apprehension of the driver.'

One wonders if perhaps Matt, Eva, Darren and Cleo are all sitting in their respective sitting rooms glued to their television sets, listening intently to this police release, feeling sick to their stomachs.

Whatever way you look at it, it would appear that the MIT have a herculean task ahead of them.

CHAPTER 12

March 2023

The Byrne family is undoubtedly the nemesis of the Watsons. They have been arch-enemies for a number of years with no suggestion of any truce on the near horizon. In fact, the recent attack on Aidan Byrne made the prospect of any kind of armistice as likely as the Pope leading the Orange Walk.

This attack was a sequel to, and a direct result of, a prior assault by the Byrne family on Billy Watson. By complete chance, they had encountered him exiting a city centre bar late one evening. They then followed him for a short while, and when the opportunity arose, dragged him into a dark lane, knocked him to the ground and gave him a sound beating. Fortunately for him, he exercised damage limitation by putting himself in the foetal position while punches and kicks rained upon him from all sides. He had no broken bones but was badly bruised and required a few butterfly stitches. One revenge attack follows another as sure as night follows day, and so the cycle of violence continues, with each faction as guilty as the other.

The Byrne family emanates from the east side of Glasgow in a district known as Bridgeton. It is, in fact, a mere stone's throw from Parkhead, the home of Celtic Football Club, the stadium affectionally known by its supporters as "Paradise". Bridgeton is typically Glaswegian and is made up for the most part of traditional tenemental properties, with several families living up the same communal "close" (passageway, stairs and landings). This housing phenomenon tended to result in the formation of very close bonds with neighbours who would ultimately become like family. Not so long ago, the residents of these tenements would not even have had their own private toilet facilities and would have been required to share a toilet in the common close with their neighbours. This district has always proved quite popular with the Irish immigrant population as a place to put down their roots. Bridgeton would be regarded as very much a working-class area.

Similar to their adversaries, the Byrne family, while maintaining a "business" presence in Bridgeton, have all moved a short distance to the more desirable town of Stepps, which offers far more in terms of facilities and community activities. Also, like the Watsons, there is a bar, in this case an Irish one, which the Byrne family frequents in Bridgeton, paying homage to their own roots. John Byrne has called a meeting there with all members of his family.

The Byrne family do also have a registered office, a not very salubrious one, upstairs in a tenement building in Bridgeton. It is decidedly pokey in size and one enters by a glass door on which is engraved: "The Byrne Family Enterprise", almost suggesting an air of legitimacy.

Cheery, atmospheric, Irish fiddle music is playing through the sound system of the Molly Malone pub in Bridgeton. The music very conveniently trumping the conversation of John, Kevin and Aidan Byrne who are huddled around an old, round, wooden table in their customary dark corner of the bar. They have already been there for over an hour, and a few pints have come their way. Their beer of choice is Guinness. With its velvety finish and unmistakable creamy white head, each perfectly formed pint is poured with a tenderness and a craft unbefitting its surroundings. With the arrival of each tray they are becoming louder, more animated and more vociferous in their disdain for the Watsons. Each member of the family seems intent upon articulating their own particular idea of the best way of exacting revenge. The most vocal of them is Aidan, perhaps not surprisingly, given that he is still enduring residual pain from the recent assault on his person.

After a few hours, and before the informal meeting descends into a drunken rabble, John draws business to a close. A decision of some sort has been arrived at. The general consensus is that they will avenge the attack on Aidan by targeting Jimmy Watson, the youngest of the brothers. It is felt that he may well be the weakest link in their family. They consider him to be not as streetwise as his elder brothers and, therefore, will be easier to catch off guard. A plan is hatched.

CHAPTER 13

Early March 2008

It is now some three weeks since the hit and run. It appears that DI Hilary Simpson and her team are no nearer to tracing the killer of Samuel Geddes. All enquiries thus far have proved to be fruitless, and she is pretty much struggling to know where to turn to next.

A member of her team has been tasked with making enquiries regarding the one and only strand of evidence, namely the fragments of blue metallic paint found at the scene. This officer checked with various garages, both mainstream and backstreet, to see if any had repaired a metallic blue car since the date of the accident, but thus far, without any success.

Adam and Sarah Goldstein are in a lengthy discussion regarding their son, Matt. They are really concerned about his behaviour of late, as it has been uncharacteristically strange. Normally very much a social animal and always out and about, he has become extremely introvert of late and has taken to staying at home. This is all the more surprising because hitherto, he would have used any excuse to take a ride in his beloved new car. In the past, this has even extended to going for the weekly shopping for his parents, just to get behind the wheel. However, the vehicle has recently been sitting stationary in the garage, simply gathering dust. More often than not, of an evening, he would be sitting in his room for hours on end. Indeed, on one such occasion, they actually thought they had overheard him crying. Naturally, as parents, it is very upsetting to experience such behaviour in one's offspring. Arguably, this situation could be deemed all the more tortuous for the Goldsteins by virtue of the fact that Matt is their one and only child. They are both in agreement that they will sit down and address the situation with him.

Matt is broken. He is experiencing very real difficulty in getting to sleep at night, and when he does, he has to endure truly hellish nightmares as he continually relives the accident. The cocktail of lack of sleep, deep-rooted guilt and intrinsic fear is proving to be a very potent and deadly one. In essence, Matt is a shadow of his former self, a walking corpse sensing that he has nothing worth living for. He is living in total dread - dread of a knock on the door by a man in a uniform or the sound of a siren.

'What if... somebody did actually witness the accident?'

'What if... the accident was caught on CCTV?'

'What if... he were to end up in prison for years?'

'What if... he were too weak to survive prison?'

'What if...? What if...? What if...?'

Matt's mind is working on overtime, always returning to that fateful evening, reliving it in graphic detail and dissecting it under the most powerful of microscopes. Over and over in his head, the evening's events are revisited in very strict chronological order. At various stages, he questions his actions:

'If only... I could turn the clock back.'

'If only... I'd chosen not to go out that night.'

'If only... I'd not taken the car.'

'If only... I'd not had any alcohol.'

'If only... I'd just waited in the taxi queue.'

'If only... if only... if only.'

These thoughts and regrets continue to race through his mind like a runaway train, which he is quite incapable of stopping. He feels totally desolate, and there seems no end to his self-flagellation.

But his concerns do not end there. He also stresses endlessly about the possibility of Darren, Cleo or Ava going to the police. Will they adhere to the pact they all agreed to, albeit with varying degrees of commitment? After all, they have so much less to lose than him. Perhaps they would simply be found guilty of leaving the scene of the crime? Also, maybe he has watched too many crime dramas on television in the past, but if one of his three co-conspirators were to "come clean" to the police, would the prosecution not be very prepared to do a deal? Would they be offered immunity from prosecution on the basis that they had offered him up on a plate?

Should he perhaps try to get in touch with them to ensure that they are adhering to their agreed code of silence? It then occurs to him that he has not actually taken Ava's number, given the unexpected premature end to the evening. However, he recalls the name of her real estate business and would probably be able to make contact. Also, he is aware that Cleo works at the Victoria Hospital. His mind then drifts to Darren, but try as he does, he is unable to remember his surname or indeed any information that would facilitate contacting him.

He further considers his situation. Would contacting them in the hope of ensuring their continued silence, be a wise move or not? His mind keeps oscillating back and forward. Perhaps they have put the sad events of that evening behind them, and by making contact, he is bringing it back into their consciousness, like opening up an old sore. On the other hand, perhaps he could use the opportunity to encourage them to have some sympathy for his plight? This indecision in itself is having an adverse effect on his already fragile disposition. On balance, he decides to simply let sleeping dogs lie, at least in the meantime.

CHAPTER 14

March 2023

Cara takes a couple of sips of her glass of chilled white wine in the evening sun. James has already made meaningful headway with his pint of shandy. Suddenly, a young man in his early twenties approaches them. He has a broad smile on his face and his eyes are fixed upon James.

'Well, Jimmy Watson, how the bloody hell are you? I've not seen you for ages!'

Cara's facial expression tells all. And if she needed any confirmation, it was there for all to see in James's demeanour.

One could almost see each of her thought processes filter through her brain, one after the other, dropping into her consciousness like watching a pinball machine, each one with quite devastating effect:

..... he's not the James Gibson she thought she knew

..... he'd lied when on the dating website

..... his real name is Jimmy Watson

..... he's probably of the notorious criminal Watson family

..... that's why he has failed to speak about his family

Everything was sadly falling into place for her.

Jimmy greets this person, gives him a quick man hug and whispers something in his ear, upon which he disappears as quickly as he had arrived. Before sitting down again, he immediately looks at Cara to see if he has been outed. It is clear as day that he has been. He is a man now in need of some robust body armour. However, rather than hurl abuse or engage in a tantrum, Cara reacts to his deception by breaking down in tears. She is quite inconsolable. She eventually regains her composure sufficiently to question him.

'Why, why, why did you fuckin' lie to me?'

Looking duly humbled, he coughs a nervous cough and then, somewhat sheepishly, responds:

'I didn't mean to. I didn't set out to, I honestly didn't. I had changed my name to register with the online dating company, long before I met you. I did so because I feared that my name would be recognised and that nobody would want to date someone who was part of a well-known criminal family. I wasn't to know that I would develop such strong feelings for you. Of course I'd wanted to tell you, but was so scared of losing you forever.'

'But surely you knew that the truth had to come out, you lyin' bastard?' asked Cara.

'Of course Cara, I probably knew it would, but I was scared of losing you and decided to say nothing.'

Once again Cara breaks down, which attracts some interested looks from other customers in the bar. James then puts his arm around her in an attempt to comfort her, but she shrugs him off.

'Fuck off and leave me alone. And what do you think our families would say if they knew, given that they're always at war with one another?'

He fails to reply and there followed a rather lengthy, awkward silence.

Jimmy then once again tries to defend himself.

'To be honest when we first met, I didn't know even know who you fuckin' were. Yeh, I know your brothers, but

I'd never heard your name before. I suppose I should have realised right away. I was just not thinking. Also, I'm not so much into the family business as my elder brothers.'

'Well, this is one fine mess you've now got us into,' said Cara.

Upon hearing this, and in particular the use of the word "us" Jimmy detects that her attitude has softened just a fraction and is thankful for small mercies. He again makes a move to cuddle her, and on this occasion, she does not resist. In fact, she even seems to take some solace from his warm, caring embrace.

'And what now?' she asks, putting the ball back firmly into his court. 'Do you still see any future with me?'

He hesitates, clearly electing to choose his words very carefully, before responding:

'Cara, not only do I love you, but I want us to spend the rest of our lives together. Maybe we can do something to stop this warring between our families.'

Filled with emotion, Cara leans forward and whispers in his ear:

'You've no idea how much that means to me because I've been dying to tell you something. I'm going to have your kid!'

CHAPTER 15

March 2008

While Matt has been on a steady downward spiral following the events of 15 February, his fellow passengers in his vehicle that fateful night have been reacting in their own individual ways.

By contrast, Darren has that type of personality that can simply pigeonhole the accident, move on and continue his somewhat blinkered life in the general pursuit of wantonness and self-gratification. That is not to say that he does not feel any remorse for the victim of the hit-and-run. It is not as if he knew him personally, and so any feelings of sympathy or empathy have been, at best, very transient. If Darren were to be brutally honest, he very rarely gives much thought to the accident. Also, despite having been sworn to absolute silence regarding the night in question, he has already mentioned it to his brother, Paul, with whom he still shares a fairly unique bond.

As for Ava, she was truly traumatised following the accident. Of course, being the front seat passenger, she had witnessed it at very close hand. The almighty, deafening, sickening sound of the thud as the man was struck by the car will live long in her memory. Also, she will never forget the gut-wrenching image of the body being involuntarily propelled upwards, thumping against the front windscreen before dropping lifelessly at the side of the road. Nor will she ever forget the expressionless face of the victim and the flow of red blood emanating from the corner of his mouth before forming a pool, a deep red halo around his head.

Ava has also experienced great difficulty sleeping since the accident and lies awake for hours on end, reliving the events of that horrific evening. This insomnia is also taking its toll on her health in that she is constantly feeling worn out and devoid of any energy. Similarly, it is adversely affecting her appearance. She looks desperately tired, grey and almost ghost-like. Sadly, given that she is self-employed, due to financial restraints, she does not have the luxury of being able to take time off work to recharge her batteries.

Any casual observer may be forgiven for thinking that Cleo, like Darren, was taking the aftermath of the hit-and-run very much in her stride. It is true to say that compared to Ava, she appears to be coping quite well. Perhaps one contributory factor is that she works full-time in a hospital, and while predominantly in an administration role, it is not unusual for her to be surrounded by trauma.

Also, shortly after the accident, Cleo met a certain John Sinclair, with whom she has had an ongoing relationship. Sinclair is fairly well known in Glasgow circles as being a bit of a wheeler dealer, with fingers in lots of pies. Suffice to say that some of these pies might be of questionable legitimacy. In any event, within a relatively short time their relationship has become quite intense, seeing one another four or five times per week. In retrospect, this new romance probably goes some way towards explaining how she has largely managed to put thoughts of that devastating evening behind her. Her mind is now almost entirely occupied with matters of the heart. One evening, after a few glasses of wine and in direct contravention of their joint pact, Cleo had shared with John Sinclair the events of 15 February 2008.

CHAPTER 16

April 2023

Brian Kelly is the eldest of six children brought up in one small tenement flat in Bridgeton. When he was a mere fourteen years of age, his womanising, alcoholic father walked out of the matrimonial home, never to be seen again. As a direct result, Brian had no choice but to mature very quickly and adopt the role of a father figure in helping provide for his mum and five younger siblings. This he had to do alongside attending school. By virtue of necessity, Brian became extremely resourceful. Although still a youngster, he was a well-known figure in the local pub, where he would earn some ready cash by running to and from the local betting office, placing bets for patrons. If they happened to win, he would often earn an attractive cash bonus for his efforts. His mother would always be greatly appreciative of such contributions to the family's weekly purse.

On weekends when Celtic FC were playing at home, there was also another opportunity to earn. Parkhead, where their stadium is situated, has always been considered a fairly deprived and run-down area where crime is an everyday occurrence. Wealthier supporters, who had the luxury of arriving by car, understandably had some concern for the welfare of their vehicle whilst attending a match. This in itself created a financial opportunity for young urchins, such as Brian Kelly, whose mantra became:

'Hey, Mister, can I mind your car for you?' It was in effect a tacit blackmail situation, because if this offer were declined, Brian might be disposed to remove the wheels and sell them on to a local garage! Alternatively, the owner might return to find his car badly scratched, to encourage him to pay up the next time! The reality of the situation is that Brian, and others like him, would not actually be looking after the car. Instead, they too would be watching the match for free, having persuaded a supporter to lift them over the turnstile - a custom that existed at that time.

This was in the days when there were pound notes in circulation rather than coins, and some of Brian's customers could be equally resourceful. Upon parking their car, they would offer Brian a pound for looking after it - a very attractive rate of remuneration in those days. The "customer" would tear the pound note in half and tell Brian that he would receive the other half upon returning to his car. This was, of course, on the basis that the vehicle was found to be in the same condition when he returned to it. Brian secretly admired their entrepreneurial spirit, but yet would merely leave the football match a few minutes before full-time to ensure he was by the car when the owner returned.

Perhaps inevitably, by the time Brian had turned seventeen, he had turned into a small-time criminal. His fairly minor street cons had developed into more serious crimes, and he had drifted into a knife and drugs culture that was prevalent in the east end of Glasgow. By the time he had reached his eighteenth birthday he was a hardened young criminal, someone not to be messed with. He had also been recruited to the Byrne gang, to which he had taken an oath of allegiance. By doing so, he automatically recognised the Watson family to be his arch-enemy. Ironically, although already recognised as a Glasgow "hard man", he nevertheless made his mum's welfare his number one priority and always ensured that he and his siblings were supported, both financially and morally.

Brian has now been working for the Byrne family for many, many years. In fact, he is even contemplating retirement. It is no surprise to him when he receives a call from the family, letting him know that they have a "job" for him. Being a dutiful and obedient member of the gang, he immediately arranges to meet them in the Molly Malone bar in Bridgeton, and upon arrival, John, Kevin and Aidan are already in situ. John sets up some beers and then they promptly get down to business. Basically, Brian is to be used as a modern-day hitman. It has, however, been determined that his victim is to be kneecapped, namely the act or practice of shooting at and disabling one's knee. This injury would typically be inflicted by a low-velocity gunshot to the area of the knee with a handgun, and such an injury would normally involve a recovery period of three to four months and could well involve a full knee reconstruction. It is a form of punishment that, over many years, has been favoured by both the Mafia and the IRA.

John slips a package under the table to Brian which contains a handgun that he is told to dispose of in the river after the deed is done. Also in the bag is a recent photo of the target and a note of his current address, both of which he is also asked to destroy. John is a bit of a stickler for detail and pre-planning is very important to him. Another example of John Byrne having truly done his homework becomes clear when he tells Brian to shoot him on the right kneecap. Brian questioned why he was so specific, only to be that the target is very skilled at football and harbours ambitions of turning professional. He is right-footed. Very little more is said other than Brian is told to report in on a burner phone whenever the job has been done, and then he is to lie low for a while until the dust settles.

CHAPTER 17

May 2008

Adam and Sarah Goldstein's concern for their son's physical and mental health has truly peaked, and they have decided to address the situation with him once and for all. Within a couple of minutes, he breaks down uncontrollably in front of them and is virtually incapable of speaking due to the torrent of tears running down his stress-lined face. His parents immediately realise there is something very seriously wrong. It has also become clear to them that he now wishes to share his burden. He mumbles almost inaudibly through a sea of tears:

'I've done something really, really awful, worse than you could possibly ever imagine. I'm really ashamed. If it got out, it would totally ruin my life. I'm so, so sorry, it was a terrible accident...' He once again breaks down.

'Look, son, we love you unconditionally, there's nothing you can have done that could change that.' Says his Dad while his Mum nods enthusiastically in agreement. Then again, they don't for one second anticipate the words that Matt is about to verbalise, just three words that will suddenly turn their almost perfect world upside down:

'I've killed someone!'

For a minute or so, there is the eeriest of silences as Matt's words penetrate the numbed brains of Adam and Sarah Goldstein. Of course, they totally understood the words uttered by their son, but the ramifications of what he has said are almost beyond their comprehension. Immediately, their minds are awash with questions:

'Whatever has happened to their precious son, whom they had nurtured since birth?'

'Where have they gone wrong as parents?'

'Is this a terrible nightmare, or is it really happening?'

'How could their son, Matthew Goldstein, possibly be responsible for killing someone?'

'What about his future law career?'

'Could their son be going to prison for several years?'

The whole scenario is almost beyond their comprehension.

Adam then hugs Sarah so tightly she is almost struggling for breath. They both take some crumbs of comfort from their deep embrace - some shelter from the storm. They continue to hold one another for a few minutes as they allow the reality and severity of the situation to truly sink in. It is almost as if being united in grief is in some way further strengthening their already close bond. In the meantime, Matt, a shadow of his former self, sits sobbing uncontrollably.

Eventually, Matt's parents collect themselves and invite their son to tell all and not hold anything back. As the words trip from Matt's mouth, the relief he feels is akin to the gradual release of a pressure valve. The proverb "a problem shared is a problem halved" comes to mind, but magnified a hundred times over.

Matt makes a massive effort to pull himself together and collect his thoughts. He then proceeds to narrate in detail the events of Saturday, 15 February, and the early hours of the following morning. He opts for a very full disclosure with nothing left unsaid. He speaks of driving to The Lair with the intention of leaving his car to uplift the following morning. Of meeting with Ava and later Cleo and Darren and to enjoying a few drinks in their company. Of the four of them leaving the bar to go to the nightclub and having a few more drinks. Of them intending to go back to their house, but being unable to secure a taxi. Of him insanely offering to drive them - a decision he is to regret for the rest of his life.

At this point, Matt again breaks down in tears and is quite inconsolable for a few minutes. Once he has regained his composure, he then admits that he had not been concentrating sufficiently on his driving. He talks of a figure suddenly appearing out of the darkness in front of him and not being able to react quickly enough to avoid striking him. He also tells of how they left the vehicle to attend to the motionless man, realising that he was dead and, in a panic, drove off, abandoning the scene of the accident.

Adam and Sarah Goldstein sit in complete silence for a few moments, totally numbed by what they have heard and desperately wondering how best to respond. In a few words, the bottom has well and truly fallen out of their lives.

CHAPTER 18

April 2023

Brian had spent a couple of hours per day covertly watching his target's movements. Jimmy Watson did not give the impression of being a man who felt he should be going about his business in a careful and cautious manner. While observing him, he had never once glanced over his shoulder to check if he was being followed. Had it been either of Jimmy's elder brothers, who are more streetwise and generally more criminally active, then the task he had been set would have been infinitely more challenging.

Brian is of the mind that the intended assault will take place in the evening, under the cover of darkness. By so doing, it should not be necessary to wear a mask, and he can quickly vanish into the night, hopefully completely undetected. Brian decides that tonight's the night. The adrenaline is pumping through his veins as he visualises the violent act and his quick getaway. The thought of actually doing the hit excites him and provides him with an energy rush, without sparing a single thought for his poor unfortunate victim.

 It is about 9:30pm as Jimmy Watson leaves his house. Brian follows his target on foot, but at a safe distance. Initially, he has no idea where Jimmy intends to go and then realises he is heading for the local taxi stand. There is nobody else in the queue, and about four or five taxis are standing in line. As his target jumps into the first cab, he has to think on his feet. Should he attempt to follow or wait for another day, another opportunity? Mentally, he is geared up for it tonight, so he elects to hop into the second taxi.

'Where to, mate?' asks the driver.

'Could you just follow my pal in that taxi in front?' responds Brian, all the time hoping the driver would not question him as to why they would not just have shared a taxi. He has elected to wear a baseball cap, and upon entering the vehicle, strategically pulls the brim of the cap down over his eyes. As the taxi in front heads towards Glasgow city centre, Brian fears he may have lost his opportunity.

Before long, the taxi pulls up in what is known as The Park District area, just west of the city centre. It is an affluent area of the city located around Park Circus and overlooking the stunningly beautiful and scenic Kelvingrove Park. It is generally made up of very large townhouses built in the mid-nineteenth century, which sometime later were mostly converted into offices. While the majority of them remain in office use to this very day, it has now become quite a trendy place to live, and increasingly more and more of them are being changed back into residential use. The area tends to be very quiet at night, with just a couple of bars and restaurants in the immediate vicinity.

Jimmy's taxi pulls up at a dead end where the street is blocked by concrete bollards, thereby only permitting pedestrian traffic to continue onwards, to where a small, select cocktail bar is located. Jimmy gets out and walks in the direction of the bar. His taxi promptly starts up again, does a U-turn and sets off, just as Brian's own taxi arrives. He quickly hands the driver a twenty pound note and, very generously, tells him to keep the change - perhaps tacitly paying for his silence! Then, assuming that Jimmy is heading for the cocktail bar, quickly jumps out of the taxi in hasty pursuit.

At this point, Jimmy, who is engaged on his phone, is only a few yards ahead. Brian decides he should confront him now as the street is empty, rather than wait until he is in close proximity of the cocktail bar. As he approaches him from behind, he shouts out his name, upon which Jimmy turns around and Brian floors him with a right hook. Jimmy's mobile is sent crashing to the ground, its case parting ways with the phone. With Jimmy lying on the ground, Brian takes his pistol from his waistband and, in a very cold and calculating manner, fires a shot directly into his right kneecap. With Jimmy's terrifying screams ringing in his ears, Brian sprints off into the night. Within minutes, he is walking casually at Charing Cross, where it meets Sauchiehall Street, mingling with evening revellers - completely incognito. The next job at hand is to dispose of the handgun as directed and then report back on a mission successfully accomplished.

CHAPTER 19

May 2008

Matt waits very anxiously to hear his parents' response, and fears the worst. He has visions of being frogmarched down to the police station, losing his liberty, his career and a large chunk of his young adult life. However, he is truly astounded by his father's reaction.

'Were there any witnesses to the accident?' Asks his dad, carefully using the euphemistic term 'accident', rather than "hit and run" or even worse "killing".

'No,' replies Matt, just beginning to find a grain of composure.

'That's, of course, apart from the three passengers in my car.'

'Who were they? Are you in touch with them?'

'I only met them that night for the very first time, and have not been in contact with any of them since. My memory isn't great, but I think I suggested that we should just leave the scene and the other three all agreed, albeit maybe reluctantly. That evening we all made a pact that we would go to our graves without saying to anyone what had happened.'

'But do you honestly believe you can trust them?'

'I think so, but as I said, I only just met them that one night.' (Matt thinks for a moment that in normal circumstances he would have genuinely liked to have seen Ava again at some future date. He does recall feeling a very genuine fondness for her. However, even if she had been agreeable to seeing him again, it would drag up too many distressing memories. He then, just as quickly, abandons any such thoughts.)

'Do you know if there are any CCTV cameras in the vicinity?' asks Matt's father as his mother sits with her head in her hands, quietly sobbing, but occasionally nodding approvingly whenever her husband speaks.

'No, I don't think there are. That part of the road is pretty quiet.'

'And is there any damage to your car?'

'Very slight, and as you have probably noticed, my car has barely been out of the garage since.'

Matt is somewhat surprised that his dad is going into so much detail, when the bottom line is that he is guilty of drink driving, of killing a man and of fleeing the scene.

'Was the victim conscious after you struck him?'

'No, I'm pretty sure that he died instantly upon impact. There was a smell of alcohol from him. He may well have staggered out in front of me. I can't be too sure, it is all a bit of a blur because I'd been drinking and was also distracted at the time.'

'What do you know about the victim?'

'Only what I have heard on radio and TV. He was a down-and-out who lived on the streets, a loner with no known relatives.'

'And you have not been contacted by the police?'

'No.'

'As far as you are aware, they have absolutely no knowledge of your involvement?'

'Yes, I think so.'

There is then a brief interlude in the questioning, during which time Matt has the opportunity to assemble his thoughts. He has always respected and looked up to his parents, despite them being somewhat more old-fashioned than the parents of his peers. They are very much viewed as pillars of their local community, and true stalwarts in terms of raising funds for various deserving charities, both regional and national. Basically, they are viewed as being very principled, a couple who live their lives by a fairly strict moral code. Given this background, Matt is more than a little shocked at the line of questioning from his dad and is curious about where it is all heading. His feeling of surprise changes to utter bewilderment as his father continues:

'Ok, one thing that we will have to do is have your car repaired. I have a friend who runs a small panel-beating garage not too far from here. He owes me a big favour, which he will be only too keen to repay. He will not ask any awkward questions. As far as he is concerned, the work was never carried out. However, we will wait until the heat is off. In the meantime, do not under any circumstances drive the car.'

Matt's dad had uttered these words in a cool and calculated manner and Matt was momentarily speechless. It is abundantly clear from what he has said that it is not intended that he give himself up to the police. On the contrary, his father is actually helping conspire to cover up the crime! This leaves Matt with a bitter-sweet taste. On the one hand, he is very relieved that he is most likely not going to be charged and possibly go to prison. On the other hand, he feels a tinge of disappointment that his parents are suddenly betraying the very principles that were so prevalent throughout his upbringing. And why? To save their precious offspring from incarceration? Or perhaps, as he rather suspects, to avoid tarnishing the precious Goldstein name.

His dad continues: 'The facts of the matter are that we cannot undo what has already been done. What would it achieve by going to the police? Absolutely nothing - but it would entirely ruin the rest of your life. Nothing we can do will bring this man back from the dead. If this person was of no fixed abode and has no known relatives, then there will be nobody hounding the police to make an arrest. Furthermore, there will not be any relatives desperately seeking closure. Indeed, will anyone be mourning his loss?' (At this point, Matt wonders if his dad is actually trying to convince himself with these arguments.)

'No, son, the best thing for you to do is try to put this entirely out of your mind and get on with your own life. And consider yourself very lucky that there were no witnesses.'

Matt could not have been more shocked than if his dad had said that he was leaving his mum to go live with a twenty-year-old lap dancer!

Despite his dad's words, it was suffice to say Matt did not feel in any way lucky. Indeed, his overriding emotion at this precise moment in time is one of deep disappointment, disappointment at his parents for their total insensitivity towards the victim. Would they have felt differently had he not been a 'tramp'? A life is a life!

His father then continues, again with his mum tacitly in agreement:

'In any event, as I understand the situation, this man was drunk and wandered out in front of your car and was therefore largely to blame for his own fate. Who is to say that even if you had not had a couple of beers beforehand, that the outcome would have been any different? So, all things considered, there is nothing to be achieved or gained by speaking to the police. Why on earth would you wish to ruin a very promising legal career for the sake of one drunken tramp, about whom nobody appears to give a jot?'

For the very first time in his life, Matt sees his parents in a completely new light, and he finds it incredibly disarming. Throughout this, he has remained largely silent. However, from his mum's body language, it is abundantly clear that she is in total agreement with his dad's line of thinking – namely, protect their son, whatever the cost. This conversation constitutes a crossroads in Matt's life. His relationship with his parents is irreparable from this moment onward. He now has two overriding and unshakable sentiments.

Firstly, he has lost all respect for his parents, parents whom he has always held up on a pedestal for being good-living, responsible and very righteous human beings.

Secondly, a deep-rooted feeling of shame and guilt for not having the guts to speak openly to the police about the truth of what happened on the night of 15 February - and accept the consequences, however painful. He is remaining silent for reasons of self-preservation, but the fall-out from this decision is that he will have to live the rest of his life wrestling with his conscience.

Matt also has one other recurring question in his head that is constantly niggling away at him. Are his parents actually taking this stance out of genuine love for their son? Or rather, as he very much suspects, are they simply trying to avoid the spotlight shining on their family and the public shame they might have to endure?

CHAPTER 20

April 2023

Cara has just arrived at Carriages Wine Bar and looks around for Jimmy, but there is no sign of him. He is normally extremely punctual, but then again, she has arrived a fraction early. Not feeling particularly comfortable walking into a bar on her own, she very quickly seeks out the sanctuary of a corner table where she has a view of the door for his impending arrival. She is particularly looking forward to seeing him today as she is keen to discuss the exciting topic of potential baby names. She has only just had time to order a drink when she notices a call coming in from him.

'Sorry I'm a bit late, babe. I've just got out of a taxi and will be with you in a few minutes.'

'No probs, I will order up a beer for you.'

No sooner has he spoken than she hears another, more distant voice, then a really loud bang. Almost instantaneously, this is followed by a truly blood-curdling scream, indicative of someone experiencing the most excruciating pain. This scream causes a cold chill to go right through her body. Total silence then follows. She frantically calls his name - no response! In a state of extreme panic, she grabs her handbag and runs out onto the street. Within minutes, she spots in the distance a body writhing on the pavement and hears accompanying groans. Instantly, she realises it is the father of the baby she is carrying. Consumed with fear and apprehension, she rushes towards him and immediately notices the ever-increasing pool of blood around the area of his right leg. She instinctively looks around for help, but there is nobody in sight. She then telephones the emergency services before cradling his head in her arms. At this point, he loses consciousness. Her distress is palpable as she weeps inconsolably, and her imagination goes into overdrive. Despite his lack of consciousness, she continues to whisper in his ear that she loves him while at the same time regrets not having told him before.

Sometime later, she is sitting by his side in the ambulance. Until now, her mind has been in total turmoil, and her imagination has been on overdrive. Only now, in this moment of relative calmness, does it occur to her that this is most probably an act of retribution at the instigation of her very own family. Her tears start to flow once again. She is constantly wiping her cheeks, choking on her sobs and mumbling incoherently to herself. Her eyes are puffy and bloodshot, and she feels as if her world is at an end.

CHAPTER 21

July 2008

In Glasgow Division Police Headquarters, DI Hilary Simpson has called another meeting of her team. High on her agenda is the death of Samuel Geddes by a hit-and-run. She invites her team to provide a progress report. On reflection, a better term for it might have been a "lack of progress" report.

At the end of it, DI Simpson sums up the somewhat dire situation in concise, bullet-point fashion:

- There are conclusively no CCTV cameras at the stretch of the road where the hit-and-run accident took place.
- There are no private houses with security cameras that might lend assistance.
- Despite a public appeal, no witnesses to the crime have come forward.
- We have carried out a door-to-door enquiry, which has also proved to be fruitless.
- As you know there were very tiny particles of blue metallic paint found at the scene. Having checked with all known garages there is no record of any bodywork repair having been carried out to a car of that colour. Also, unfortunately the toning in question is not limited to any one make of car, so we cannot even tie it down to a particular manufacturer.
- Very little is known about the deceased, Samuel Geddes. He was very much a loner, and no known relatives have been able to be traced. We did provide representation at

his funeral. This was partly out of respect, but also, experience has shown that for some macabre reason, killers sometimes turn up at their victim's funeral. However, this too proved to be a blind alley as there were insufficient numbers present to even carry his cardboard coffin.

- All the forensic evidence has gone under the microscope, literally and metaphorically, and absolutely nothing has been turned up.

- Finally, we now have the benefit of the post-mortem report. We were already aware that the victim is a certain Samuel Geddes of no fixed abode and aged 64 years. He was of slight build. The injuries he sustained were consistent with having been struck by a vehicle. There was general bruising to his torso, but the fatal blow was to the side of his head. As a result of this blow, his head was severely fractured and he would have died instantaneously. In respect of the toxicology report, despite his clothes smelling strongly of alcohol, all tests proved negative, having checked for alcohol, heroin, marijuana and amphetamines. So, in essence, any perception that this was a case of a drunken man staggering out onto the street in front of an oncoming car is totally unfounded.

DI Simpson then continues. 'So, unfortunately, we have absolutely no leads to go on at this moment in time. While the case is not technically closed, pending any fresh information coming to light, we will no longer be allocating specific resources to the solving of this crime.

CHAPTER 22

April 2023

Jimmy is taken by ambulance to the A&E department of Glasgow Royal Infirmary. Their first task is to make him feel comfortable and give him morphine. This is administered intravenously and takes about twenty minutes to take full effect. At this stage, no visitors are permitted access to the patient. Once settled, Jimmy is then moved to a very small four-bedded general ward, and at this point, Cara is allowed access.

She is so very relieved to find that he seems comfortable and no longer appears to be in any pain. Although now conscious, he is extremely tired and looks as if he might fall asleep at any moment. In addition, he is pretty much talking gibberish, obviously a byproduct of the morphine.

'Jimmy darling, how are you feeling, are you in any pain?'

'I'm fine,' he responds. 'What happened to me?'

'Do you not remember, you were on your way to meet me in Carriages, and some bastard shot you in the leg?'

'Why would someone...?' And then his eyes close involuntarily, and he is quite incapable of finishing his question. At this point, a nurse comes into the ward, quickly appraises the situation and speaks very politely but firmly to Cara.

'It is very important that Mr Watson is now allowed to sleep. The police have also just been here with a view to questioning him and I told them they will have to return later once he has had the opportunity to gain some rest. I will have to ask you to do the same or alternatively go to the waiting room.' Cara chooses the second option.

Sometime later that evening, two uniform police officers call back to the hospital and are allowed access to take a statement from the patient. It comes as no surprise to them that he claims not to remember anything about any assault or indeed anything at all about how he was injured or ended up in hospital. This reaction is rather romantically referred to as "the code of honour between criminals". The irony of this situation is that the police know that James knows who attacked him. Also, James knows that the police know that he knows who attacked him!

CHAPTER 23

May 2009
(15 months after the hit-and-run)

Fact - Matt will obviously never be able to wipe from his mind the events of 15 February 2008, which were, of course, life-changing. However, time is inevitably a great healer, and with every day, week and month that passes, he relives the memory of the hit-and-run that little bit less frequently. That said, he is still experiencing horrendous nightmares, usually resulting in him waking up in a cold sweat, hoping it has merely been a dream or nightmare. Was he really driving the car under the influence of alcohol? Did he really run a man down? Then, intense disappointment follows as he has to come to terms with the reality of his situation.

After very serious consideration, Matt eventually opts to study law at Edinburgh University. Although Edinburgh is only about an hour's drive from Glasgow, it makes practical sense for him to move out of his parents' house. He is keen on the sense of independence that this provides him. Although his parents have offered to buy an Edinburgh flat for him, his preference is to stay at the University residences. He feels that staying here will enable him to mingle with and befriend other students. He also does not want to feel beholden to his parents, especially given that their relationship has deteriorated somewhat.

Matt has met a fellow student whom he has been seeing romantically for a few months, by the name of Liz Hamilton. She is also studying law and hails from Glasgow as well, so they instantly have a great deal in common. Furthermore, by coincidence, she was also born within a few weeks of Matt. Liz is slightly built, with shoulder-length auburn hair, blue eyes that sparkle when she speaks, an endearing smile and two trademark dimples. Matt is besotted, and it appears that the feeling is mutual. Not only do they see one another most evenings, but they also walk to and from each class together and sit side by side in the lecture theatres. In his occasional down periods, he thinks to himself: 'If only Liz knew that I had killed someone!'

Not only is Matt relishing university life, but he is also flourishing. His exceptional test results thus far show him to be one of the brightest stars in his year. He has scored particularly well in criminology - an area of the law in which he has a really keen interest. Befitting their make-up, his parents are never reticent about mentioning his academic achievements when at dinner parties with their hoity-toity friends and neighbours.

All in all, life for Matt has improved so much over the last fifteen months or so. Sadly, though, he will never be able to rid himself completely of a deep-rooted feeling of guilt. However, no matter how much he would like to, he is unable to turn back the clock.

CHAPTER 24

April 2023

Cara is tired, weary, worried and distressed. She has been sitting in the hospital waiting room for just over two hours. It is located close to the nurses' station, which has been a hive of activity since she arrived. On two separate occasions, she approached the nurses' desk, enquiring about Jimmy, but in truth she simply wished to remind them that she was still waiting. They were brief, if apologetic, in saying they had no more news to dispense.

Another half hour or so passes before her attention is drawn to male voices at the nurses' station. In particular, she hears mention of Jimmy's name and a nurse directing them to the waiting room while commenting 'his partner is waiting in there also.' The waiting room is only about twelve metres square, and there is nobody else present. Seconds later, a father and his two sons enter the room, and she knows intuitively that this is the notorious Watson family. (She later discovers that when Jimmy was first admitted to hospital, he had provided details of his next-of-kin, and they were then immediately contacted.) She suddenly feels extremely tense, wondering how best to deal with this somewhat surreal situation. As they take seats in the row opposite her, she decides to grasp the nettle and take the initiative:

'Hi, I assume you are Jimmy's family members? We haven't met, I am Cara, his girlfriend.' She wants to also say her surname, but is not quite able to get her mouth around the word.

'Hi there,' says the older man, obviously Sid. The other two just kind of grunt. Then he continues, 'Don't you worry darlin', we'll sort out those Byrne bastards for doin' this to oor Jimmy.'

Cara immediately feels a sickness deep in the pit of her stomach and has an urge to run out of the waiting room. Having decided to come clean about her family connections, she then does a complete U-turn and says absolutely nothing to reveal her true identity. We didn't know that oor Jimmy was going out wi' anyone. How long have you two been seein' one another?'

'Quite some time now.' She responds, being deliberately vague.

'And were you there when it happened? Did you see who did this?'

Cara went on to explain that she had arranged to meet Jimmy in Carriages, about his subsequent phone call and about finding him bleeding on the pavement.

She is dreading them asking any more questions, when thankfully, a nurse comes into the waiting room.

'Sister has said that you can all now go in to visit Jimmy. However, you are limited to only ten minutes because he has lost a lot of blood and is extremely tired. Also, I should point out that he is on a fairly large dose of morphine, and so might not be particularly lucid. He is going to be alright in time. He may or may not need surgery, but at the moment, more than anything, he needs total rest.' The nurse then leads all four of them to Jimmy's bedside.

In his hospital bed, Jimmy looks much smaller than normal and somewhat frail. He also appears slightly vague and is slurring his words, the medication obviously has taken its toll. His voice sounds a little different, an octave higher than usual and oscillating. It is blatantly clear to all that he is a little delirious. The Watsons congregate on one side of his bed while Cara takes a seat on the other. With some difficulty, Jimmy strains his neck, looking from one side to the other as if observing a tennis match. Suddenly, there is a look of absolute astonishment on his face. Cara fears the worst, and not without justification.

'By the way, that's brilliant seein' you all together,' says Jimmy in a slurred voice.

Cara, in fear of what he might say next, interjects, asking him how he is feeling.

'Fine, but a bit sore.' He responds, looking towards his father and brothers, before continuing:

'It means so much to me that you can just accept Cara for who she is.'

The Watson family are completely in the dark. Jimmy laughs and adds jokingly:

'The next thing you will all be going to support Glasgow Celtic!'

At this point, Sid Watson and his sons simply assume that Jimmy's girlfriend might be from the other side of the divide, a Catholic. This in itself would be fairly unpalatable, but little did they know there was even worse to come.

'Who'd have thought that I would have teamed up wi' a Byrne girl, and she'll be the mother of my baby.'

For a couple of moments, there is deafening silence as the impact of these words hit home. Then there is an outburst, an outpouring of vitriolic, bigoted bile by Sid Watson towards Cara, with his son's backing.

'You fuckin' Fenian bitch! How d'you have the fuckin' nerve to sit here after what your bastard brothers have done to oor Jimmy. I hope you and your fuckin' baby rot in hell. I'll see to it that you will be attending your fuckin' brothers' funerals before this month is out.'

At this point, the nurse returned, accompanied by the sister in charge of the ward, who told the Watsons to immediately leave the hospital or security would be called to eject them. Cara was secretly pleased that she had not also been asked to leave as she would have had very genuine concerns for her safety.

'Don't worry, we'll leave,' Sid Watson responds. 'We'll be glad to get away from this fuckin' bitch. And Jimmy, you need your fuckin' head examined. You shouldn't want to be seen dead with any one of that bastard Byrne family.'

The three Watsons then storm out of the hospital ward. Cara is trembling with fear. Jimmy looks totally bemused as if to say: 'What just happened there?'

From that day onwards, Jimmy finds himself completely ostracised by his family. When Cara comes clean about her liaison with her own parents, she receives an equally frosty reception. While she is given an option, it is one which holds no appeal. She is told very bluntly that if she wishes to remain a part of the Byrne family, she must terminate her relationship with Jimmy Watson with immediate effect. For Cara, there is no decision to be made.

CHAPTER 25

The year 2015

Matt Goldstein had sailed through his law degree course at Edinburgh University with flying colours. Unlike many students who decide to go for an honours degree, Matt opted instead for an ordinary degree, being eager to qualify and practice as a solicitor as early as possible. That was then followed up with a mandatory one-year diploma course. This rendered him eligible to complete a two-year traineeship in a legal firm, which in turn qualified him as a fully-fledged solicitor. Given his excellent university results, allied with an air of self-confidence and positivity, he had no lack of suitors when it came to securing a legal traineeship. In fact, he was in the fairly unique position of being able to pick and choose his employer. He opted to join Meldrums, a Glasgow city centre criminal practice that enjoyed an enviable reputation for attracting the best graduates and, more importantly for transforming them into competent and successful criminal advocates.

Things have moved forward for Matt on various fronts. His relationship with Liz has gone from strength to strength, as evidenced by the fact that they are now engaged to be married with a wedding at the initial planning stage. Liz has also chosen to complete an ordinary degree in law so that they can both qualify at the same time. She, too, has excelled in her studies, but unlike Matt, has elected to pursue a career in commercial law. The legal company she has joined for her traineeship has been sufficiently impressed by both her intellect and application that they offered her a permanent position - one she is happy to accept. Her mum has not been keeping too well and has been suffering from the early onset of dementia. Not surprisingly, this has been causing Liz great distress and has certainly been a contributory factor, not only in them advancing their wedding date, but also in them choosing to secure traineeships in Glasgow, rather than Edinburgh.

Perhaps not surprisingly, not only has Matt been offered a permanent position with Meldrums, but they have also dangled the carrot of a partnership within a relatively short timeframe. Matt is flattered by this offer and the fact that they are keen to retain his services. However, having experienced criminal law through the eyes of the defence, he now has a hankering to cross the big divide and prosecute offenders instead. Accordingly, he opts to join The Crown Office and Procurator Fiscal Service (COPFS) and is accepted with open arms. Within a very short period of time, he becomes responsible for putting a not inconsiderable number of criminals behind bars.

CHAPTER 26

April 2023

At the time of Jimmy's shooting, unknown to either family, Cara had actually moved into Jimmy's house - except it was not technically Jimmy's house. Rather, his father had gifted a house to each of his offspring, but the title to each of them remained in the name of their dad, Sidney Archibald Watson. Following the revelation regarding the relationship between Jimmy and Cara, it became fairly public knowledge that they were cohabiting. Sid announced to his wife, Nancy, that he was 'putting Jimmy out on the street.' Nancy's maternal instincts instantly came to the fore:

'C'mon Sid, he's just a young lad. Remember, you were young once, too. He didn't intend on upsetting you, he obviously loves the girl. Is it not enough that he has been shot?'

'Look, Nancy, of all the girls he could have gone out with, he had to choose that Byrne bitch!'

'But you can't throw them out of the house when the girl is expectin' a bairn!

'Just watch me!' replies Sid, who has always had a very stubborn streak. While Sid clearly always had a soft spot for Jimmy, it was evident that this was just a bridge too far for him. So Nancy is well aware that there is only going to be one winner in this argument. The only concession Sid is prepared to make is to give them one month to vacate the house - and even that took some persuasion on Nancy's part.

Cara had chosen Jimmy over her family, and so she, too, has been shunned by her family. Financially, things are now looking pretty bleak for the couple. Due to his injury, Jimmy is unable to work, and yet they are expecting a baby in December. The only better news for them is that the kneecapping has only caused soft tissue damage. There is no fracture of the joint, nor has there been any neurovascular damage, which could have resulted in several weeks in hospital and intensive outpatient physiotherapy.

Somewhat ironically, their respective family's reaction to their relationship has only served to further strengthen the already strong bond which existed between the couple. They share this feeling of "us against the rest of the world" and are happy in their little cocoon. They promptly apply to the City Council to rent a house in another area of Glasgow and are pleased to hear that this application will receive a degree of priority due to the impending birth of their child. When one door closes...

CHAPTER 27

The year 2015

Paul Alexander's general mood and mental health have been on the decline in recent years. During this period, he has been no stranger to a police cell, and on occasions, a prison cell. The majority of his offences have involved theft in a vain attempt to feed his ever-increasing drug habit. Breaking into houses tends to be his staple diet.

When committing these crimes, he is usually in an intoxicated state, so it should probably be no surprise that this pursuit normally culminates in a period of incarceration. Paul has never been, by nature, a violent man. Yet he has been convicted of a couple of armed robberies, albeit while using an imitation gun. This is an indication of how desperate he has been for money to feed his drug habit. Indeed, on one such occasion, he robbed an off-sales shop in broad daylight while customers were present. One of the staff members behind the fully enclosed counter simply pressed the silent alarm, and he was arrested while still on the premises. A true amateur at work!

Whether it be through drink or drugs, Paul is, by any standard, an addict. He drifts aimlessly from day to day and week to week. He spends precious little of his state benefit handout on food, and as a result is becoming painfully thin. It is perhaps not surprising, therefore, that the trademark Alexander glint in the eye is barely evident. On a normal day, he can be spotted wearing out the footpath, walking back and forth between his local pub and betting shop. If successful on the horses, any winnings tend to go towards drugs, initially cocaine, more recently heroin. If unsuccessful, he will either borrow or thieve to achieve his next fix. And so the cycle continues.

A couple of years earlier, his parents, Henry and Mia, eventually decided to completely disown him, but this was very much as a last resort. Perhaps any casual observer might mistakenly have considered them to be very heartless, but there is a limit to just how much pain and suffering any parents can endure. For many a year, whenever in financial difficulty, Paul would make tracks to his parent's house, very much cap in hand. Upon listening to his latest sob story, they would inevitably bail him out with cash - money they could barely afford themselves. They then told Paul that each handout was to be considered as a loan, but despite assurance after assurance, these loans were never repaid. Very quickly, hundreds of pounds grew into thousands as Henry and Mia eventually put themselves into severe debt and had to remortgage their house as a result. It is shortly after this that they choose to draw a line under their relationship with their errant son. They were able to justify this decision by convincing themselves that they had to be cruel to be kind. In essence, giving into his desperate pleas for money was simply assisting him to buy more drugs, which in turn was precipitating his demise.

Given his addictive state of mind and the fact that his parents were no longer of any use to him, he stopped all contact, not even acknowledging birthdays or Christmas. Despite not hearing from him, being typical parents, it did not stop Henry and Mia from worrying and fretting about their son. It almost goes without saying that if he were to mend his ways and cease taking drink and drugs, they would welcome him back into the fold with open arms.

Paul has long since lost contact with his elder brothers, Brian and Bobby. There had been a mutual disconnect as they had no time or sympathy for his way of life, whether self-inflicted or otherwise. In any event, Paul's only interest was in feeding his habit. It is a very sad indictment, but if Paul were to pass his nephews or his niece on the street, he would not even recognise them.

However, the bond that had always existed between Paul and his younger brother Darren has remained intact throughout this period, despite being strained to almost breaking point on many an occasion. While in some ways Darren is unreliable and irresponsible, his blind allegiance to his wayward older brother is quite atypical and indeed almost touching. One could easily be forgiven for mistakenly assuming that Darren was the older of the two siblings, certainly more responsible.

On countless occasions, Darren has helped out Paul in a variety of ways. Over the years, Paul had become a bit of an itinerant, often couch surfing with various friends, before eventually being thrown out due to his unacceptable or antisocial behaviour. On such occasions, he would normally arrive at Darren's door seeking refuge, a request that would never be refused. Of course, this would be when he was not otherwise a guest of Her Majesty.

In addition to looking for accommodation, Paul would regularly seek financial assistance from his brother, particularly after his parents' well had run dry. Darren would usually be sympathetic to whatever sad story Paul might concoct, but he, too, was becoming increasingly concerned that he was merely facilitating his drug habit. So, he decided to change his approach. More recently, Darren has assisted his brother, but only in terms of taking him out for a wholesome meal or shopping with him for clothing. He is no longer willing to provide him with ready cash.

Paul, at the behest of his brother has tried rehabilitation on a few occasions, but with a quite distinct lack of success. Darren feels he lacks sufficient motivation to be cured and that if the will is not there, the chances of him being reformed are very remote. And of course his addiction is not restricted to drugs, but also gambling and alcohol - a quite damaging, if not lethal, cocktail.

It has been a fairly normal day for Paul, wandering back and forth between his local pub and the adjacent bookmakers. Or rather, it had been a normal day, until his luck changed quite dramatically - for the better.

Paul's favoured 'punt' on the horses is referred to as a "yankee" or "accumulator". Basically it is a question of selecting four horses all on the same bet. The real attraction of this type of bet is that you have the potential to win a very sizeable sum of money for a relatively small investment.

On this particular day, the first three of Paul's horses win - and all at reasonably good odds. He has already won a substantial amount, with the potential for a great deal more if his fourth horse, 'Jumping Jack Flash' should win the 3:40pm race at Cheltenham at the very attractive odds of 16/1. Paul is both excited and nervous. This race is a National Hunt Race that requires horses to jump over fences and ditches - a fact which only adds to his state of anxiety as one slip or bad jump could be fatal.

Given that he is in this "bookies" shop virtually every day, he is very well known by both staff and patrons alike. On this occasion, they are all very aware that Paul has the very real potential to win big. The staff are particularly supportive because if he is successful, they might just receive a tip for their services. His fellow 'punters' in the shop are also cheering on 'Jumping Jack Flash' in anticipation of Paul buying them a couple of pints in the local pub by way of celebration.

There are twenty-three horses in the race. Paul's breathing becomes noticeably heavier and his hands increasingly sweaty as his selected horse makes steady progress through the field. With one full circuit of the track still to be negotiated, Jumping Jack Flash has gone from third last place to tenth and is still making up ground. Every muscle in Paul's body is tightening and his eyes are fixated upon the TV screen. His selection continues to catch up on the leading horses while approaching the final bend. Negotiating the second last fence, he quite brilliantly and successfully jumps into third position. The feeling of expectation within the bookies is almost tangible. However, at this stage the favourite 'Lucky Jim' and the second horse 'Fancy a Flutter' then both accelerate leaving a substantial gap between themselves and the rest of the field. The atmosphere immediately becomes more sombre, and Paul is feeling deflated. His body language tells the whole story.

And then it happens - like a minor miracle of sorts. The race favourite, belying its name, hits the last fence, stumbles and falls. He, in turn, also severely obstructs the second horse, and while it does manage to negotiate the fence, it virtually comes to a halt and loses all momentum. In the blink of an eye, Jumping Jack Flash sails past Fancy a Flutter' to secure the race. Legend states that Paul Alexander's cheers could be heard in Edinburgh. His win was so emphatic and his pay-out so substantial that for security reasons, he was asked by the management to make an appointment for the following day to pick up his winnings! In the meantime, they gave him an interim payment of £1,000 in cash to tide him over.

ONE SAD DAY

Yes, of course, Paul could have chosen to use at least a portion of his substantial winnings to repay his parents, or even his brother, Darren. However, he elected otherwise.

CHAPTER 28

The year 2016

Rather ironically, Paul's win on the horses has proven to be a poisoned chalice in that it has merely further accelerated his decline. Yes, he was able to party hard for a few weeks, maybe even months and during this period everyone in his local pub became his friend. However, not surprisingly his pot of gold evaporated all too quickly, as did his so-called friends. Not only did he almost drink himself into oblivion, but he also further indulged his drug habit. In addition, his large win on Jumping Jack Flash had somehow mistakenly lulled him into the misapprehension that this was a feat capable of repetition. He, therefore, persisted in throwing more and more money at this senseless pursuit.

It is now a few months since his momentous gambling win, and suffice to say that the small fortune he received has all been frittered away on drink, drugs and gambling. In addition, there have also been occasional women, usually with pound signs in their eyes. Perhaps not surprisingly, when the money disappeared, so did they.

This downward trend continues, but now he no longer has the benefit of financial support from his family. His impassioned plea to his elder brothers, Brian and Bobby, falls on deaf ears. Both of them resent the fact that he has not shown the remotest interest in their families over the years. In fact, their kids do not receive so much as a Christmas or birthday card from their absent uncle. And so, in desperation, he reverts to his "drinking friends" to whom he has been disproportionately generous following his win on the horses.

However, sadly for him, they neither have the means nor the inclination. At the end of the day his only option is to turn to crime once again.

CHAPTER 29

May 2023

Archie Watson has been planning an armed robbery for quite some time, in fact, since he was last released from HM Prison Barlinnie. During his three-month spell inside, he had shared a cell with an inmate called Tommy Turner, known affectionately to all his friends as 'Tea Leaf', being rhyming slang for 'thief'. He is just over five feet, four inches in height, with a slim but very wiry frame. In fact he does not appear to carry any excess fat. In evidence of this, his party piece in the pub is to challenge someone to punch him as hard as they can in the stomach without him flinching. This little bit of theatre usually manages to secure him the odd free pint of beer. Tea Leaf is particularly well known among the criminal fraternity of Glasgow as well as being very popular. He is one of those people who always has a joke or a quip at hand and a generally happy disposition. Basically, he is a petty criminal. However, he is quite remarkable in one respect - that he is so bad at his 'trade'! To his detriment, he has never been one with an eye for detail. Hence, he tends to spend more time behind bars than at large. On this most recent occasion, fingerprint evidence caused his downfall as he simply forgot to wear gloves. This time around, he was incarcerated for quite a long spell due to having accumulated a lengthy string of previous convictions.

Archie has become quite close with Tea Leaf whilst sharing a cell together. Inevitably, their conversations get around to talking about "jobs" they have done in the past or indeed plan in the future. In respect of the latter, there is one potential job that Tea Leaf mentions that peaks Archie's interest.

Tea Leaf has a distant cousin who had, until very recently, been employed as an assistant in a petrol station in the outskirts of Glasgow. Never one to pass up an opportunity, Tea Leaf had shown interest in their working processes. It transpires that every day, all the takings from the till are stored in an onsite safe, and then a heavy-duty security vehicle collects all the cash early each Monday morning. Tea Leaf's intention, had he been at liberty, was to rob the petrol station on a Sunday evening, for the maximum return.

However, his problem is that he is not due for release for another five or six months. By this time, the working systems within the petrol station could well have changed, obviously making the job too risky. So, when Archie shows some interest, an agreement is reached between them. Basically, when released in a few days, Archie will immediately plan the robbery with an unwritten agreement that Tea Leaf, as the facilitator, will be entitled to a percentage of the takings. Archie is keen on this proposed venture, especially as the police would never be able to connect him with their former employee, who had imparted the key information.

So, upon his release, he contacts one of the youngest members of his gang, Andy Wilson, to assist him on the job. He is known within the gang as "Handy Andy" having learned his apprenticeship as a pickpocket. Andy is keen to move up the criminal chain and is flattered to have been approached by one of the Watson brothers, even though his role is a relatively minor one - as a lookout and getaway driver.

CHAPTER 30

December 2020

The years have rolled by, and looking in from the outside, life seems pretty good for Matt and Liz. Of course, the reality is quite different. Although Matt's nightmares might be less frequent, it seems that they will continue to live with him until his dying day.

Matt and Liz are also now proud parents of two-year-old, Daisy, who is without any shadow of a doubt, the apple of their eye. Like so many couples in their situation, their lives and priorities have totally changed, as Daisy now takes centre stage. From Matt's perspective, Daisy also represents another very welcome distraction from ruminating about the events of SAD Day 2008.

The arrival of Daisy prompts a house move to something a little larger. Fortunately, their new domain, a luxurious four-bedroom detached villa in an upmarket and residential Glasgow suburb, appears to tick all the necessary boxes. It transpires that a number of their new neighbours have toddlers of a similar age to Daisy. In turn, this not only provides them with a ready-made social network, but also immediately gives Daisy play pals on tap. In addition, there is the very practical convenience of being able to share car runs with other parents.

Not only has Matt's domestic life moved on, but his work life has as well - by leaps and bounds. Very early in his career in the COPFS, he was identified as a rising star, someone earmarked for a glittering career. Even now, at still a relatively tender age, he is entrusted with prosecuting some quite major cases. Matt is enjoying the challenge of locking up the bad guys as opposed to defending criminals, some of whom he now considers to be the lowlifes of society.

In the early summer of 2017, Matthew Adam Goldstein and Elizabeth Jean Hamilton were married at a very lavish ceremony at Marr Hall Golf & Spa Resort, a truly luxurious, grand, nineteenth-century mansion just a few miles from Glasgow city centre. Set in a 240-acre ancient woodland estate, the lavish bedrooms offer breathtaking views over the River Clyde and Old Kilpatrick hills.

The Goldsteins, having just the one child were determined that this event would be virtually unrivalled, and they elected to contribute a larger proportion of the cost of the event than would normally be expected of the parents of the groom. Suffice to say that the 150 very entitled guests were treated to a wedding experience extraordinaire. As well as a sumptuous wedding breakfast and a complimentary hotel stay, guests could avail of a complimentary round of golf on Marr Hall's very own golf course. What's not to like?

Two years earlier, Mother Nature had not been quite so kind. Adam Goldstein had been diagnosed with lung cancer and had to undergo both radiotherapy and chemotherapy. While the treatment was deemed to have been relatively successful, he is now a shadow of his former self. In addition to the physical impact, it also took its toll on the mental state of both Adam and his wife, Sarah. And while Matt obviously has some sympathy for them, his relationship with his parents has never returned to what it was pre-February 2008. While this saddens him, he realises that it is something that cannot be forced.

Equally, while he and Liz are naturally very appreciative of the substantial wedding contribution made by the

Goldsteins, they are under no illusions that his parents' primary motivation is probably not the happiness of the wedding couple. Rather, his parents view the occasion as a somewhat rare opportunity to flaunt their affluent lifestyle before an audience containing many of their peers. This theory is probably best evidenced and endorsed by the number of personal guests invited by Adam and Sarah relative to the friends of the bride and groom.

As originally intended, the date of the wedding was advanced due to the ill health of Liz's mum. While Liz was delighted that her mum was able to attend, very sadly, she was present in body only. Nor did she have any recollection of the wedding after the event. However, Liz took great comfort from being able to show her mum the wedding photos afterwards, even if they did not rekindle any memories for her.

CHAPTER 31

03 June 2023

Sunday evening duly comes around and, as pre-arranged, Archie meets Andy, (Handy Andy), in the Tavern. No alcohol is partaken as they both require clear minds for the task at hand. They are both wearing dark coloured hoodies and jeans. Archie is a fairly hardened criminal, and for him, this is just another job. However, for Andy, this is a pretty big deal and very much a step up from his previous life as a pickpocket. He is extremely apprehensive. While as a juvenile, he had experienced the judicial system, he has not yet tasted the inside of a prison. Having only been in the bar for about fifteen minutes, he has already had to make two trips to the toilet. Adrenaline is pumping through his veins. Archie is not oblivious to this and tries to put his mind at rest by assuring him that the first job is always the hardest and it will get easier with time.

After these words of reassurance and some causal preambles, they get down to business. Archie has supplied the vehicle for the job. It is a recently stolen, nondescript, white, eight-year-old Ford Focus, a car which should not attract any unwanted attention and one they plan to abandon and set fire to later that evening.

The petrol station closes at 11.00pm. So the plan is to arrive there about 10.30 to 10.40pm. According to the ex-employee, there will only be two people on duty on a Sunday. Apparently, it is company policy to have a minimum of two employees at all times. The intention is for Andy to drive Archie there, who in turn will only access the petrol station when there are no other customers present. Andy is then to park up at one of the petrol pumps, appearing to be a customer, while Archie will enter the shop. Andy is told that he is not to leave the car. If another vehicle should enter the forecourt he has to beep the horn as a warning. Archie is to wear a balaclava and will be armed with a sawn-off shotgun, whereas Andy will be unarmed and unmasked. Archie will also take a bag in which the cash will be deposited.

They arrive at the petrol station shortly after 10.30pm, both with their hoodies up to conceal their features. It has been a typical dull, grey day in Glasgow, and they are now covered by a cloak of darkness. Fortunately, there are no cars in the forecourt, and it also appears as if there are no customers in the shop. Conditions are looking good. As directed, Andy pulls up at the petrol pump nearest to the shop. Having already visited the petrol station on a previous reconnaissance trip, Archie is aware that this pump is the least visible from the security cameras that are in situ. Also, it will provide him with cover as he replaces his hood with a balaclava. He then very hurriedly takes the few steps from there to the shop entrance, looking to have the element of surprise on his side. He succeeds.

There are, in fact, only two staff members present. One is a grey-haired woman probably approaching pension age. Somewhat surprisingly, given the circumstances, Archie notices her identity badge. Her name is Marjorie. Rather weirdly, the quite inane and most arbitrary thought flashes through his mind that she is a woman who very much suits her name. Perhaps this robbery business is becoming too routine for him!

In addition, there is a much younger man, maybe in his early twenties, who does not appear to merit a name badge. Perhaps this is due to lack of service or perhaps he has simply forgotten to wear it today. Once again - a very random thought! It is later discovered that this second employee is a certain Gary Conway, a student merely looking to earn a bit of extra cash during his summer holidays. He is currently crouched down stocking the shelves, probably just idling away his time until he can finish up for the day.

Perhaps Archie has been watching too many American crime films, but he adopts their policy of putting the fear of death into innocent members of the public by creating chaos and generally shouting and swearing in an extremely loud voice. While wielding his sawn-off shotgun, he demands that they listen very carefully to what he has to say. Without even being asked, Gary immediately lies face down, arms and legs outstretched. He has presumably adopted this pose to ensure that he could never be asked to identify the robber, despite the fact he is masked. Perhaps he has seen too many movies!

'Don't either of you fuckin' move. Touch an alarm button and it will be the last thing you will ever do.' He then directs his attention to the more senior assistant:

'Go into the back office and open the fuckin' safe - now!' He yells at her.

Both she and young Gary are completely fear-stricken. Neither of them can believe this is actually happening. But Marjorie is long enough in the tooth to appreciate that absolutely nobody in her situation is remunerated sufficiently to be a hero. So, in the interests of her own salvation, she is going to do exactly as she is told and hopefully then be able to look forward to her impending retirement.

Archie positions himself behind the counter in a location where both employees are within his line of vision. Having said that, he does not anticipate there is any danger of Gary even moving a muscle. As Marjorie enters the security code, Archie throws a shopping bag in her direction, telling her to empty the cash contents of the safe into it.

In the meantime, in the getaway car, Andy is becoming increasingly edgy and agitated, furiously biting at his cuticles until they start to bleed. He is also tap, tap, tapping with his foot and feels a desperate need to relieve himself, yet again. Being a pickpocket was so much easier, he thinks to himself. Also, it did not involve all this hanging around, expending nervous energy. Why was he really needed anyway, not a single car has entered the garage? What is taking Archie so long? What if the staff have pressed a silent alarm? Has something gone wrong? The more his imagination runs riot, the more worried and agitated he becomes, and the more his fingers bleed. He decides to be proactive and switch on the ignition to facilitate a more rapid getaway.

PC Adam Yardley has just finished his shift, somewhat belatedly and is on his way home. He had been due to finish a few hours earlier, but reality dictates that criminals do not always oblige him by accommodating his time schedule. He is thirty-five years of age and has been married for over nine years to his part-time teaching assistant wife, Susan. They also have two boys, aged three and five, whom they totally adore. He had been hoping to be home before they fell asleep, but that luxury was denied a few hours ago. On a positive note, at least his overtime pay will go some way towards repaying the hefty mortgage payments they had saddled themselves with a couple of years earlier upon buying their first home together. He had phoned Susan earlier that evening to let her know that he was having to work late. She was disappointed but understood that it went with the territory. By way of consolation, since neither of them was working the following morning, they could have a late dinner. They agreed that she would take a couple of steaks out of the freezer, and they would then put their feet up and watch a film. Susan had also already said to him that morning that she wanted to further discuss the celebration plans for their upcoming tenth wedding anniversary. Adam's only role in this well-intentioned plan was merely to stop off en route home to buy a bottle of red wine.

Andy is now so tense and unnerved that he is in danger of throwing-up. His eyes are affixed on the entrance to the shop trying to will Archie Watson to emerge with his bag of swag. He thinks to himself that perhaps he is not cut out for this criminal life after all.

Perhaps it is because he is so focused on staring at the shop door that he forgets the actual task he has been set. Or perhaps it is due to him being so overcome with nerves. In any event, he neither hears nor sees the car enter the forecourt. Nor does he hear or see the uniformed officer exit his marked police vehicle and walk in the direction of the shop. Although to be fair, having just come off duty and looking forward to a relaxing night, the officer has a noticeable spring in his step and perhaps covers the ground more rapidly than he might otherwise have done.

CHAPTER 32

December 2020

As the years slip by, Paul Alexander's life continues to spiral in a downward direction. He is simply surviving on a day-to-day basis as he uses almost any means possible to feed his addictions to drugs and alcohol. And, of course, to do so, he is continuing to engage in a life of petty crime, which is in turn leading to regular, albeit short, periods of incarceration. Given that he is very often under the influence of one substance or another whenever committing acts of theft, the end result usually tends to be a bungled job. If one were searching for a positive, at least he is making the task of Police Scotland just that little bit easier!

The truth be told, in recent times Paul is not entirely opposed to being apprehended and jailed. At least when inside, he is assured of hot meals and a bed for the night, such luxuries are not always available to him when at liberty.

In order to feed his drug habit, and when in desperate need of ready cash, he has become increasingly dependent upon short-term loans - obviously not of the bank variety. For years, illegal money lending operations have existed in the streets of the poorer parts of Glasgow. They are run by criminal gangs who prey on the weak and the vulnerable, often low-income families and individuals. Loans are readily made available to them at prohibitively high interest rates, and the penalties dished out for non-payment do not tend to be of the financial variety. The funds provided by these "loansharks" are inevitably from unidentified sources. They do not require background checks or credit reports and will often lend relatively large sums of money with a view to securing high levels of interest within a short period of time.

This is a "facility" that Paul has occasionally had to avail himself of when all else has failed. Like his addictions, it started in a very modest way and over a very short period. Initially, for example, he would perhaps borrow only one hundred pounds. He would then repay this with interest the following week upon receipt of his state benefits. Provided this was repaid timeously, the repayment amount inclusive of interest might be one hundred and forty pounds. If there were any delay in repayment, however, then the rate of interest would become exorbitant, and suddenly a small debt would turn into a quite substantial one.

Paul was becoming increasingly reliant upon this method of borrowing, and for a time, it was working satisfactorily in terms of it helping him feed his habit. However as his level of borrowing increased, he was struggling to meet the repayments. It then became a vicious circle for him. Failure to meet these repayments ultimately has violent repercussions, which in turn puts pressure on him to thieve more.

Very recently, Paul fell foul of these "dodgy" lenders on one particular occasion, and he desperately does not wish to repeat the experience. In this instance, he had continually failed to meet a repayment as more and more interest was added. Basically, he kept promising to pay but failed. One day he was suddenly grabbed off the street by two "heavies" and was quite severely beaten. Such an eventuality has a tendency to focus one's mind! Within a week Paul had robbed a local corner shop and repaid all sums due. Once again, he has a clean slate - but for how long?

CHAPTER 33

03 June 2023

When PC Yardley enters the petrol station shop, he is certainly not in police mode, is not armed and has no reason to be on any state of alert. Rather, his thoughts are simply on which bottle of wine he should select for dinner. Accordingly, he is all the more surprised and shocked to see a young man lying face down on the ground and hear an angry, raised voice coming from the direction of the counter. As he stands frozen in the doorway, he witnesses a man in dark clothing, wearing a balaclava and wielding a sawn-off shotgun.

Upon spotting PC Yardley blocking his exit, Archie, in a frenzied state, drops the bag he is carrying and without any warning, fires one single shot into the chest of the officer, who immediately collapses to the floor. Archie Watson then rushes out of the shop, leaping over his victim's body en route. However, to his absolute horror, there is no sign of his getaway driver, Andy, or his car!

Andy, upon eventually spotting the marked police vehicle and the uniformed police officer entering the shop, had frozen on the spot. In a state of complete shock, he panicked and went into flight mode, driving off at top speed. Upon doing so, he heard one single shot and is instantly consumed with dread. He has a mental picture of Archie lying in a pool of blood with bank notes scattered around him.

Shaking like a leaf, he drives at a frantic pace, eager to distance himself as quickly as possible from the scene of the crime. He then remembers the specific instructions he had been given regarding the disposal of the car. So he duly takes the vehicle to a nearby quarry site, throws a can of petrol over it, sets light to it and then disappears swiftly on foot into the darkness, all the time trembling with abject fear. He simply cannot come to terms with what has just happened. Has he been responsible for Archie's death? How did he not notice the police car entering the forecourt? Looking for just a grain of consolation, he comforts himself in the knowledge that Sid Watson will not know that he has bungled the job. His mind is in a state of complete turmoil as he makes his long walk home. For whatever reason, it does not seem to occur to him that the victim might have been the policeman rather than Archie. Had he done so, then he would have had even more reason to be concerned.

One week later, Andy's pickpocketing days are over.

CHAPTER 34

03 June 2023

Susan Yardley has set the table for two, pending her husband's imminent return from work, including tall, thin stemmed crystal glasses for the much-anticipated wine. Her attention to detail extends to replacing the everyday cutlery with steak knives. In addition, she has placed at Adam's side of the table a brochure for the Sheraton Grand Hotel & Spa in Edinburgh as a potential venue for their forthcoming anniversary celebration. In short, she is very much looking forward to their "date night". While she has anticipated that her hubby would have been home by now, she does not risk putting the steaks on yet. She recalls one of the TV chefs saying that the most common error is overcooking. Apparently, it should be a question of simply, 'flashing them in the pan". So, on balance, she decides to hold off until he comes home. She secretly curses the fact there is no wine in the house, as she would have relished a glass while cooking. However, when doing her weekly shop she had wandered past the alcoholic drinks section in a bit of a daze thinking instead about some recent event that had occurred in her school and completely forgot.

She hears the doorbell. Her instinctive feeling is one of relief that Adam is at last home, albeit feeling just a tad irritated that he has forgotten his key. Then, in a flash, she remembers that his car keys and house keys share the same keyring. In any event, complete with flowing apron, she heads for the front door with a welcoming smile to greet her tardy husband, whose uniformed reflection she can see through the frosted glass.

As Susan opens her front door, her jaw almost falls to the floor. The uniformed officer is not, in fact, her husband. In addition, he is accompanied by a policewoman. If the image of these two figures on her doorstep was not enough to give her cause for alarm, their facial expressions most certainly did. Her fears are instantly confirmed by their introductory remarks:

'Mrs Yardley, I am PC Walter Jones, and this is my colleague PC Anita Watters. There has been an incident concerning your husband Adam Yardley, may we please come in?'

Almost subconsciously, Susan ushers them into her sitting room. The officers notice in the background the dining table set up for dinner for two.

'Mrs Yardley, your husband has been an innocent victim of an armed robbery that has gone wrong.' Susan Yardley is immediately totally inconsolable and collapses lifelessly onto the sofa.

'When I say, "an innocent victim", I would explain that he was off duty at the time in question and called into a petrol station. Very sadly, he was simply in the wrong place at the wrong time. I have to tell you that he was shot in the chest and was thereafter immediately conveyed to the Royal Infirmary, where he is currently being treated in their intensive care department.'

Everything else said by either of the officers was pretty much of a blur as one thought ran through her brain time after time, like a lengthy train with every carriage bearing the words in bold letters:

Why did I forget to buy the wine?

As if in a trance, Susan Yardley half-listens to the police instructions as she makes sure everything in the kitchen is turned off and then picks up her house keys. She does, however, take heed of the fact that PC Watters will pop upstairs to check on their kids (aged three and five) and will remain in the house until she returns from the hospital. However, she does insist on seeing them before leaving. She is on automatic pilot as she kisses each of them on the cheek. She thinks to herself that they appear even more cherub-like than usual. Susan wonders if either of these little darlings will ever set eyes on their beloved dad again. This thought produces yet another avalanche of tears as she hurriedly makes her way back downstairs to accompany PC Jones to the hospital.

CHAPTER 35

June 2023

The nearby woods provide welcome cover for Archie as he makes his escape on foot, his adrenaline levels reaching an all-time high. He is grateful for the torch facility on his mobile. One of his obvious priorities is to conceal the shotgun. He eventually chooses an area of clearing which fits the bill. In an almost canine-like style, he bends over, and with his large hands shovels the loose earth backwards between his legs. He then covers the area with vegetation before making a mental note of the spot for future reference. His intention is to return to recover the firearm at a future date once the heat is off.

Fortunately, when he was young, he had a school friend who lived nearby, and when invited to sleepovers, they would play together in these woods. As a result, he is fairly well acquainted with the paths and lanes in the area.

He is breathing very heavily but making good progress when he is alerted to the sound of police sirens in the background. At the moment all his thoughts and efforts relate to getting as far away from the petrol station as possible. After a little while he is forced to rest for a moment. Bending over, hands on knees, he attempts to recapture his breath. At that very moment, the stark reality that he may have actually killed a cop sinks in and a cold shiver engulfs his fatigued and bone-weary frame.

He eventually reaches a road where he manages to hail a taxi. Something deep inside his brain is telling him that going home is not the best plan and so he decides to go to his parents' house.

His parents are immediately aware that all is not well as they open the door to their beleaguered, dirty, and obviously very agitated eldest son. Sid immediately asks Nancy to put on the kettle. This is his less-than-subtle way of telling her that he needs a quiet word with his son. Nancy takes her cue, all too aware that their lavish lifestyle has been financed by "dodgy dealings" and that it is not always plain sailing. Wherever possible, he prefers to spare her the specifics, and that is absolutely fine by her. And so he ushers Archie into their sitting room where he listens with grave concern about the events of the evening.

Having been fully updated, Sid tells Archie to immediately take off all his clothes and burn them. Like his son, he is livid about the cowardly behaviour of Andy and promises that there will be consequences. However, in the first instance, the priority is to check with him that the stolen car has been destroyed as directed. He quickly phones his son, Billy, to seek reassurance on this front.

Billy immediately goes around to Andy's house only to find a quivering wreck of a man. It has not been explained to Billy that Andy had taken fright and abandoned his brother Archie at the petrol station, thereby endangering his life. At this point in time, Sid has considered this to be on a purely need-to-know basis. When it has become clear that it is the policeman who has been shot, and not Archie, Andy's legs buckle at the knees. He is one pathetic soul, crying pitifully at the feet of Billy, who does not at this time quite appreciate the reason for such dramatic and subservient behaviour. Billy's sole task is to ensure that the stolen vehicle will not in any way incriminate the Watson family, and he eventually leaves Andy's house satisfied that this is so.

ONE SAD DAY

Two days later, two balaclava-wearing men abduct Andy from near his house and throw him into the back of their transit van. They then drive off to a remote part of the countryside - specifically chosen to ensure that nobody will be able to hear Andy's blood-curdling screams. One attacker, almost double the weight of Andy, restrains him while the other slowly and systematically fractures all ten of his fingers, one by one, with a pair of pliers.

He is then bundled out onto the side of the street, a bloody mess. This has not only been an act of retribution, but also a silent and deadly warning to others not to dare double-cross any member of the Watson family.

CHAPTER 36

June 2023

The police investigation into the shooting at the petrol station is now in full flow. The premises have been closed for business and declared a crime scene. Several police cars are in evidence, and the area is a hive of activity with uniform police, plain-clothed officers, dog handlers with their trusted canines and white-coated forensic specialists scouring every square inch for evidence. It has become clear very early on to the forensic team that the perpetrator was wearing gloves, and this is borne out by the staff on duty.

Police officers Hardy and Khan have been charged with interviewing Marjorie Simpson and Gary Conway, the two employees at the petrol station. They decide to interview them separately.

Marjorie is to be first. It is fair to say that she is a quivering wreck of a woman following her ordeal. She is a spinster and lives a relatively quiet life on her own with just one tiny Yorkshire Terrier (Ted) for company. Her primary purpose in taking the job four years earlier was to get out of the house in order to socialise and meet new people. The remuneration element was most probably secondary. In the time she had worked there, she had become very popular with the patrons, always greeting them with a warm, inviting and very genuine smile. Much as she would like to help the officers with their enquiries, she was so paralysed with fear that it was all pretty much a blur to her.

'Just take your time, Marjorie, and try to tell us everything that you can recall about the robbery.' Said

Officer Khan, having just provided her with a cup of tea in an attempt to calm her nerves.

'Firstly, what time of day did the robbery take place?'

'About 10.30pm.' Marjorie responded, clutching a hanky so tightly in one hand as if she were trying to rinse it out.

'And what were you and Gary doing at the time?'

'I was standing behind the counter, ready to serve any remaining customers before closing up. Gary was out in the shop area filling up shelves.'

'And then tell me exactly what happened, in as much depth as possible, as sometimes the smallest detail can prove to be very significant.'

'I'll try, officer, but it all happened so quickly, and I was absolutely terrified. I've never had a gun pointed at me before.'

'We totally understand,' says Officer Hardy, trying to put her at ease.

'All of a sudden, a man came rushing into the shop brandishing a shotgun, and he was shouting and swearing. He told me to open the safe, and I was so scared I would have done anything that he told me to.'

'You absolutely did the right thing,' responded Officer Khan, trying to provide some reassurance.

'And what about this man's accent?'

'Just normal,' replied Marjorie.

'When you say normal, what exactly do you mean?'

'Well, Scottish, Glaswegian, I suppose - and not posh, a bit rough-spoken.'

'And what did he look like?'

'I don't know, he was wearing a balaclava.'

'Yes, but what kind of height would he be?'

'Quite tall, about your height,' she said.

'Ok, so about six foot then.'

'And what kind of build was he fat, thin, toned, flabby?'

'He was not fat. He was quite well built and looked reasonably fit.'

'And what about his clothes?'

'All I can remember was that he was wearing very dark clothes, probably black, and yes, I think black jeans.'

'And what about gloves?'

'Yes, he was definitely wearing gloves. I think they were also black.'

'Now, Marjorie,' said Officer Hardy, 'I would like you to think quite hard about this and imagine him holding the shotgun. Was your assailant right-handed or left-handed?'

Marjorie took a few moments before responding, obviously trying to envisage the situation.'

'Left-handed'

'Are you sure?'

'Yes, I think so.'

'And was he on his own, or was he accompanied?'

'He was on his own.'

The officers both thank Marjorie for her time. They then give her a card inviting her to call should she remember anything else regarding the robbery, no matter how trivial. A police car is then organised to give her a lift home. She has already assured them that she would be absolutely fine staying on her own. When pressed on this, she assures them that should she feel in the need of any company, or just someone to talk to, her next-door neighbour is extremely supportive, thoughtful and kind.

The officers then arrange to interview young Gary Conway, hopeful that his levels of observation might well be greater than his co-employee. They are to be sadly disappointed as they discover that throughout the course of the ordeal, he was lying face down on the floor. Accordingly, his statement does not provide much additional information apart from one small point. From his situation, lying on the floor throughout the attempted robbery, he observed that the perpetrator was wearing a pair of black Doc Marten lace-up boots. He is very confident and assured about this as he also owns a similar pair, which he had treated himself to with some recent birthday cash from his parents. When questioned further if his assailant had small or large feet, he suggested about a size 10, which is probably pretty standard for a man of that height. Officers Hardy and Khan then conclude the interview feeling that it has perhaps not been entirely in vain.

Summarising what they had heard, they were looking for a left-handed man from the Glasgow area, who is approximately six feet tall, has a sturdy build, is fairly broadly spoken and wears Doc Marten boots. The needle in the proverbial haystack comes to mind!

CHAPTER 37

15 February 2023
(SAD Day)

It is fifteen years to the very day that Matt had first encountered Ava, Cleo and Darren, although Matt is quite oblivious to this fact. A great deal has changed in the lives of Matt and Liz Goldstein in the intervening years, the most recent being the sad passing of Liz's mum in 2022. However, it had been considered to be a blessing in disguise as her quality of life towards the end was virtually non-existent. Latterly, she was unable to even recognise her own daughter, and Liz found this to be extremely distressing.

In addition, that same year Matt's dad, Adam, eventually succumbed to cancer, which by this time had spread to most of his vital organs. His wife Sarah was by his side and was acting nurse, companion and beloved spouse. Stubborn to the very end, he downright refused to go to the local hospice, insisting that he wanted to die at home. This placed a massive and quite unfair burden on Sarah. Matt did visit, but not with any great regularity. This caused his mum a fair degree of hurt, especially since he was their only child. However, he was present the day he actually passed away, having temporarily relieved his mum at his bedside. Although by this stage heavily sedated with morphine, he was still able to have a conversation with his son, however laboured. In fact, his clarity of thought was truly remarkable and took Matt somewhat by surprise:

'Hello, son, thanks for coming to visit.'

'No problem, Dad.'

'I know I don't have long to go now, and I wanted to say something to you.' He was so very weak and frail and had to rest for quite a few seconds to recover sufficient breath or strength to continue.

'Our relationship has not been great since what happened in 2008, and it so saddens me to say this. In fact, it seems to have deteriorated with every year that has passed. I just want to say that what your mum and I did was out of love for you and that if we had the whole situation all over again, we would behave in the same way. I am sorry if you think any less of me or your mum. But now as a parent yourself, I can only hope that you can maybe see our point of view. Would you resign Daisy to a potential prison sentence on a point of principle?'

At this point, his bony, heavily veined hand reached out, and Matt took it, with tears in his eyes. He was now really struggling to speak, and as Matt leaned in more closely, his dad murmured his very last words:

'Please forgive me, son.'

Matt's dedication to his work is such that he very regularly works weekends. To be fair, his excessive workload demands it, and furthermore, it is actually expected of him at his level of seniority. However, this weekend is different as Liz has made him promise that he will spend it with her and Daisy, who is now in her sixth year. Matt and Liz would have loved to have had a little brother or sister for Daisy, but Mother Nature seems to be dictating otherwise. It transpires that in this respect, they may be in the same position as Matt's parents - a one-child family. Each of them is probably more disappointed about this than they would openly admit to the other, but they are both so eternally grateful for the beautiful gift they have been given - Daisy.

Yes, she has proved to be a dream of a daughter, extremely open, friendly and ever-smiling. She is one of those children who seems to bring light into the lives of anyone with whom she comes into contact. This morning she is in a particularly good mood, for a couple of reasons. Firstly, yesterday afternoon, when opening her school desk, she discovered no less than three hand-made valentines from boys in her class. Although none of them had actually written their name, it was very obvious to her by the writing as to who her 'secret' admirers actually were. Upon receiving them, the thought ran through her head that her mum had always said that at Daisy's age, girls were more intellectually advanced than boys, and perhaps this is borne out by their feeble attempt at anonymity. This was swiftly followed by a second thought. Perhaps Mum is wrong and is only trying to humour me. Maybe the boys are cleverer than my Mum is giving them credit for by pretending that they wish to remain anonymous. What if the reality of the situation is that they secretly do wish to be identified as being an admirer? Either way, she is very flattered. Yes, for her age, Daisy does have a creative little mind.

She has another reason to be happy this fine Saturday morning. For her recent birthday, Daisy was promised that she could have a canine friend. After much discussion and studying of books on the various breeds of dogs, they decide upon a Golden Retriever. It is determined that this breed ticks all the boxes, being biddable, intelligent, easily trained and good with children. The fact that they have the most adorable, dreamy eyes eventually tips the balance. The only negative is that they shed a lot of hairs about the house. However, whenever this is mentioned, Daisy conveniently changes the subject. This young lady is also smart beyond her years. In any event, the decision has been made, and today is the day they are heading down the Ayrshire Coast to visit a breeder who has an available litter for sale.

En route, they visit a pet store and purchase the essentials, such as a bed, collar, lead and some doggy toys. In respect of the collar and lead, they have chosen a neutral colour as they are yet undecided whether to opt for a boy or a girl. And rather conveniently, Daisy, who had asked to be able to name their pooch, had gone for the name "Goldie", which in itself is fairly unisex. When her parents asked how she had decided upon this name, which they considered to be more apt for a goldfish, she replied.

'Well, our surname is Goldstein, and our pup is a Golden Retriever.' Matt and Liz saw no reason to argue with their child's logic.

A few hours later, the very excited Goldstein family were in the car, heading back up the road. Driving is Matt, while Liz and Daisy are in the back seat taking turns at cuddling Goldie, a gorgeous, little, creamy-golden bundle of cuteness. They finally decided to choose whichever pup showed the most interest in them irrespective of their sex. When they got down on the floor to play with them, Goldie was the very first out of the traps as he waddled towards them demanding a tummy rub. Goldie was a little boy, and the Goldstein family were already completely smitten.

Soon, they are almost home, absolutely enthralled with their new family member. Matt and Liz have a great feeling of inner warmth in seeing their daughter so happy and content. Liz is particularly pleased that Matt has actually agreed to take a weekend off work, and they are able to enjoy some rare, quality time together.

All in all, everything is good for the Goldstein family. That is until they open the door of their family home, and Matt's very worst nightmare comes to light exactly fifteen years to the very day since his life last fell apart.

CHAPTER 38

June 2023

A meeting of the Major Investigation Team (MIT) has been urgently called by Detective Chief Inspector Karen Orr to discuss progress in relation to the attempted armed robbery.

'Right, let's get down to business,' said DCI Orr, setting the scene and clearly indicating a no-nonsense approach to proceedings.

'Ok, we are going to start by looking at the facts and evidence we have thus far, identifying what questions they raise and then setting out some clear action points for us to take away.'

'As we know, the attempted robbery took place at approximately 10:30pm on the evening of Sunday 03 June. I believe this to be significant. It is probably no coincidence that I have confirmation from the owners of the petrol station that the cash for the week is uplifted on a Monday morning. And so it seems very convenient that the offence happened just before closing time the evening before. Accordingly, this raises a fairly obvious question. Was it an inside job?'

'As we know, the robbery was unsuccessful in that no money was actually taken. The female member of staff was in the process of filling a bag with cash when PC Yardley entered the shop and was tragically shot. There is every likelihood that the assailant had not intended violence, the sawn-off shotgun being intended simply to intimidate staff. He also brought with him a bag to carry the cash. This was later recovered at the scene of the crime. It is a standard issue strong, cloth, reusable, supermarket bag, with very distinctive Aldi branding.'

'It seems pretty certain that he left the scene of the crime on foot. Assuming this to be so, the question remains as to how he actually got there. It also raises a second question as to whether he was working alone or in concert. If the latter, did he abandon a vehicle nearby, or was he driven there? We need answers to these questions.'

'From the information we have to hand, it appears that the perpetrator of this crime is white, aged probably in his thirties, about six foot tall and of good build. He was wearing dark clothes, we think a hoodie and jeans. He was also wearing a black balaclava. We also have good reason to believe that he hails from Glasgow, or at least the West of Scotland. Oh yes, and he is left-handed, wore gloves and owns a pair of Doc Marten boots!'

'That is a brief summary of where we are at. Let's now try to secure answers to all these questions. DC Smyth will identify the tasks which need to be carried out urgently and asks that you apportion them amongst your team:

'Firstly, please have a very detailed look at CCTV cameras in the petrol station. I understand they are not state-of-the-art, but perhaps it might give us a clue as to whether there was also an accomplice.

'Secondly, I would like you to secure a list of all employees of the petrol station, past and present, and then do background checks on them. In particular, check if any of them have any criminal records.

'Finally, and again, we are perhaps clutching at straws, but I would like a list of the addresses of all Aldi stores within the Glasgow area.

Thank you all for your attention. Now, let's do this for Susan Yardley. Let's get out there and catch this bloody guy who shot one of our colleagues in cold blood. We will have a catch-up meeting in a couple of days, when there will hopefully be some meaningful progress to report.'

CHAPTER 39

15 February 2023
(SAD Day)

There is a real buzz of excitement as Matt, Liz and Daisy Goldstein open the door to their house, very keen to show their eight-week-old puppy his new, forever home. It is one of those days that should happily linger in one's memory bank for years to come. It is certainly a day that Matt will never forget, but for quite different reasons.

They hurriedly remove their coats before choosing an appropriate place in the kitchen for Goldie. They then introduce him to his lovely, new, thick, warm doggy bed, his own little sanctuary for years to come. It is so gratifying for Daisy's parents to witness the pleasure that this little pooch is already bringing to their daughter's life. It is also extremely reassuring for them to know that as a single child, she will have this devoted companion by her side during her formative years.

Both Daisy and her Mum are on the floor rolling a tennis ball back and forth between them with Goldie in hasty pursuit - when it happens, the bottom falls out of their lives. Matt lets out a loud shriek and runs to the toilet, where Liz can hear the sound of violent retching. He had been absolutely fine a few moments earlier whilst opening the mail, and they were playing with their new arrival. She knows instantly that something is desperately wrong, and rushes into the bathroom after him. When Matt is no longer capable of being physically sick, having emptied the contents of his stomach, he washes his face in cold water as Liz looks on, concern etched on her face.

'Jesus Christ, shit, I can't bloody believe it! I don't know what to do. I just feel so sick.'

The colour has completely drained from his face and Liz knows immediately that there is something dreadfully wrong. What could possibly be so bad as to affect him in this way?

Liz asks Daisy to leave Goldie in his bed as he will be exhausted and tells her to go to play in her room while she chats to her Daddy. Daisy is not too happy about leaving Goldie behind but can tell from her mother's stern tone that she means business, so does what she is told. Liz then ushers her quivering wreck of a husband into the lounge in fear and trepidation of what he is about to tell her.

Matt is sitting on their lounge sofa, his head cradled in his hands. Liz sits down next to him, her arm around him. Eventually, Matt takes a handkerchief to wipe his tear-stained face, then mumbles something inaudible before removing from his pocket a letter which he slowly passes to her. The envelope itself has a Glasgow postmark and is addressed to Matt Goldstein and is hand-written in fairly large, random capital letters, almost as if written by a child. Nervously and very tentatively, she slowly opens the envelope almost as if in fear that something might jump out at her. Inside is a sheet of standard white A4 paper containing a letter of sorts - one made up of individual letters cut out from a newspaper, all of varying fonts, styles and sizes - the type one would only normally see in a TV crime drama. Liz is also now feeling physically sick as she begins to read its contents.

Hi MaTt

*I KnOw wHat **You** Did oN 15 FebRuaRY 20o8*
yOu thOughT yoU'd goT awAy WitH iT - BuT yOu hAven'T!
I knOw tHaT yOu kILLed a MaN.
iF i TeLL ThE pOlicE YOur caREer iS finIsheD, anD yoU
wiLL gO to PRIsOn FOr a verY lOng TImE.
i wIll Be iN tOuCH verY sOOn.

The Observer

Now Liz is the one who needs to be consoled as the tears flood down her cheeks, taking refuge in her lap. Her mind is like a tumble dryer with a multiplicity of terrible thoughts jostling for position.

How can this possibly be?

Who is the victim?

Who sent the letter?

Is this really happening?

My lovely husband, a murderer?

'There's something I've never told you.' He begins. 'It was before I knew you, and I was very young and immature. When I met you and fell in love with you so quickly, I was scared to tell you for fear of losing you forever.'

'Who was it, and how did it happen?' Asks Liz, now speaking quite abruptly.

Matt then speaks at some length about his night out all those years ago. He talks of being very young and immature, of having been drinking, of not intending to drive, of a drunk suddenly wandering out in front of his vehicle, of not being able to avoid hitting him and of panicking and driving off.

He adds that as far as he is concerned, the police have not made any headway in their investigations, nor are they aware of his presence at the scene of the accident. (Perhaps understandably, Matt has massaged the truth a little when relaying his account of events, although in fairness, he was not to know that the victim was not, in fact, under the influence of drink at the time of the accident.)

Liz listens attentively to every word that has dropped from her husband's lips, choosing to allow him to finish without interruption.

'Oh holy fuck!' said Liz, who never normally swears. She is then deep in thought for a while before she continues by addressing the elephant in the room.

'Think very carefully and tell me the names of absolutely everyone who was aware of your involvement that evening.'

'Ava, Cleo, Darren who were in the car with me, and of course, my Mum and my Dad.'

'Are you sure that is all?'

'Yes, that is all, assuming, of course, that none of these people have leaked the information to anyone else, but we all made a pledge to say that we would take the events of that evening to our grave.'

Liz looked at Matt somewhat sceptically before responding:

'Well, it is a pretty safe assumption that you're Mum or Dad did not tell anyone.'

'One hundred per cent,' replies Matt.

'And how well did you know the passengers in your car?'

'I only met them for the very first time that evening and I have not seen them or indeed spoken to them since.'

Liz frowned upon hearing this response, before continuing.

'Ok then, can I also take it as definite that you have not let it slip to anyone, perhaps even after a few drinks?'

'I honestly don't think so, except for my parents, and now of course, you. I have been trying for years to obliterate it from my mind, the last thing I have ever wanted to do was resurrect thoughts of that bloody evening.'

Somewhat strangely, Matt is actually now taking some tiny crumbs of comfort from the fact that his wife is starting to take part-ownership of the situation, and approaching it in a methodical and logistical manner.

'Well,' she continues, 'the hard facts of the matter as I see it are that you are being blackmailed by either Ava, Cleo or Darren, or somebody one of them has blabbed to. The only other possibility is that, perhaps after a few drinks, you have let it all out to some third party who is now trying to capitalise on your situation.'

Just then they hear a high-pitched whining from the kitchen. Given the way matters have unfolded they had both completely forgotten about their new canine family member. Liz goes to lift him up to comfort him and is greeted with a puddle at the door - just what she needs at this moment in time! Matt is slightly relieved that the spotlight has been removed from him, even if only momentarily.

CHAPTER 40

June 2023

There is still a heavy presence of police officers within the vicinity of the petrol station as they actively hunt for clues. One particularly diligent police sniffer dog, a spaniel that goes by the well-earned name of "Snout", has followed a trail that leads into the nearby woods. She then becomes particularly agitated and excitable at a spot where the ground appears to have been recently disturbed. Snout's handler, PC John Stanton, does not have to dig too deep before being rewarded - a sawn-off shotgun is discovered, buried about a foot and a half below the surface. Snout is also duly rewarded for her diligence and is the very enthusiastic recipient of some tasty chicken morsels. Her tail wags so appreciatively that it looks in severe danger of becoming detached from its torso.

Needless to say that the discovery of this weapon is a major breakthrough. However, there has been other significant progress. As is customary, the police had made a public appeal for assistance in the case. They received quite a number of responses, but almost all were completely fruitless. Some were from the usual suspects, simply craving the limelight, others were simply from well-known nutcases. However, one call from the owner of a Hackney taxi cab, a certain John Barber, most certainly piqued their interest.

Barber tells of having picked up a man on the night in question at a point not far from the petrol station. The location was very close to an exit from local woods, but at the opposite side of the woods from the crime scene. John

Barber felt there were sufficient unusual, if not suspicious, aspects to this taxi fare, which gave rise to him reporting the matter to the police. Firstly, the location of the pick-up. It was a very quiet street, with no residences in the immediate vicinity. Secondly, when the man entered his vehicle, he noticed that his clothes were very dirty. Finally, the man was severely out of breath, as if he had been running, so much so, he struggled to give the driver directions. Barber added that not only was he breathless, but he also appeared extremely agitated.

This evidence from John Barber was of great interest to the police as all things pointed towards his passenger being the assailant. At least it was a line of enquiry well worth pursuing. John Barber was also able to advise them as to the location of the drop-off point, which was at the junction of Greenland Road and Maitland Road. Apparently, apart from stating where he wanted to be dropped off, the passenger did not speak at all during the fifteen to twenty-minute taxi journey. Also, and sadly from a police perspective, he settled the taxi fare in cash, as opposed to a card.

The not-so-good news is that John Barber felt he would be unable to identify this passenger because throughout the relatively short journey, he had kept his hood up and his face down, most probably so that he could not be recognised. The best he could do was state that he was white, reasonably tall, well-built and dressed in all black, or at least very dark clothes. Also, from the few words he did utter, when advising of his destination, he was definitely a local lad.

On a positive note, it transpires that the area where the sawn-off shotgun had been located in the woods was about halfway between the petrol station and the point of the taxi pick-up. Another piece of the jigsaw appears to fit into place.

CHAPTER 41

February 2023

A cloak of darkness has descended over the Goldstein family. Only the merest glimmer of light is allowed in when either Daisy or Goldie is in the immediate vicinity. From Matt's perspective, Liz has not reacted quite as explosively to the incident of February 2008 as he might have feared. Rather, she is quite pragmatic about it, almost accepting that he was so much younger then, and now he is almost like a different person. She is also truly astonished that his parents had reacted in the way that they did. Liz is a very sensible, matter-of-fact type of person. In her world, everything tends to be black and white, with no room for grey areas.

'OK,' said Liz. 'We have to look at the facts of this situation and face this problem head-on. Whatever it takes, there is no way we are having you going to prison and having Daisy denied her dad for years. One thing we do know is that the blackmailer will be back in touch with us, and probably very soon. Let's not sit back and wait for that to happen when we can try to do something positive.'

Matt hangs on to her every word, hoping that they can impact the situation positively and feels just a smidgen better now that he has shared his burden, and they are looking to try to address the situation.

'Matt, first of all, we need to do some background work to find the whereabouts of the three passengers in your car. This might not be straightforward, given that we are talking about some fifteen years ago. Any of them could have moved overseas, but if that is the case, then they can almost definitely be written off as a suspect. Then we need to try to eliminate them, one by one. Let's start with your partner for the evening, I think you said her name was Ava? Don't suppose you would have any idea of her second name?

'Sorry, no idea. She owned her own estate agency business in the centre of Glasgow, although I have no idea of the name of it.'

Liz is now on a mission and instantly enters "Glasgow Estate Agents" in Google and obtains a full listing before accessing the "about us" section on the website of each one in turn. She is just about through the list and beginning to lose faith when the name 'Ava' pops up as the owner of "Select Estate Agents" in Glasgow city centre. Bingo! She says enthusiastically, almost giving the impression that she is relishing the task at hand. She shows a photo of her to Matt and despite the lengthy passage of time, he recognises her. Her distinctive large olive-green eyes are unmistakable.

Matt decides not to contact Ava by phone. He fears she might not want to speak to him and have to relive thoughts of that harrowing night. Rather, he elects to simply call into her place of work, completely unannounced. Asking for her at the reception, he simply gives his first name, saying it is a personal matter, hoping this might be enough to spike her curiosity. This approach proves successful as within a couple of minutes she enters the waiting room. Very obviously not recognising him, she invites him into her office. When he identifies himself, she is visibly shaken. It is abundantly clear that she would never have ushered him in had she known who he was. After all, why would she wish to dredge up such truly horrid memories? But now she is cornered.

They first of all exchange a few pleasantries, during which he discovers that Ava has been happily married for a number of years and has three young children, all of whom feature in individual photo frames on her office desk. Right away, it seems perfectly clear to Matt that she is not the guilty party. This is even before he tells her about the blackmail letter and the reason for his visit. She is visibly shocked and unless she is an actress extraordinaire, knows absolutely nothing about the letter. He is just about to thank her for her time and leave when he casually asks:

'Did you, by chance, mention to anyone else about the events of that evening?' As she goes into think mode, it becomes instantly clear to Matt that she has forgotten completely about their pledge of silence, which admittedly means far more to him than her. He cannot help but feel a shade disappointed.

She then responds, 'I started going out with someone very soon afterwards for two or three months. Because it was obviously very fresh in my mind at the time, and pretty major, I possibly told him. I cannot be absolutely sure.'

'Do you know if you mentioned my name?'

'I honestly cannot remember.'

'Would you happen to have his details?'

'God no! I have not seen him since. It transpired that he was involved in the drugs scene in Glasgow, and so I decided to cut loose. I think his name was Dave, and he lived in the south side of the city, but beyond that I don't know anything else. Also, a few years ago, my mobile phone was stolen and so I would not even have his number now. Sorry, I know that this is not much help.'

At that, Matt asked her not to mention his visit or their conversation to anyone else - she heartily agreed. He thanked her and then left with a view to return home to report back to Liz.

'And what do you remember about the guy Darren?' Asked Liz.

'Virtually nothing. Again, I don't know his surname. I recall he was a few years older than me, and I think he was in sales of some description. Sorry, Liz, but it was so, so long ago and we had all been drinking.'

'Well, how about Cleo? If we can locate her and she was with Darren, maybe they continued to go out together, or if not, perhaps she can recall something about him that would enable us to trace him.'

'Cleo was Caribbean or Afro-American, or at least of that origin. I specifically recall that she worked in what is now the Victoria Hospital, but not in a nursing capacity. It is highly unlikely that she is still there, but at least it might serve as a good starting point.' Liz responds:

'I have a good friend who works in the personnel department of the Royal Infirmary,' said Liz.

'Given that both hospitals are managed by the same umbrella organisation, NHS Greater Glasgow and Clyde, I might just be able to ask her a little favour.'

A couple of days later, Liz receives a return telephone call from her friend within the Royal Infirmary and her investigative efforts had proved fruitful. She is keen to share the content of the call with Matt.

'Matt, the bad news is that Cleo left employment within the hospital service some three years ago. However, the better news is that my friend has checked into her records and has confirmed to me, strictly unofficially of course, that she had apparently been offered a position as the manager of an osteopath practice in Glasgow. She is not at liberty to divulge any more specifics, but there are not that many osteopaths in the Glasgow area large enough to have a dedicated manager. A little more detective work is required!'

Matt once again feels very fortunate to know that he has Liz in his corner.

CHAPTER 42

June 2023

Having allocated her team various tasks, DCI Orr organises a catch-up meeting to ascertain what progress has been achieved. She specifically invites DC Alan Smyth to bring her and her team up to speed.

'Well Ma'am, we have had two very recent and fairly major breakthroughs, as I believe you are now aware. The first of these relates to the taxi driver, John Barber, who came forward in response to our request to the general public. It would appear almost certain that he picked our man up after the attempted robbery and we now know where he was dropped off.

Secondly, thanks to the sterling efforts of one of our police dogs, we have managed to recover what we now believe to be the weapon used, a sawn-off shotgun found buried in the woods not far from the crime scene.'

'Excellent work,' said his boss enthusiastically.' DC Smyth continued:

'Following on from these discoveries, we are now checking for any CCTV coverage for the area where the taxi passenger was dropped off to try to determine where he was heading. Also, the shotgun has just been passed to forensics, and we've asked them to report back ASAP.'

DC Smyth then addresses the tasks that were set at their last meeting:

'We have been looking very closely at the CCTV coverage of the petrol station. I am afraid it has not been very helpful. However, there is some evidence of one other vehicle in the forecourt at the time PC Yardley drove in, which appears to have left about the time of the shooting. However, it is located at the very edge of a blind spot on the camera, so for the most part is obscured. This could be a coincidence, or perhaps, and much more likely, is yet a further indication that it was an inside job. We certainly have no number plate recognition, but whatever little footage we do have I have passed to our forensic team in the hope that they might be able to come up with something.'

'As requested, we have carried out detailed security checks on all employees of the petrol station, past and present, but so far, we have had no success. It is clear that the owners of the establishment have very rigorous HR procedures in place that encompass carrying out criminal record checks on all potential employees. What we can say at this stage is that we have totally dismissed the possibility that the two employees on duty on the night of the offence were involved - they are both squeaky clean. We are, however, continuing our enquiries into past employees.'

'As you asked, Ma'am, we also looked at the location of Aldi Stores in the Glasgow area, but I honestly feel this line of enquiry is not worth pursuing further. To be honest, anyone living in the Glasgow area is within reasonably short driving distance of an Aldi Store. Also, it was impossible to secure any fingerprint evidence from the bag. To be fair, I think we should park this line of enquiry in the meantime. I suppose it was too much to hope for that there might be a discarded credit card slip lying in the bottom corner of the bag!'

The meeting concludes on this slightly lighter point. DCI Orr thanks them once again for their ongoing efforts and commitment.

CHAPTER 43

June 2023

A couple of weeks have now passed since the robbery. DCI Karen Orr receives a phone call from the police constable stationed outside the private ward where PC Yardley is being treated. When the call comes through, she is rather hoping that it is to announce that he has regained consciousness and will be able to provide a statement. Sadly, the message is not to this effect.

'DCI Orr, it is PC Paul Evans calling from the Royal Infirmary. I feel I should inform you that PC Yardley's health has taken a severe turn for the worse, and the attending doctor has said that there is now very real cause for concern. His wife is currently by his bedside with their two children, and not surprisingly, she is in a state of great distress.'

DCI Orr thanked for the update, concluded the call and ordered a car to take her immediately to the hospital. She arrives there some thirty minutes later, but sadly, five minutes too late. She is met by a very distressing scene that will live long in her memory. Susan Yardley is draped over the body of her now-dead husband, wailing and screaming with uncontrollable anguish. One nurse is trying in vain to console her, while a second nurse ushers her two children out of the ward to a nearby waiting room, their angelic little faces smudged from recently wiped tears. DCI Orr immediately conveys her sincere apologies to Susan Yardley, who stares back at her with hollow eyes in total bewilderment, obviously not absorbing a single word that is being said.

DCI Orr has encountered this type of situation on numerous occasions throughout her career. She thinks to herself that it never gets any easier. She feels personally engulfed in a veil of sadness, but at the same time is striving to appear stoic and resolute. She feels so much compassion for Susan Yardley, whose grief is a nakedness laid out for all to see. In this case, it is even worse as it is one of her own, a fellow officer, who has passed away. The futility of this particular loss of life in this case is almost unthinkable. A young man on his way home from work just happens to be in the wrong place at the wrong time - a simple, but very cruel twist of fate. As a result, his young wife is now a widow, left having to bring up their two very young children on her own - so very tragic.

Only one month earlier, DCI Karen Orr had lost her own father in this very same hospital after a long battle with cancer. Inevitably, memories of this add further to her feelings of desolation. Yes, she is a policewoman, and yes, she is of course expected to cope in such situations, but first and foremost, she is a human being with very real feelings and emotions like everyone else. She pulls herself together and then, under her breath, but in a very determined voice, she utters a shrill warning to the killer:

'You absolute bastard! Whoever you are and wherever you are, I am going to hunt you down like a dog. I won't rest until you're put away for this.'

Her resolve has not improved her mood, but has certainly heightened her determination to progress the case. Upon returning to the police station she is met with some very encouraging news.

'There is a God!' She thinks to herself as she is brought up to speed by her subordinate:

'Ma'am, I've just heard back from forensics, and they have managed to find some fingerprints on the shotgun, in fact two sets. We already have a match for one set, and they are identified as belonging to one of the notorious Watson family, more specifically, Archie Watson. DCI Orr is so absolutely over the moon that she involuntarily responds. 'DC Smyth, I could kiss you!'

One of her worst-ever days has just taken a very dramatic turn for the better. Her mind is now working overtime. She recalls the statement provided by the taxi driver, John Barber. The Watson family are well known to the Glasgow Police, indeed as is their arch enemy, the B family. She has a mental picture of Archie Watson, tall, probably about six feet and with a good physique. She then asks PC Smyth to check out where Archie Watson lives.

Some fifteen minutes later, he returns, but her hopes are temporarily dashed as he provides her with his address, which is not close to where John Barber dropped off his passenger on the night in question, namely Lenzie. She then asks him to check out the addresses of the other Watson family members. A short time later, she spots DC Smyth approaching, and notices his beaming face, she is instantly aware that they have struck gold. It transpires that Sid Watson, the so-called "godfather" and the father of Archie lives with his wife in Maitland Drive in Lenzie, just around the corner from where the taxi was asked to stop. Result!

As in any murder case, a Major Investigation Team (MIT) had been set up to lead the investigation. Their first priority is to organise a warrant for the arrest of Archie Watson in addition to warrants to search the houses of both Sid and Archie Watson.

CHAPTER 44

February 2023

Matt and Liz continue their detective work by checking up on local osteopaths, both online and also occasionally by calling them and asking to speak to Cleo. They consider themselves fortunate that it is not a common name. Eventually, they are successful and manage to locate her. They barely have the opportunity to enjoy this small win when the inevitable happens. It is what they both have been secretly dreading. Another letter has dropped through their mailbox and they both recognise the almost childlike writing of the envelope. Instantly, they are paralysed with fear, terrified of reading its contents, but knowing that they have no option. They simply cannot ignore it. Almost ceremoniously, Liz takes a knife and slices open the envelope, very slowly extracting the all too familiar-looking, white A4 sheet of paper with a note constructed of letters extracted from newspapers.

> Hi aGaIn MatT
> I GUeSS You KnEw yOu woUld Be hEAriNG fRoM mE aGaiN.
> YOuR siNs will alwaYS CAtcH Up wItH yOu!
> i wiLL bE baCK in tOucH sHORtlY - bE rEady.
> ## The Observer

Matt and Liz are stunned into silence. How had they deluded themselves into thinking for one second that they would not hear again from "The Observer".

'Who is this evil, vindictive, despicable person?' asks Matt. 'Why is he or she not saying what they actually want?'

'Whoever it is, they appear as if they are revelling in their role.' Responds Liz.

Once again, they decide to be proactive rather than sit back and await the arrival of the next dreaded letter. As he had done with Ava, he now decides to pay Cleo a visit. Once again, he is not recognised, and she appears totally shocked when he identifies himself. Weirdly, it is almost as if she has never ever given a thought to the events of 15 February 2008. The reality is that immediately after that fateful night, she disbanded "The Calendar Girls" and no longer attaches significance to any particular dates. In essence, fifteen "SAD days" have passed without as much as a nodding acquaintance from Cleo.

She appears very genuinely shocked and sympathetic upon hearing that Matt is potentially being blackmailed. It transpires that she was married in the summer of 2010 but was subsequently divorced. She does not have any children. As was the case with Ava, Matt is absolutely convinced that Cleo is not the blackmailer. Rather tentatively, he also asks her if she has told anyone else about what happened that night. Similar to Ava, she responds somewhat casually:

'No, not at all, apart from my ex-husband, of course.'

Inwardly, Matt wonders what part of them not telling a living soul, did she not understand? But she had responded so openly and honestly that he simply could not be annoyed with her. She obviously thought that telling her husband was absolutely OK. That very same husband from whom she is now estranged and could be blackmailing him! He truly wants to remind her of the pact they had made, but appreciates there is little point.

In the course of the general conversation, Matt deduces that her current relationship with her ex is non-existent and that the break-up had been very acrimonious. Apparently, unknown to her for a very long time, he was a serial gambler. Their relationship had been floundering for some time, in fact since she discovered that he had dwindled away their life savings. However, it not surprisingly came to a head when they were forced to sell the matrimonial home.

But why on earth would he choose to blackmail me? And why after all this time? It simply just doesn't make any sense. On balance, rightly or wrongly, Matt also decides to exclude Cleo's ex-husband from his non-existent list of suspects.

Before leaving, he enquires if Cleo has any information on Darren, the third passenger in the car. He is disappointed, but not surprised to hear that there has been absolutely no communication between them since the evening they first met. Nor does she have any idea as to where he may now be living, or indeed working. However, strangely enough, she does recall that his surname was Alexander. Matt was curious as to why she would remember this and so he decides to probe a little further.

'The reason this stuck in my mind was that he spoke of his brothers, and she had a vague recollection that her parents used to listen to a folk-music duo from the Glasgow area known as the "Alexander Brothers".

'Is there anything else you can remember about him, no matter how trivial, that might provide me with some assistance in finding him?'

'Somewhat strangely, given that I obviously had been drinking, I can actually remember a couple of very small points, which may or may not be helpful. For example, I recall at the time him saying that he was living in a small flat in the Shawlands area, although he will undoubtedly have moved long since. I also recollect that he was employed in a sales capacity within a recruitment company. The only reason is that I recall joking that I had always wanted to be headhunted. And I still do!' said Cleo laughing, and then suddenly remembering the seriousness of Matt's situation.

Matt duly thanks Cleo and says his goodbyes. It crosses his mind that in his conversations with both Ava and Cleo, intentionally or otherwise, neither had made the slightest mention of the accident itself nor, indeed, of the tragic death of Samuel Geddes. 'All a little surreal,' he murmurs to himself as he makes his way home to once again update Liz.

CHAPTER 45

July 2023

'Archibald Watson, I am arresting you for the murder of Police Constable Adam Yardley. You are not obliged to say anything, but it may harm your defence if you do not mention when questioned something that you later rely on in court. Anything you do say may be given in evidence. Do you understand?'

'Yes,' said Archie Watson, somewhat gruffly. Being a relatively hardened criminal, he is no stranger to such cautions and tends to always follow the same strategy, "when in doubt, say nowt."

While determined not to show any emotion, inwardly, he is totally devastated, for entirely selfish reasons, to hear the news that the policeman has actually died. He is also very intrigued as to how they have managed to link him to the offence.

As the caution is read out by DCI Karen Orr, with DC Alan Smyth in attendance, Meg is wailing and shouting profanities at them, claiming that "her man" has done nothing wrong.

'Murder a cop, you must be fucking joking - absolutely no way.'

Meg is not stupid. Of course, she appreciates that her lavish lifestyle is largely financed by such nefarious activities as theft, moneylending, money laundering, gambling, protection rackets, drugs and prostitution. However she is unaware of the specifics and likes to keep it that way. Also,

Archie prefers to keep her in the dark, especially when acts of violence are involved. This choice is not in any way based on any notion of sentiment. Rather, he operates on the simple premise that the less she knows, the less she is able to talk about.

Archie is then handcuffed and is about to be removed from the house. At this point, Meg's screaming moves up a few decibels. Archie's patience is wearing thin, and he very unceremoniously puts her down:

'For fuck's sake woman, will you bloody shut up? I'll be back in time for ma tea. Make yourself bloody useful and phone ma solicitor.'

Meg stands at her front door as her husband is led from the house to the awaiting police car, Meg cannot help but notice the curtains twitching in some of her neighbours' houses.

'Nosey fuckin' bastards,' she shouts at the top of her voice and then slams the door closed in anger. Suffice to say, there is absolutely no chance that Archie will be home for "his tea".

The Watson family have used the services of the same solicitor to look after their criminal affairs for many years. Devlin Delaney, referred to as "Double D" by his loyal clients, is very much a courtroom wheeler and dealer. It has been said of the man that if you are to shake hands with him, you would be well advised to count your fingers afterwards! He is extremely smart in a streetwise kind-of-a-way, a good person to have by your side in the proverbial trenches. Over time, he has gained a substantial reputation, largely for keeping his criminal clientele on the streets as opposed to behind bars. Devlin does not come cheap, but then again, neither do his suits!

Aged in his early to mid-sixties, he has the appearance of having been born in a bygone era. He is a man who does not know the meaning of the word 'modesty', the absolute antithesis of a shrinking violet. In his mind, and probably in his mind only, he is a snazzy dresser. His trademark, Al Capone-style pinstriped suits are accompanied by immaculately ironed, coloured shirts with contrasting crisp white collars and large cufflinks. To complement this rather outdated look, he has greased-back hair. While it is unnaturally black for his age, there are some errant, giveaway grey hairs evident at his temples. In court Devlin wears a pair of very fine, wire-rimmed spectacles, perched very perilously on the tip of his nose, looking as if they might slip off at any moment. It would be no surprise if the lenses were actually plain glass and his spectacles were merely to add an air of respectability. To complete the ensemble, he sports unfashionably pointed but pristinely polished shoes and ultra-colourful socks.

CHAPTER 46

February 2023

Matt becomes more and more convinced that both Ava and Cleo can be discounted as being his potential blackmailer. They both seem so genuinely surprised, if not shocked, to hear from him after such a lengthy period. Unless, of course, one of them has truly amazing acting skills, which seems very unlikely. Moreover, in his job as a prosecutor, over many years, he has perfected the art of identifying when a witness was lying or telling the truth. Searching desperately to find a positive, at least he is now able to eliminate the two of them from suspicion.

But there is still something niggling him. They have both confirmed that they divulged information about the hit-and-run incident to their partners. Then again, he keeps coming back to the same old question. Why now? What would prompt them to blackmail him so many years after the event? And who are these people anyway?

Matt shares these thoughts with Liz, and she is in total agreement with his assessment.

'There is, of course, another option, namely Darren. We need to locate him - and quickly. Unfortunately, "Alexander" is not an uncommon name in the West of Scotland.' Said Liz, not intentionally meaning to add further to Matt's woes.

Ever since receiving the very first letter, Matt has been having great difficulty falling asleep. Furthermore, when he does eventually drop-off, he is having to endure horrific nightmares. These inevitably feature him being imprisoned and thereafter being subjected to violent, revenge attacks from fellow cellmates, whom he had previously successfully prosecuted and put behind bars in the first instance.

He is also really struggling to cope with his day to day job, lack of concentration being the major issue. His colleagues at work have been showing genuine concern for him, observing that he appears to be losing weight and also seems to be very distant and remote. He simply responds with a part truth - that it is all due to lack of sleep. If only they knew why!

Matt and Liz have discussed their ruinous situation ad infinitum, but they seem to be simply going round and round in circles. The thought of the events of 15 February 2008 coming out into the open are, on every level, unbearable and unthinkable. Yes, he would lose his career and his freedom, but also what effect would it have on Liz, on Daisy, on them as a family? Any time Matt lets his mind run off in this direction, he feels physically sick and, on occasion, it even results in vomiting. The only time he seems to be able to concentrate is when he is on "detective duty", trying to identify his blackmailer. However, he and Liz have never once discussed what approach they would take if they did eventually identify him or her.

They have, however, had discussions regarding how much money they could afford or indeed be willing to pay. They decide that if need be, they would sell their house - perhaps a small price to pay for freedom. But for Matt, the very thought of them having to sell the family home fills him with guilt. His wife does not deserve to be treated in this way, after all she has done nothing wrong. And what of Daisy, who is so happy and content in this house and has her little friends living nearby. They would both be compromised, all due to his utter stupidity in driving whilst under the influence of alcohol all those years ago.

Another option for Matt is to seek financial help from his mum. After all, she became a fairly wealthy woman upon the death of his dad. However, he would feel very hypocritical, given that he had not shown much love to either of his parents in recent years. So, he has a moral dilemma. Either he sells or remortgages their house, obviously causing an even greater degree of emotional distress to his own family or else he swallows his pride and approaches his mum. To some degree, he feels he can justify the latter given that, as an only child, his mother's estate will naturally come to him at the end of the day anyway.

But then again, until he hears further from "The Observer," he has absolutely no idea how large the financial demands will be. In his more pessimistic moments, he fears the worst. Firstly, whoever is blackmailing him must know the very extreme lengths he would be prepared to go to, to avoid being detained in prison for years on end. They might also be aware that he is from a relatively wealthy family.

Another matter is also causing Matt genuine anguish, one which exists in so many blackmail situations. Namely, if the blackmailer names his price and it is paid, how do you stop them coming back looking for more? And what if the well runs dry? In theory, he could bankrupt himself in the hope of retaining his liberty, and his past could still be exposed. The more he deliberates over this, the more depressed he becomes.

In the meantime, the detection process continues and as usual, Liz is at the helm, the master of operations.

'OK Matt, let's set about finding this Darren Alexander on social media. What do we know about him apart from his name? Going by what you said, he is now approximately forty-three years of age. Also, he lived in Shawlands all those years ago. Now, assuming he has not emigrated, let us assume he still lives south of the River Clyde, on the basis of the old saying "once a south-sider, always a south-sider". We also know that he has other brothers. Finally, the likelihood is that he still works in a sales capacity or at least we need to work on that presumption.

After several hours of trawling both Facebook and Instagram, they hit the crossbar on a few occasions, in that they located "a Darren Alexander" as opposed to "the Darren Alexander". They are beginning to feel quite demoralised when Liz suggests that they try using a slightly different angle of approach.

'Matt, we must remember that he is no longer a young lad, we are talking years ago. Yes, he may well be working in a sales environment, but if he had any ambition, by this stage in his life he is likely to be at management level now. Also, a number of people I know prefer to stay clear of Facebook because they find it very invasive. Why don't we try LinkedIn?'

Bingo! Within a few minutes they find an ideal match - a Darren Alexander who currently lives in Newlands, on the south side of Glasgow. He was educated at Shawlands Academy and is currently employed as a manager with a well-known national double-glazing company. Most importantly of all, having studied the photograph, Matt is fairly confident that it is the same Darren Alexander from all those years ago.

CHAPTER 47

February 2023

The Observer is seated at his kitchen table. Scissors in hand and surrounded by bits and pieces of newspapers and a small bottle of glue, he almost gives the appearance of enjoying his creative work. He is also enjoying that perverse pleasure which emanates from having unbridled power over another individual, one who is at his mercy, completely at his beck and call. This feeling of omnipotence is all the more satisfying given that his victim is such a very prominent figure within the legal fraternity. He simply knows that his quarry will be squirming more and more with each letter that drops through his letter box. With every word he meticulously forms on the page, his pleasure intensifies. This is a one-off opportunity that has fallen so very conveniently onto his lap, and he is going to milk it for all it is worth.

He stops for just a moment as something vaguely approaching a conscience, blurs the lines. However, just as quickly as it came, the thought vanishes as he elects to justify his actions to himself. After all, he is not the guilty one. It was not he who, in an intoxicated state, knocked down an innocent man before driving off, leaving him lying dead at the side of the road. Yes, of course, he has a modicum of sympathy for Matt's wife, who is no doubt suffering because of the actions of her husband, but she is merely collateral damage. So, refusing to allow these thoughts to linger, he once again puts on his rubber gloves and then applies more letters to the page.

CHAPTER 48

February 2023

Before Matt and Liz Goldstein have the opportunity to pursue their investigation into Darren Alexander, yet another envelope drops through their letterbox. Of course, they both know in their heart of hearts that the blackmailer was not going to go away. Nevertheless, the physical reality of seeing the envelope once again consumes them with dread and fear. They so wish that they could just bin it without opening it in the hope that their problem would somehow disappear. If only that were so. But knowing they simply have to face the music, Matt duly opens the envelope. He does so very tentatively as if the contents are some lethal, poisonous resin, deadly to the touch.

> Hi mAtt
> tHE tIMe hAs Now COmE!
> I neeD YOu TO dO sOMeTHinG foR Me.
> thERe is a CasE cOMinG uP VeRy sooN iN tHE hIgh COUrT
> In gLasGoW.
> HMA V ARCHIBALD WATSON
> (Ref no. sCs/2024-0554985)
> IF HE Is fOuNd NoT GUIlty theN YouR sEcrET wIll rEmAin
> sAfE wITh mE.
> iF FouNd GuilTy yOu WilL bE gOInG t0 PrISoN foR a VeRy
> loNg tiMe anD yoU will Not bE abLE tO sEE yoUr littLe
> dAUghteR gROw Up.
> TEll AnYoNE aBouT mY leTtERs aNd tHE pOlice wiLL bE
> kNOckIng AT youR dooR.

Don'T dO anYtHiNg STupID!
I wILL BE iN TouCh sooN.

The Observer

Their mood has plummeted to new depths. In many respects, Matt would probably prefer it if the blackmailer had actually demanded money. But no, he is asking Matt to compromise himself professionally - as if he were not already in enough trouble.

What is the possible connection between this forthcoming trial and the events of that evening all those years ago? There simply has to be one. And who is Archibald Watson, although the name does ring a vague bell with him?

He shakes his head in utter dismay as these questions remain unanswered. Having recovered a fraction from the shock, they try to pick themselves up and attempt again to be proactive in trying to identify their blackmailer. Matt decides to visit Darren Alexander at his place of work, the double glazing company.

Upon arrival at his office, Matt immediately identifies him as one of the passengers in his car on 15 February 2008. This is a positive start. Matt asks to have a private word with him and is ushered into his office. As with the girls, it is abundantly clear that Darren does not recognise him and Matt very much has the advantage in this respect. When Matt does identify himself, Darren could not be more pleasant and friendly. Matt watches his body language very carefully whilst Darren thinks back to that fateful evening, as if for the very first time. He appears to have very genuine sympathy when Matt tells him about the fact that he is being blackmailed. (Matt does not make any mention of the actual blackmail demand, nor does he allude to the nature of his own employment). Darren, one would think, will merely assume that the demand is a financial one. Given his professional skills in terms of reading people which have been honed to perfection over many years, Matt would bet his life on the fact that Darren Alexander is not The Observer. It would appear that he has reached yet another dead end.

'Thanks so much for your time, Darren. I'm sorry to have brought this up after all these years.

'It's OK,' said Darren, secretly worrying in case it affects him. Out of interest, why do you think it is suddenly raising its head at this late stage?'

'I honestly have no idea, I only wish I knew. May I just ask you a couple more questions before leaving? Have you ever told anyone else about what happened that night?'

'No, I seem to recall that we all agreed to keep quiet about the whole episode. To be honest, I kind of compartmentalised the events of that night and have purposefully chosen not to revisit them in my mind.'

'And one further random question, does the name Archibald Watson mean anything to you?' As Darren shook his head, it was abundantly clear to Matt that he had never heard the name before.

Before saying their farewells, Darren casually enquired about what had happened to the two girls who were also in the car, obviously not recollecting either of their names. Matt provides him with the briefest of updates before leaving.

He is now back in his office and contacts both Ava and Cleo again to enquire whether they know anyone by the name of Archibald (or Archie) Watson. However, these approaches do not bear any fruit, and so he is left with only Darren as his final ray of hope.

Careful not to attract any attention, he then accesses the file pertaining to HMA v Archibald Watson. No sooner has he done so than he realises why the name was familiar to him. Of course, the accused is one of the infamous Watson family from Glasgow, a family that has been terrorising the streets of Glasgow for many years. It then comes to him that this is the cop killer case that he had, of course, heard about in the most general of terms. He feels sick to the pit of his stomach.

'How in God's name did I get myself into this situation? Either I go to prison for a very long time, or I help get a cop killer off a murder charge. What the hell am I going to do?'

His mood descends to unprecedented depths.

CHAPTER 49

July 2023

DCI Karen Orr has arranged for searches of the houses of both Sid Watson and his son, Archie Watson. Upon arrival at Sid Watson's house, the officers receive an extremely hostile response, not only from Sid but also his wife, Nancy. In fact, she is the more vociferous of the two, her language leaving a lot to be desired. She becomes all the more irate as she watches on as her house is turned upside down. To be fair, the officers concerned, who know the Watson family all too well, are being more cavalier than usual in their approach and are quite revelling in the task. As they empty drawers and cupboards, clothes and personal belongings are thrown about without a care, as Nancy Watson becomes visibly more and more agitated:

'What the fuck do you think you are doin' wi all oor stuff?

How would you like this done to your hoose? You are deliberately makin' as much o' a mess as possible, you absolute bastards!'

'Sid, why don't you stop them? We've done nothin' wrong.

You're nothin but polis scum and you can stick that fuckin' warrant where the sun don't shine.

Is it not enough that you have locked up ma boy for something he's not fuckin' done in the first place? Just because a polis has been killed, you don't need to take it out on us.'

By this point, the three police officers have decided that they are not prepared to take any more abuse and warn her that if she does not keep quiet, she will be arrested. To their surprise, her husband, who has probably got a headache by this point, speaks up in support:

'Nancy, for fuck's sake, will you just bloody shut up?' And she did!

The officers eventually leave the house about three hours later, and it now has the appearance of having been struck by a bomb. Nancy Watson, since receiving the public rebuke from her husband, has quietened down, but is permanently scowling, her face wrinkled up like an ageing prune.

While the officers did remove some items and clothes from the house, they were ultimately all returned, being deemed not to be of any real evidential value. However, the officers concerned have absolutely no regrets about having carried out the exercise and having caused the Watsons such emotional distress.

Their next port of call is the house of Archie and Meg Watson, and the reception they receive there is equally frosty. Once again, they remove various articles and items of clothing for forensic investigation.

In the meantime, a post-mortem of Adam Yardley has been carried out. The body is known to be that of a 35-year-old well-developed, well-nourished male and was found to have been in a state of general good health, with no significant past medical history. There is no evidence of any tattoos or obvious scars.

Death was ultimately caused by one single gunshot wound to the chest area. There was clear evidence of damage to the soft tissues at the point of entry, accompanied by the presence of a rim of bruising in the vicinity of the entry wound. Given that the shot was fired from relatively close range, the wound was characterised by the presence of a gunpowder tattoo, namely particles of gunpowder embedded in the skin and also burning due to hot exhaust gases from the barrel. From an examination of the trajectory of the entry wound, it can be deduced that the victim and his assailant were both in a standing position at the time the shot was fired. There was no evidence of any exit wound.

The toxicology report proved negative. There was no evidence of any alcohol or drugs in the victim's system.

A few days later, the funeral of Adam Yardley takes place. In anticipation of the inevitable, and as encouraged by Police Scotland, Adam had actually made certain plans in the event of his death. In spite of his relatively tender years, he had legislated that he wished his funeral to be a celebration of his life. Furthermore, he had requested that those in attendance dress accordingly, namely in colourful attire.

Having said that, given it was the death of a police officer, certain formal protocols were observed.

A full service funeral is normally only arranged by the local police force if the death has occurred in the line of duty. Strictly speaking PC Yardley, while in uniform, was not on duty at the time of the shooting, but Police Scotland made an exception given the unusual circumstances of his death. Susan Yardley was extremely appreciative of this gesture on their behalf and considered it to be a great honour.

As a result, in attendance at the funeral were a number of senior officers as well as uniformed officers to carry the coffin. There was also a formal printed Order of Service and a police force flag draped over the coffin. A very moving eulogy was also delivered by one of Adam's senior colleagues

158

as he spoke of his dedication to the role and his popularity among his fellow officers.

The Yardley house is a very short distance from the church where the service is taking place. It is also particularly poignant, emotional and heart-warming to see the uniformed officers lining the streets as well as a host of friends and neighbours. Immediately behind the coffin walks Susan, as if in a kind of trance, perhaps partly due to the strong sedatives she had prescribed by her local GP. She is walking hand in hand with her two young children, neither of whom can completely comprehend why they will never see their loving dad ever again.

Throughout the funeral and the days leading up to it, Susan had shown quite remarkable resolve and resilience, seemingly coping admirably with all the slings and arrows fate had hurled at her. It was only a few days later that she truly buckled under the pressure and the reality of life without the love of her life. Perhaps the fact she was no longer taking sedatives was a contributory factor. Perhaps also because she was no longer surrounded by friends and family. For Susan, this was now the quiet after the storm.

CHAPTER 50

December 2023

The more Matt gives consideration to his situation, the more indecisive he becomes. This indecision, in turn, leads to more enhanced stress levels, increased anxiety and unfathomable bouts of depression. At home, he is now in an almost permanent state of irritability and tetchiness and is constantly functioning on a very short fuse. For a while, this behaviour only surfaced in front of his wife, Liz. It is, of course, not at all uncommon for the nearest and dearest to have to bear the major brunt. Fortunately, Liz has been particularly long-suffering and accepting of him, given these very extreme circumstances. However, there has been a more recent trend developing, whereby he has been also directing his abject intolerance towards young Daisy, who is now six years of age and is becoming increasingly aware. This has proved to be one step too far for Liz, and she has relayed her views to Matt in no uncertain terms.

Even Goldie has been spotted running out of the room with his tail between his legs whenever Matt makes an entrance!

In the meantime, Matt's mental health continues to deteriorate as the trial now looms on the not-so-distant horizon. Sleep is at a premium, and he appears to have aged immeasurably in a relatively short time. Perhaps not surprisingly, he has also lost his appetite, and this is evidenced by the fact that his suits appear as if they have been borrowed from a big brother. As a consequence, his shirt tail is regularly spotted making a break for freedom from his waistband. That, coupled with his now apparent reluctance to shave, culminates in a very unkempt and dishevelled appearance.

Also, there are murmurings within his workplace. These are not generally gossip per se but rather expressions of genuine concern for his wellbeing. The most popular theory doing the rounds, based solely on conjecture, is that he must be experiencing matrimonial issues. If only they knew of the real demons at play in the mind of Matthew Goldstein.

On a more positive note, for better or worse, he has finally forced himself into making a decision as to his best way forward. For weeks on end, he has been weighing up both the options currently available to him, namely, whether to admit his guilt or leave his fate in the hands of his blackmailer. Indeed, during particularly low moments, he has briefly considered a third option - namely taking his own life. However, he soon dismisses this route due to a lack of courage rather than the more laudable consideration, namely that it would be selfish in the extreme and grossly unfair to his wife and family.

The logic used by Matt to finally reach a determination is simplistic in the extreme, and entirely based on self-preservation. If he were to defy the blackmailer and confess to his crime, then there would be absolutely no dubiety regarding his fate. He would be incarcerated for a very lengthy period, his career and family life both totally destroyed - fact.

However, the alternative option leaves a chance, however remote or infinitesimal, that he might remain at liberty. When considering this option, he tries to convince himself of potential scenarios whereupon the trial against Archie Watson might go his way:

e.g. the jury simply returning a not guilty verdict

e.g. loss or displacement of material evidence by the Crown

e.g. death of a key witness

e.g. legal or constitutional error on behalf of the Crown Office

e.g. the blackmailer not going through with his threat

  etc., etc.

Also, such a disposal does not allow for any influence Matt might be able to bring to bear. So his bottom line is that, on the balance of probabilities, the latter option holds much more appeal. He decides to roll the dice.

Having arrived at this decision, and in the interests of preserving his own sanity, he has deliberately blocked one crucial point from his mind. That is the very real possibility that even if Archie Watson were somehow to be acquitted, there is no guarantee that he will never hear again from The Observer.

Having at last been decisive, all he can do now is to try to influence his future by acquainting himself as best as possible with the case file. Thankfully for him, he is in a position to do this remotely by studying digital files. By so doing, he does not arouse too much curiosity or suspicion as to why he appears to have an almost unnatural or unhealthy interest in one particular trial. This is especially so, given that it is already in the capable hands of the highly respected Henry Worthington and his very able assistant, Angela Fraser. So, on a daily basis, he is charting the progress of the case online and is able to read all the witness statements at his leisure. Matt elects to go through the file with a very fine tooth comb, painstakingly taking meticulous notes along the way. As a result, his nine-to-five job is now very much taking a back seat. His attention to detail is so extreme that he is almost able to recite by heart some of the witness statements and can list off all the exhibits. But then again, the stakes could hardly be higher for Matthew Goldstein.

CHAPTER 51

August 2023

The turf war between the Byrne family and the Watson family is never likely to end. In fact, it will most probably transcend generations, as bigotry and religious divides so often do. However, recent circumstances have resulted in inactivity on this front, albeit it is very far short of an armistice.

From the Byrne point of view, they dealt the last blow in terms of the shooting of young Jimmy Watson. Now, they are concentrating their efforts on their illegal pursuits and the further expansion of their criminal empire. They are also pursuing an interest in a couple of legal businesses with a longer-term strategy of going legitimate and not always having the threat of jail sentences hanging over them.

By contrast, the Watson family have not been actively pursuing their rivalry with their arch-rivals for quite different reasons. They have been feeling somewhat depleted in their ranks of late. Sid was only just released from prison in January and since then, there has been effectively the expulsion of young Jimmy. Also, now there is a large shadow over the family and a general feeling of unease as Archie, the oldest son, is potentially going to be locked up for the rest of his natural life. In short, they are too preoccupied with internal matters to concern themselves with any thoughts of revenge against the Byrne family.

The location is booth number eight, The Tavern, Springburn. It is a Friday evening. There are only two occupants. Both are successful within their own fields of activity. Yet, that is where the similarities end.

One is wearing an extremely dapper pinstriped suit with a gaudy yellow and red tie, the other a once-white tee-shirt and an old pair of blue Levi jeans which have the benefit of an elasticated waistband to accommodate an ever-expanding and over-indulged belly. While many who have been incarcerated for a lengthy period of time tend to leave prison much trimmer than before they entered, others do not. When you are in HM Prison Barlinnie and are considered or reputed to be a prominent figure within the Glasgow hierarchy, then food and treats are never in short supply. There are always fellow inmates trying to endear themselves. Also, some of the less scrupulous prison officers are very acutely aware of the influence a crime lord can have beyond the prison walls. They know that they can secure "favours" in the outside world on a quid pro quo basis.

On this occasion, Sid Watson and his criminal lawyer do not bother with any niceties or preambles and get straight down to business. By necessity, there is only one item on the agenda.

'OK DD, what are we up against here?' asks Sid.

'I am afraid, Sid, it is not looking at all good for Archie at the moment. The Crown appear to have a very strong case, and the evidence is looking pretty damming. Some of it could be viewed as being pretty circumstantial, but when you put together all the various small pieces of the jigsaw, then I am afraid a clear picture emerges. I am not meaning to be all doom and gloom, I am just trying to be a realist. Given that it was a cop who was killed and not in the line of duty, the public awareness is sky high, and they are not going to rest until they have nailed someone for this. Sid, you absolutely know that I will do whatever it takes to try to keep Archie out of prison, but I wanted you to know that it is going to be a real uphill struggle.'

Although it is something which remains unsaid, Devlin Delaney knows that Sid will stop at absolutely nothing to prevent his son from being convicted. In the past, he has been aware of acts of intimidation against both witnesses and jurors in order to achieve the right outcome in a trial. While Delaney is mindful of these situations and could be deemed complicit, in the interests of preserving his legal practising certificate, he remains completely passive and detached. In this respect, perhaps it is the words that do not pass between them that are the most significant. Devlin Delaney has, in effect, painted an extremely bleak picture, which is tantamount to telling Sid that Archie's defence team are going to lose, and so the only real hope you have of winning is to revert to dirty tactics.

Sid has taken from this meeting exactly what was intended by his Defence Counsel. He is entirely focused upon protecting his first born and keeping him at large. His mind is already working overtime as to how this can best be achieved. Little does he know that an opportunity is going to land on his lap, and from a most unexpected and unknown source. Fate works in mysterious ways!

CHAPTER 52

September 2023

The MIT team have been working around the clock in order to build a water-tight case against Archie Watson and is feeling confident that everything is coming together quite nicely. They are so incredibly determined and focused upon securing justice for the death of one of their own and also obtain some degree of closure for Sue Yardley, his grieving widow and her two young children.

More evidence has become available incriminating Archie Watson as the search of his house had not been in vain. Among the articles removed were a pair of size nine Doc Marten boots, which Gary Conway, the petrol station assistant, will confirm are very similar if not identical to the pair being worn by the accused.

Furthermore, during the search, they also discovered a black balaclava which contained the accused's DNA. Unfortunately, they are unable to tie it in with the headwear worn at the attempted robbery, but it constitutes yet another strand of evidence incriminating the now accused.

A member of DCI Orr's forensic team has been studying in great detail the CCTV footage taken from the petrol station. Unfortunately, the system installed is fairly antiquated and not only are the images very sketchy, but they are also only available in black and white. This, coupled with the fact that the cameras do not cover the whole of the forecourt, has made the task for the forensic team a very arduous one. However, they have managed to shed a little light on the case. The vehicle that had been partially seen leaving the forecourt just about the time of the shooting is confirmed as being a Ford Focus Mark 4 model, hatchback style, a model which has been available in the UK market since April 2018. Unfortunately, they are unable to identify the number plate, nor can they be specific about the colour. However, this additional information is sufficient for MIT to further progress their enquiries. It transpires that the evening before the attempted robbery, a grey Ford 2019 version of this very model was stolen in the East End of Glasgow. Even more significant is that in the very early hours of the morning after the offence, a burnt-out Ford Focus was discovered by a quarry a mere twenty minutes from the petrol station. Bingo!

So it appears that Archie Watson had an accomplice, the driver of this Ford Focus. The search is now on to locate him or her. Strictly speaking, in the eyes of the law, the getaway driver is as guilty as the person who pulls the trigger.

CHAPTER 53

December 2023

Matt is at least grateful that he can immerse himself in the case file. This provides him with a sense of purpose and, somewhat ironically, a welcome distraction from simply contemplating his future or lack of one.

By contrast, his wife, Liz, does not have that luxury. While she is a stay-at-home mum, it is not necessarily entirely by choice. She is keen to return to work, even to return part-time as a teaching assistant, but has been actively discouraged by Matt. He harbours a slightly old-fashioned view of marital life and prefers that Liz is at home for Daisy. Liz can see the sense of this while Daisy was still full-time at home, but now that she is at school, this is a different matter. She has talked about returning to employment a few times in recent months, but somehow, the subject always seems to be changed. The bottom line is that she is at home most days - alone with her thoughts – and, of course, Goldie, to whom she is becoming increasingly attached. Had her issues and concerns related to almost anything else, she would have been able to share them with a friend. That said, more recently, she has tended to isolate herself from her friends, doubting her ability to disguise her feelings of consummate desolation. In any event, she would be quite incapable of mouthing the very words: 'My husband has killed someone.'

It is a Friday. Although recently all days are pretty much the same in Liz's world. The only difference a Friday offers is the impending companionship of her husband for the next couple of days. On reflection, perhaps the word "companionship" should be replaced with "company". The Oxford Dictionary definition of the former states: "The pleasant feeling that you have when you have a friendship with somebody and are not alone." By comparison, the word "company" enjoys a certain neutrality in that it may be either good or bad.

In anybody's language, Liz has had one hell of a week. Apart from walking Goldie, she has not been out of the house since Monday, with too much time to think. Now, she is desperately trying to just pass away the hours until she can go to pick up Daisy from school. She will then cuddle her and not want to let go, drowning in that beautiful fresh smell that only young children have, that unforgettable and cherished scent of nature and unashamed innocence. She so wishes she could drink it in endlessly. In the meantime, she just has to reap the benefits of whatever creature comfort her canine friend has to offer.

It is still mid-morning, and Liz cannot take much more of the solitude and extreme stress, and yet, there are still a few more hours until she will again see her daughter's smiling, angelic face. She feels a desperate need to confide, to lighten the immovable burden she is carrying, like a millstone around her neck.

Liz has an older sister who now lives just outside Edinburgh along with her husband and three young children. She and her sister used to be very close before she moved to the east of Scotland. Nevertheless, they enjoy that kind of relationship whereby, even if they have not been in touch for a few months, they can instantly pick up where they last left off. Liz has inwardly (as she could never tell Matt) mooted on a number of occasions the possibility of confiding in her and now the urge is stronger than it has ever been. She can no longer resist and picks up the phone. As fate would have it, at that very instant, she hears the one sound that she now dreads more than anything else in the world - that familiar "thump" of mail landing on their wooden entrance hall floor. All thoughts of phoning her sister immediately evaporate. Consumed with apprehension, she very slowly and painstakingly approaches the bundle of mail, as a lion would stalk its prey - but with no potential reward at the end.

Her worst fears are realised. The top couple of envelopes have windows. Who would have ever thought that she would feel a sense of relief to receive household bills! However, nestled among them is, regrettably, one that is all too familiar to Liz and Matt.

> Hi mAtT
> YOu WiLL bE eXPeCTIng tHis!
> I DO hOpE tHAt yoU aRE prePaReD.
> If NoT, yOu wIll SUFFeR ThE cOnSEquEnCes.
> I mIGhT EvEN be iN coUrT, bUt DonT tRY To
> LoOk fOR mE!
> YoUR fAtE Is IN yoUr Own HanDs.

The Observer

Liz simply cries and cries. When will this ever end? She feels so desperately lonely, and so phones her husband pleading that he return home.

CHAPTER 54

October 2023

DC Alan Smyth has been tasked with trying to locate the getaway driver. If successful, then they feel that it would virtually seal the fate of Archie Watson.

To this end, DC Smyth has made contact with an informer or "grass" that he has used very successfully in the past. Any information he may obtain relating to recent crimes is then covertly relayed to the police in return for a handsome payout in ready cash. While this is obviously a very dangerous occupation, it can also be very financially rewarding.

DC Smyth had requested inside information regarding the Watson case from his informer and has arranged to see him in their usual meeting place, a dark and dingy backstreet pub in Glasgow city centre. To ensure his anonymity, DC Smyth is wearing a t-shirt, sweatshirt, jeans and baseball cap, blending perfectly into the less-than-salubrious surroundings.

Mitch is already in the corner of the bar waiting for him, and he eventually arrives with a pocketful of cash. There is a deal to be done. Mitch is not actually his real name. Although DC Smyth has been using his services for a number of years, he does not actually know his real name. In the interests of his personal safety, this is for the best. It was in fact DC Smyth who eventually christened him Mitch, or rather, "Mitch the Snitch".

'Well, Mitch, what do you have for me?'

'My sources have given me the name of someone who almost certainly is your getaway driver in the petrol station job.'

He hesitates at this stage, not wishing to give away any meaningful information until the terms of the transaction have been negotiated. Having then done so, and the cash having changed hands, he continues:

'He is a young lad by the name of Andy Wilson, a very small-time criminal whose only talent to date is pickpocketing. Somehow, he got caught up with the Watson gang, which I bet he regrets now. He seemingly messed up big time, and when the polis arrived, he drove off leaving your man Watson high and dry. The reason I heard about him is that a day or so later, he had every one of his fingers broken. It certainly does not pay to mess about with the Watson family.'

DC Smyth thanked Mitch for the information before asking where he could find this guy Andy. They then leave the bar separately, both equally satisfied with the terms of their transaction.

CHAPTER 55

November 2023

Matt Goldstein has very recently been elevated in the COPFS to the esteemed position of Procurator Fiscal in charge of the Homicide and Major Crime Team, which does what it says on the box. Inwardly, he is somewhat surprised at his latest promotion, given his distinct lack of application in recent times. He can only assume that it was based on his past record, prior to his absolute preoccupation with all things relating to the Archie Watson case.

Basically, he is now answerable to one of five Deputy Crown Agents, who are very much at the top of the tree. Normally, in his elevated post, he would have no involvement whatsoever in the preparation or indeed overseeing of any particular trial. Having said that, he would tend to know about the existence of specific cases, especially the more important ones. Rather, the Principle Depute, with his or her own team, would be keeping an eye on how the more serious cases are progressing.

The irony is not lost on Matt that had he not been granted his latest promotion, he would have been in an infinitely better position to influence the result of the Watson trial.

Matt's anxiety levels rocket as he discovers that the trial date in the case against Archibald Watson, having been already fully prepared, has been advanced to the upcoming sitting of the High Court. This is due to the fact that the accused parties in two or three other trials scheduled for that sitting have opted to change their pleas to guilty. Also, the fact that there are so few witnesses involved in the Watson case makes it relatively easy to squeeze into the schedule. A veil of depression engulfs Matt as the true reality of his situation hits hard.

Upon enquiring further, Matt notes that the case has been allocated to a certain Senior Advocate Depute whom Matt knows only too well. By any standards, Henry Worthington is a man of some pedigree. His father before him was also an advocate of standing, and it was always his destiny that he would follow in his father's footsteps. His grandparents were reputed to be landed gentry, and his mother was also deemed to be of "good stock". Yes, Henry Worthington is very much a legal thoroughbred. Befitting his heritage, when addressing the court, he exhibits almost unparalleled loquacity. Despite being viewed universally as being extremely privileged and, in essence, an archetypal toff, he is also very well respected as being a really decent fellow and a very fair, able and accomplished Counsel for the prosecution.

In the trial, Henry Worthington is to be assisted by a relatively young but very competent and extremely enthusiastic Member of the Faculty of Advocates, namely Angela Fraser. Angela hails from Edinburgh, is single and extremely driven. The saying, "living to work, not working to live" was perhaps devised with Angela in mind. In short, Henry is fortunate to have such a committed and industrious assistant by his side.

As far as the defence is concerned, Matt notes that the solicitor acting for the accused is none other than the flamboyant and irrepressible Devlin Delaney, someone known to all in the profession. He, in turn, has instructed his favourite Senior Counsel, Charles Melvin. Melvin is very much in demand and, therefore, one with a very congested diary. Indeed, Delaney is exceptionally fortunate to have been able to avail of his services at relatively short notice. He is favoured by Delaney for being very much '"a man for all seasons". He enjoys a quite unique talent for being able to converse very comfortably at all levels. Whether taking instructions from some lowlife criminal being tried for the most heinous crime, advising grieving parents regarding the loss of their offspring or addressing a High Court judge, he is an ace communicator. Unlike many of his colleagues, he is also willing to bend, but not break, the rules if to the ultimate benefit of his client. To this extent, he often walks a very thin and dangerous line between the acceptable and the unacceptable, the legal and the illegal, the reverent and the irreverent, the conventional and the unconventional. It is these aspects of his personality that appeal so much to Delaney and are exactly why he was so keen to have him in his legal team to represent and defend Archie Watson. All in all, Charles Melvin is an extremely capable adversary and not one to be underestimated.

The High Court in Glasgow is to be the stage where Henry Worthington and Charles Melvin will be verbally jousting, somewhat like feuding stags. And the stakes are so very high - one man's freedom. The trial date has been determined - 08 January 2024.

Now that the date of the trial has been scheduled, Matt takes a crumb of comfort from the fact that he will soon know his fate. That is, of course, unless he decides to confess to the hit-and-run prior to then. He is well aware that if he were to confess, he would be charged, albeit belatedly, with the statutory defence of causing death by careless driving when under the influence of drink or drugs, a statutory offence under Section 3A of the Road Traffic Act 1988.

In terms of this statute, sentencing is based on two distinct factors. Firstly, the culpability of the offender. Culpability is generally determined by both the standard of driving and the level of intoxication. In this respect he appreciates that things do not look so great for him. Even in the very unlikely event of the matter proceeding to trial, his passengers under oath might conceivably confirm that at the time of the accident he had only one hand on the wheel and the other on Ava's leg. In regards his level of intoxication, the overall evidence would be pretty damming.

The second factor taken into account is the amount of harm caused - and the death of a victim is obviously at the very top of this scale. As either or both of these factors increase, so may the seriousness of the offence. In short, if the truth of what actually happened in 2008 does come out, matters look extremely bleak for Matthew Goldstein.

When passing sentence, the court would also take cognisance of various aggravating and mitigating factors. Matt has already considered these in relation to his own situation. In respect of the former:

- leaving the scene of the accident

- not reporting the accident

- victim being a vulnerable road user, namely a pedestrian

- failing to show any remorse

- the passage of time since the accident

- being a member of the legal profession

In respect of the mitigating factors, one solitary factor:

   - no previous convictions (although very young at the time).

Matt knows all too well that, technically speaking, the maximum sentence under statute is actually life imprisonment! However, that would be imposed only in the most extreme cases where there has been a lengthy series of similar convictions, and the accused has persistently displayed a total disregard for human life. Matt is of the view that in his situation, the sentence would likely range from 4-8 years in custody, depending largely on the judge. The actual length of any jail term is also likely to vary dependent upon whether he confesses to the crime, or whether it has only come to light by the actions of his blackmailer. In addition to the major charge of causing death, there would be separate charges of failing to stop and failing to report, which would also impact on his sentence. All in all, a very bleak picture!

CHAPTER 56

November 2023

Archie Watson is currently in remand in Barlinnie prison. It is certainly not for the first time. Having said that, perhaps not surprisingly, he has never been on such a serious charge. While he still exudes a hard man image to other inmates, he is still only human and as his trial date approaches, his insides resemble a tumble dryer. The stakes are so very high this time around.

Today, he is having a visit from his solicitor, Devlin Delaney, together with his Counsel, Henry Worthington. After a few quite unnecessary pleasantries, they get down to business. It fairly soon becomes clear to Archie that his Senior Counsel is there primarily to manage his expectations as to how the trial might go - and these expectations are not set very high. The atmosphere changes when Henry Worthington is involved in discussions, it is far more formal. Also, Archie cannot help but notice Counsel's very posh Edinburgh accent and contemplates for a moment the lifestyle he might enjoy. He then considers how different it must be to his own, and yet fate has thrown them together, both striving towards a common goal.

Archie decides he would welcome the opportunity to have a private word with his solicitor at the end in order to investigate "less official" ways of trying to secure a not guilty verdict. Such methods would normally involve intimidation or blackmail or bribing of witnesses or jurors - certainly not for the ears of learned Counsel!

'I am afraid to say, Mr Watson, that your situation is looking far from healthy. Your solicitor and I were discussing the case prior to this meeting, and we are both on the same page on this matter. Furthermore, given that the victim is a police officer, there is absolutely no possibility of a plea bargain in this case. To be completely honest with you, Mr Watson, in these circumstances, I would not even dare suggest one on your behalf. There is substantial public interest in this case, and forgive me for being blunt Mr Watson, but the prosecution are under great pressure to hang you out to dry. Despite this, Mr Devlin and I will, of course, do my very utmost to try to secure a not guilty verdict on your behalf, or more likely a not proven, but it will be a mammoth task. I would also make mention at this preliminary stage in proceedings that I do not for one minute anticipate putting you on the stand to present evidence in this matter.'

Then, glancing at his instructing solicitor, he continued:

'I trust Mr Delaney that you and I are also in accord on this particular point?' It was, however, more of a statement than a question as he was clearly not wishing to invite a response.

"As regards the evidence against you, it is by no means insubstantial. The most damning is the fact that they have your fingerprints on the murder weapon. This, Mr Watson is obviously a difficult one to explain away. Not only that, but the location where it is found, very close to the petrol station, is further incriminating.'

Archie decides not to respond to this until he has managed to have a word with DD on his own.

'To be fair, the prosecution do not require a great deal more than this in order to secure a conviction. In addition to this they have a balaclava found in your house, similar to the one used in the attempted robbery.

A certain amount of weight will be given to the evidence of the taxi driver, and while it seems he may not be able to positively identify you, the fact that he drops his passenger off very close to your parents' house also does not look so good for us.'

Archie is intrigued by his use of the word "us" and thinks to himself, somewhat whimsically, that it will not be 'we' who might be locked up in a cell for the rest of our lives! Counsel then continues:

'Then again, we also have the evidence from the petrol station assistant regarding the Doc Marten boots - yes, very circumstantial, but the prosecution will suggest that this is yet another little arrow of guilt pointing in your direction.

Obviously, there are some other elements of the evidence to be led by the prosecution which are flimsy, if not dubious, and it will be my task to expose them, and do that I most certainly will. However, in the meantime, I will bid you farewell and leave you in the capable hands of your solicitor, Mr Delaney, to take specific instructions from you in relation to the evidence we have discussed.'

With those parting words ringing in Archie's ears, Senior Counsel departed the interview cell, and instantly the atmosphere lightened as Archie let out an almighty sigh.

'Jesus Christ DD, he was all doom and gloom! When I listen tae him an' his posh voice and big words, I may as well go and hang myself right now!'

Delaney responds and tries to put his client's mind at rest.

'Counsel will always err on the side of caution and will tend to paint a pretty bleak picture. It is all a question of expectations; expect the worst and then anything else is a bonus.'

'Well, that's OK then. That has fair cheered me up!' responded Archie in a very sarcastic voice, followed up with a hint of a smile.

Devlin then takes his client through the evidence and discusses how they would try to combat each strand of evidence against him, which in the case of the murder weapon, will not be straightforward. Aware that there are no listening devices in the interview room they then begin to discuss potential "alternative" methods of securing Archie his liberty. More specifically, they have some discussion about how they might "get at" one or two of the witnesses. They also discuss how, a little further down the line, they might be able to bring some pressure to bear on jurors. Yes, the bold Devlin Delaney is not a man known for having many scruples. But yet he is a survivor.

CHAPTER 57

December 2023

> *Hi MaTT*
> *It Is gEttInG VerY clOSe nOw*
> *SOOn Your WoRRiEs cOuLd BE aLL beHinD yOu*
> *PrInt It ouT aND pUt iN aN EnvELopE and piN On NoTicE bOarD of AsDa SupERmaRKet on MarKEt sTReet aT exActLY 1:00pm toMorRow (TUesDay) - Or yOU kNoW whAT wILL hAPpen!*
> *I wiLL Be waTcHiNg yOu. tEll NobODy aNd gO alOne*
> *Do noT unDereStimAtE ME!*

The Observer

Matt has passed the point of no return. He has sold his soul to the devil, or in this case, The Observer. There is no way back. He feels like a puppet, with his every move being determined by the puppeteer. He has to do exactly as he is told, he has left himself with absolutely no other option.

Matt has easy access to the jury list online and does exactly as he is told by printing off a copy. One significant word in this latest note is "potential". Some of the jurors on the list may well be assigned to another case, others may be dismissed by the prosecution as part of their mandatory objections. However, the jurors in the Watson trial will come from this global list and at the end of the day, probably only one or two jurors need to be targeted to achieve the desired result. However, in order to achieve this goal, initially the net has to be spread a little wider.

The Observer sits in the Asda cafe bar nursing a cup of coffee while awaiting the arrival of his hapless victim. Almost exactly on the due hour, he spots a man approaching the public noticeboard. A relatively young man, unshaven, slightly unkempt, with a tired face and laboured gait. Perhaps not all that surprising, thinks the onlooker to himself. Even before he removes the envelope from the inside pocket of his jacket, he identifies Matt Goldstein from his online photo, albeit a poor relation of his former self. As requested, Matt pins the envelope to the noticeboard before trudging in the direction from which he had come, all the time looking straight ahead. Moments later, The Observer checks the contents of the envelope, and allows himself a slight grin.

Matt and Liz have observed something different about the latest note that they received. The previous ones had all been posted from the centre of Glasgow, whereas this last one had simply been hand delivered through their letterbox. Had they known, they would have installed a video doorbell. They also question the change of tactic and, after some discussion, simply put it down to the urgency of the situation, in terms of them needing the jury list urgently. But why would their blackmailer risk being seen? Matt then said that even if they knew who it was, did it really make any difference? After all, they could never ever report him to the police anyway! The only way out would be to kill him, and for this Senior Prosecutor, one death is quite enough! Nevertheless, they both agree to be in a state of alert should either of them hear the letter box closing.

Devlin Delaney is seated on his rather grand, red leather Chesterfield swivel office chair with his feet on his antique walnut desk within the offices of Delaney, Watt and Partners, Solicitors. As it happens, there is no Mr or Mrs Watt, and there never has been, but the illusion of grandeur goes hand in hand with his persona. Nor are there or have there been any partners. Image is everything to Devlin.

His receptionist dutifully delivers a handwritten envelope addressed to him marked 'Strictly Private'. Upon opening it, a note drops out, which reads as follows:

I thought this might help you in the Watson trial.
There might be more help coming soon.
Until then ⋯

The Observer

Also in the envelope is a list of potential jurors for his forthcoming trial. He is more than curious as to the identity of The Observer, but at the end of the day he is just grateful that this Good Samaritan has ventured forward. The best surprises always come when you least expect them, he thinks to himself. In the past, he has, on the odd occasion, been able to use a juror list to very good effect. This "gift from the gods" has truly lifted his spirits. Particularly so, given that when he last met with Sid Watson, they agreed on an outstandingly attractive fee for representing his son in the murder case. However, in the event that he is able to secure a not guilty verdict, Sid has agreed to quadruple the fee! Upon receiving this juror list, he conjures up thoughts of acquiring a luxury pad by the sea in the Costa del Sol. He then stops his imagination running away with him as there is still so much work to be done. Instead, he makes a call to Davy Ross his private detective of choice.

The following morning, Davy Ross arrives at Devlin's office. He is an ex-cop, a former plain clothes detective. He was "persuaded" to vacate his job by the powers that be, due to his over-reliance on the bottle. At the time he was in the force, he would have been termed a functioning alcoholic. To his credit, he never actually got into any trouble as a result of his alcohol intake. However, his superiors, and presumably others, would often smell alcohol on his breath, and thus, he was considered to be an accident waiting to happen. He was offered a financial package to leave at the age of forty-eight, which he happily accepted. It was a shame, as he was particularly good at his job and at one time was destined for the very top. For the following few months, he used his financial pay-off to drink himself into oblivion. He would often be seen wandering aimlessly about the streets. Alternatively, he would be found in a local bar, boring some unsuspecting individual with his repetitive and exaggerated stories of his time in the police force.

A year or so later, he went to rehab and has never touched a drop of alcohol since. Like so many ex-policemen, he opted to go down the private detective route - a fairly natural progression. In his case, he opted for self-employment and rented an extremely small, modest, and inexpensive rental property in a Glasgow side street, close to the city centre. Initially, in order to be able to pay the rent he would take on anything and everything. For the most part, this would mean handling messy, sometimes sordid divorce cases. Not only were these cases low earners, but they very often involved sitting in his draughty, clapped-out old car, camera in hand, trying to obtain photos which would justify sufficient evidence to establish adultery. Sometimes, he would have to sit in his car all night long, with just a flask of coffee, some cigarettes and his mobile for company.

However, his fortunes took a change for the better when one day, while giving evidence in court, he bumped into Devlin Delaney. They went for a coffee together and talked about old times and past acquaintances. The rest is history! When Delaney promised to try to send him a little business on a trial basis, little did either of them imagine that Ross Enterprises would prove to be such a valuable asset to Delaney's business.

Equally, it is very much a two-way street as Davy Ross could virtually survive solely based on business passed to him from this source and turning away all other business leads. From early on in their relationship, Devlin started to refer to Davy as 'the Badger' because he is so good at digging up dirt - on people, and that name has stuck. They work very well together. This is largely due to the fact that they share a similar moral code, in that they don't really have one. Suffice to say that Davy Ross will use whatever means is necessary to achieve the desired result. He certainly does not allow his conscience or indeed any principles (assuming he has either or both) to get in his way. This way of working suits Devlin Delaney just fine.

Delaney tells Davy Ross that he has got quite a big job for him and hands him an envelope containing a copy of the potential jury list, inclusive of their addresses. What is required of him is immediately made clear. Basically, he needs to elicit as much information as possible on the potential jurors - information that can be used as leverage against them. His task is a fairly mammoth one but not beyond his capabilities. Delaney emphasises to him that the jury of fifteen finally selected will ultimately come from this list. Accordingly, it will be necessary to do the numbers game, but to try to have the odds on our side they will pick three or four targets and hope that at least one of them is on the jury. To a limited extent, Delaney, via Senior Counsel, might just be able to influence this situation slightly by objecting to other jurors who have not been 'tapped'.

'Please get on to this right away and work around the clock as we have precious little time on our hands. However, on the positive side, you will be paid extremely well. Not only that, but should your efforts result in my client walking at the end of the trial, I will quadruple your payment.' Davy Ross nods approvingly and is out the door in a flash. He did not need a second invitation.

CHAPTER 58

November 2023

DC Smyth and an accompanying constable arrive at the door of Andy Wilson's parents' house, where he still resides. He has become a bit of a recluse since the punishment attack on his person by the Watson gang. His fingers are all still completely bandaged, and perhaps not surprisingly, he is wallowing in self-pity. Just when he thought things could not get much worse for him, he opens the door to the two police officers and, of course, he knows exactly why they are there. The Watson family had well and truly taught him a lesson about loyalty, but for fear of even more serious repercussions, there is absolutely no way that he is going to cooperate with the police, which would one hundred per cent seal Archie Watson's fate.

Andy invites them into the house, having little option. Once seated, DC Smyth starts the questioning.

'Do you know an Archie Watson?'

'No comment'

Do you know the Watson family?'

'No comment'

'Where were you on the night of 03 June 2023?'

'No comment'

'What happened to your hands?'

'No comment'

'Did the Watson family do that to you?'

'No comment'

'Andy, we know that you were the getaway driver in the attempted robbery and murder at the petrol station.'

'No comment'

'If you come clean to us and tell us everything that happened that evening, we can come to a deal with you, and you will get a reduced sentence.'

'No comment'

'C'mon Andy, look what they have done to you. You owe Archie Watson absolutely nothing. Do yourself a favour.'

'No comment'

'Ok, if that is the way you want to play it, you can get your jacket and come down town to the police station to be questioned there.'

Andy simply stood up, put on his jacket, albeit with some difficulty due to his heavily bandaged hands, and freely accompanied the officers to the police station.

Three hours later, Andy Wilson was duly released without charge.

In the police station, he underwent more rigorous questioning but continued to refuse to respond. At times, DC Smyth tried to take a tougher approach with him, but all to no avail. They even tried the 'bad cop, good cop' routine, with DS Orr taking over the reins and attempting a much more softly, softly approach - but still without success. Having endured pretty horrific torture at the hands of the Watson family, it became perfectly clear that the young lad was now totally terrified of them.

The bottom line is that they do not have one iota of solid evidence linking Andy Wilson to the offences and, therefore, have no alternative but to release him.

CHAPTER 59

December 2023

It is 10:05 on 20 December 2023 when a certain Walter John Sidney Watson enters this world weighing a healthy seven pounds and eight ounces. He has a shock of fiery red hair, which is later established as being attributable to the Byrne side of the family. Present throughout the birth is his extremely proud dad, Jimmy Watson, who is convalescing well following the shooting.

In the recovery room with baby Walter is one radiant mum, one overwhelmed dad and one other very invested party. Officially, nobody else is aware of this new arrival. Unofficially, however, Rosie Byrne has been keeping in touch with her daughter during her pregnancy, and there are tears of joy as she cradles little Walter in her arms. Neither Jimmy nor Cara have given up completely on the prospect of being reunited with their respective families. An indicator of this was their joint decision in choosing their baby's middle names, a gesture that they hope in time their respective parents might appreciate.

Rosie eventually, albeit with reluctance, prises herself away from her new grandson, but not before warmly embracing her daughter and going around the bed to embrace her son-in-law, Jimmy. Although not a word passes among them, the significance of this last gesture is not lost on any of them.

When Rosie returns home, she does not intend on telling her husband where she has been as she does not consider it wise to 'poke the beast'. However, having spent some time with little Walter, she is unable to contain herself, just bursting to share the news. Sadly, from her perspective, the feeling of elation she is experiencing is not shared by her husband, John. On the contrary, he refuses to acknowledge the birth and will not enter any conversation on the subject.

Later that day, Jimmy also tried to call his own mum, eager to share his happy news. The call went unanswered. The reason being that when Nancy saw who was calling, she blocked the call because her husband was in the room, and she did not wish to risk his wrath. However, just a short time later, she slipped out into the back garden to return the call, the first time in quite a number of months. Her maternal instincts get the better of her and she melts when she hears the news, with not a bigoted thought entering her head. Sadly, the patriarchs in the two families are so entrenched in their beliefs that forgiveness is not on their radar.

CHAPTER 60

December 2023

Davy Ross has been on the case for a few days. Buoyed by the very attractive carrot that was dangled in front of him, he has been working very long hours and has made meaningful progress. As best he could, he has been digging deep into the jurors' backgrounds and has successfully identified three potential 'targets' which he hopes will be sufficient.

Davy has a follow-up meeting with Devlin Delaney in their usual pub and after some initial pleasantries, he provides the following report:

'The first potential target from the jury list is Malcolm Scott. He is 21 and single. He's in sales and earns commission. I reckon he has a pretty bad gambling habit, maybe even an addiction. His job takes him out on the road, and he is placing bets along the way. It would appear that Lady Luck is not looking favourably on him. I had eyes on his financials, and he is pretty maxed out on loans, some of which are with dodgy lenders. DD, this guy is prime.'

Here's another, Brian Hunter, thirty-six, married to Penny with two young kids. Penny comes from good stock, and they live in a big house and her parents made him sign a prenuptial agreement. Aye, but here's the thing, he's been havin' a fling with a girl from his work, Sandra Baxter. Aye, and it's been going on for about a year. He'd be desperate to keep that quiet.

'My third one is Alice Murray. She's single, forty and flying high in her work, but she pulled the wool over her bosses' eyes. She lied and made up references. She's got a dodgy past. Miss Goody Two Shoes is not what she appears to be. She embezzled a lot of money from her previous company. So DD, you should get some mileage oot o' these three!'

Devlin Delaney is very pleased with this report. The Badger never fails to come up with the goods. He also spares a kind thought for the Good Samaritan who had anonymously provided him with the jury list and wonders for a fleeting moment about his or her identity. He then thanks Davy Ross for his excellent work and then, once again, they leave the bar separately. Devlin Delaney has a noticeable spring in his step, most probably in anticipation of a potential big payday.

CHAPTER 61

Late December 2023

Liz is sitting on the sofa, her mind drifting quite aimlessly. She is on her fourth black coffee of the morning, and she makes a mental note that she really needs to cut back on her caffeine. Then, just as quickly, she does a complete about turn and tells herself that it is justified in light of the extreme stress she is under.

It is a midweek day, so Matt is at his workplace, Daisy is at school and, as usual, she only has Goldie for company, and he does not usually have much to say for himself! As if on cue, Goldie barks quite furiously before rushing towards the hall. Looking out the lounge window, Liz observes a figure approach the front door. Goldie has become accustomed to the daily visits from the postman, and as a result, no longer barks to herald his arrival. Well aware of this, when Liz hears the familiar metallic sound of the closing letterbox, she rushes into the hallway. There it is, lying on the floor, the all too familiar handwritten envelope - her worst nightmare. She quickly opens the front door, completely forgetting that precious Goldie could potentially bolt. In fact, he merely stands in the doorway, continuing to bark at the slight figure of a male now retreating at normal pace towards their front gate. Liz instinctively yells at him, fully anticipating that he will run off, and she will then make a futile attempt at catching him. But rather, he turns around with a look of astonishment on his face. Liz is equally surprised to be faced with a very young, innocent-looking, spotty-faced youth, whom she imagines to be no more than about thirteen years of age.

'Come here, you.' She shouts to the youth.

Again, somewhat unexpectedly, he quite dutifully turns on his heels and approaches her.

'Yeh?" bearing the most innocent of expressions. Not quite the look she was expecting from a blackmailer - thinks Liz to herself.

'Did you put that letter through our letterbox?' asked Liz, pointing to the offending item on the hall floor.

'Yeh'

'Do you know what is in it?'

'No idea, Missus. I was playing football down the road, and a man came up to me. He offered to give me £10.00, and all I had to do was deliver that letter to this address.'

'Do you know this man? Have you seen him before?'

'No, don't know him, but I've seen him before. A few days ago, quite near here, he came up to one o' my pals, and he too got £10.00 for bringing a letter here - a pretty good gig, yeh?'

Liz thinks to herself, if only he knew!

'What does this man look like?' asks Liz, thinking she might be onto something.

'Just a normal kind of guy, I suppose, nothin' unusual about him.'

'What kind of age?

'Am not too good at that kinda thing, he wasne kinda young and he wasnae kinda old, if you know what I mean.'

'Not really,' she thinks to herself, but chooses not to articulate.

'It's kinda difficult to say, 'cos he had his hoodie up all the time.'

Liz thanks him anyway and apologises for having shouted at him in the first instance. "Don't shoot the messenger" comes to her mind.

She is just about to close the door when she has some inspiration.

'Sorry, I don't even know your name.'

'Mark.'

'I've maybe got an even better gig for you, Mark.' She said, deciding to adopt his vernacular.

'Interesting.'

'Do you have a mobile?'

'Yes,' he responds, reaching to his jeans' pocket.

'Ok, if you can manage to get a photo of this man, I'll double his payment. I'll give you £20.00.'

'Cool,' a cute smile lighting up his face as he goes on his way.

Liz was never to set eyes on Mark again.

Her brief exchange with Mark had side-tracked her just a little. Reality now hits her with a thump as she stares down at the dreaded envelope.

Why is this all on me? Where is Matt when I need him? After all, he caused this situation in the first place. She looks intensely at the envelope, now in her hand. Perhaps she will leave it for Matt to open when he comes home. She stares further at it, as if it were an animate object. It is drawing her towards it and saying: "Open me! Open me!" She ignores this invitation and duly deposits it on the coffee table. But her resistance lasts all of two minutes!

Hi Matt

tHanKS fOR tHe jUROr List - VErY HelPful.
I hAve AnOther TAsk fOR yoU.
I WaNT yOU tO gO tHroUGH tHe FIle anD FiND FLawS IN
tHe croWN cAsE. OnEs tHe deFENcE do'NT kNOw AbouT.
tOMMoroW sAmE pLacE - sAMe tImE.
OR elsE!

The Observer

Liz is at breaking point, and feels she just cannot take anymore. She telephones her husband and advises him of the latest demands from The Observer. Matt slumps in his chair, totally deflated. He then once again accesses the Watson file to deal with The Observer's latest request. His feeling of powerlessness is so totally all-consuming.

Of course, it is not in any way healthy to harbour regrets, and when Matt does, the pain is so much greater. He tries really hard to resist going to that tortuous place, but sadly, he seems unable to control that particular compartment of his brain. The same old "if only's" flood through his head and he does not have the defences to divert it.

'...if only I hadn't gone to the bar that night'

'... if only I hadn't gone to the SAD party afterwards'

'... if only I'd just waited longer at the taxi rank'

'... if only I'd not driven my car'

'... if only I had not invited the others back to my parents'

'... if only, if only.'

Each and every one of these "if only's" are visualised in Matt's brain as being T-junctions. Yes, junctions at which he had complete free will to choose to go left or right. Yet, on every single occasion, he made the incorrect decision. He only had to have chosen correctly once, just once and all his worries would disappear in a puff of smoke, and he could enjoy life to the full. Matt continues to torture himself by running through all these "if only's" in his head, over and over and over again. He feels he is almost going insane and, in his more lucid moments, admits to himself that he is desperately in need of therapy. However, even that route is blocked off for him. How can he possibly reveal his dishonourable past? No, there is no escape, he simply has to continue to comply with all requests made by The Observer. He has to dance to his tune.

CHAPTER 62

End December 2023

Matt knows the Archie Watson file intimately, from back to front and inside out, and is acutely aware of both the strengths and weaknesses of the prosecution case. Consequently, conforming with the latest request from The Observer is not at all an issue for him. Forever the dutiful and obedient puppy, he drafts a note. It clearly outlines two aspects of the prosecution case that, in their desperation to convict a cop killer, they had conveniently not mentioned thus far. The note is fairly brief and succinct:

Hi

As requested, here are a couple of aspects of the case that the prosecution are aware of, but have chosen not to share with the defence.

Firstly, the petrol station assistant, when interviewed, claimed that the shooter was left-handed. Is Archie Watson right-handed?

Secondly, while Archie Watson's fingerprints were identified as being on the shotgun, unknown to the defence, there was also a second set of prints. These belong to a man called Dougie Smith, who is a well-known villain in the Glasgow area. He is currently in prison on remand for another armed robbery but was at liberty at the time of the petrol station job.

Matt duly places the note in an envelope and pins it to the noticeboard within Asda at exactly the requested time. As before, his every move is being monitored.

The Observer is pleased with the content of the note. It is exactly the kind of information that could be invaluable to the defence. Yes, thus far, he is pretty satisfied with the contribution from Matt Goldstein. Without any delay, he, in turn, writes a note making mention of these two pretty crucial evidential points and places them in an envelope before making his way towards Glasgow city centre. There, he adopts the same tactic of offering a youngster cash to deliver the letter to the offices of Delaney, Watt & Partners. He took the precaution of watching him to ensure it was delivered and to the correct destination. Job done!

Not surprisingly, once again, Devlin Delaney is a very welcome recipient. What a delight to have evidence drop onto his lap in this manner. He then duly shares this unexpected gift with his Counsel, Charles Melvin.

CHAPTER 63

08 January 2024
(Day one of the trial)

The High Court of Justiciary in Glasgow hears the most serious cases in the area, including all cases of rape and murder. It is located in central Glasgow in the Saltmarket area of the city, close to the entrance to the famous Glasgow Green. In this court, there is absolutely no limit on the length of prison sentence that may be imposed.

It is the first day of the trial, and the area around the High Court is awash with the general public, members of the press and friends and relations of the accused. Jurors are also seen scurrying about, like schoolchildren, anxious not to be late on their first day. The case is extremely high profile. This is inevitably so, given that it involves the death of a member of the local police force. There is an almost tangible buzz of anticipation as this long-awaited trial is due to commence, with a lot of people baying for blood.

The courtroom is steeped in tradition and history, with its rich oak panelling and unquestionable aura. The judge presiding over the case is The Honourable Lady Fotheringham, who is very experienced. She enjoys a reputation as being extremely fair, albeit fairly severe in terms of sentencing. Her clerk of court, looking quite austere, announces: 'Court, please rise'. At this, Lady Fotheringham appears with a swirl of her robe and duly takes her seat, ready to preside over the day's proceedings.

Also in situ are Charles Melvin, Defence Counsel for Archie Watson, with his sidekick, Devlin Delaney, as always dressed very flamboyantly in one of his many pinstriped ensembles. Across the passageway, representing the prosecution, are Senior Advocate Henry Worthington and his depute, Angela Fraser. Let battle begin!

Early in the morning on the day of the trial, Archie Watson was transferred from HM Prison Barlinnie to the High Court. He has been brought up from one of the various holding cells below the court via the hidden stairs to the dock, which is surrounded on three sides by reinforced glass. Upon entering the dock the court is already assembled. Quite surprisingly, given the circumstances, he seems quite relaxed and even manages a smile and a casual nod to his family members. The public galleries are full, and the press benches are bursting at the seams, with everyone wanting their piece of the action, but with varying agendas. The air is filled with anticipation.

Amongst the public benches, blending in with the crowd, is The Observer. Having taken his seat, another man slides past him and apologises for bumping him in the process while making his way to a spare seat just a couple of yards away. The man in question is none other than his very own puppet, Matt Goldstein himself. If only Matt knew! A smirk comes over the face of The Observer as he contemplates the beautiful irony of the situation.

Matt had thought long and hard as to whether he would attend court. He eventually decides that he could not stand the "not knowing" and has also promised Liz that he will provide her with regular updates. Given that it is such a high-profile case, it is not altogether unusual for someone of his level of seniority to show an interest as a spectator -

although perhaps not sitting on the public benches. Matt is determined to draw as little attention to himself as possible.

Jury selection takes up most of the first morning. Very quickly, a couple of jurors are excluded. A young lady who is obviously in a very advanced state of pregnancy, plus another older woman who is apparently the sole carer for her elderly father, who has advanced stages of dementia. Following various exceptions on behalf of both the Crown and the defence, they finally decide upon the panel of fifteen jurors who will ultimately determine the fate of Archibald Watson.

Very significantly within this number are two of the three jurors identified by Davy Ross, namely Brian Hunter and Alice Murray, two unsuspecting jury members who both have no idea what the unscrupulous Devlin Delaney has in store for them.

It has taken a full morning to arrive at the final list of jurors who will attend the trial. It is a very lengthy and painstaking process. Each juror is questioned as to their background, general outlook on life and proclivities. They are also questioned about any preconceived views they may have as jurors in the forthcoming trial. Finally, they are asked if they have personal knowledge of any individual involved in the proceedings.

The jury is then sworn in, and the indictment is put to the accused. The Honourable Lady Fotheringham then addresses the jury:

'Good morning, Ladies and Gentlemen, although I suppose it is now technically the afternoon! First of all, may I thank you for giving up your precious time to be on jury duty. It is a very important and valuable service that you are providing. As regards the proceedings, let me make it perfectly clear that you, the jurors, are the complete masters of the facts of this case. By contrast, I am the master of the law. Arguably, you are the most important people in this courtroom. Your task is a relatively straightforward one - it is to carefully assess the evidence and deliver a verdict. It is entirely up to you to determine whether the accused is guilty or not.

While the jurors appear to be listening attentively to the address from Lady Fotheringham, the eyes of a number of them drift occasionally towards Archie Watson as if desperate to witness some reaction from him or perhaps a show of emotion. However, he continues to sit impassively in the dock.

'May it please, My Lady, Ladies and Gentlemen of the jury, I am Henry Worthington and, along with Angela Fraser, I appear for the Crown. My learned friend, Charles Melvin, appears on behalf of the defence.'

The Honourable Lady Fotheringham decides to break everyone in gently by calling a halt to proceedings after all the administrative functions and pre-trial formalities have been completed. She is inclined to the view that this will allow all of them to start again fresh in the morning.

This shortened day works quite perfectly for Devlin Delaney, as he is very keen to indulge in the extremely nefarious activity of jury tampering. He calls his partner-in-crime, Davy Ross, to arrange an urgent meeting.

CHAPTER 64

08 January 2024

Devlin Delaney and The Badger are sitting in their usual corner of their usual pub, being their usual villainous selves. In essence, Delaney uses Ross to do his dirty work, to keep the spotlight away from him and stop his own hands from getting dirty. Together, they are hatching a plan.

Penny Hunter is surprised to see her husband return home quite so soon. It is still early afternoon. She is pleased because he can then pick up their two young boys from nursery, a task that she normally undertakes. She welcomes him with a quick kiss and then invites him to tell her all about his first day at court, knowing that he was looking forward to the experience.

'God, I've been chosen for jury duty. You'll not believe it! Remember that petrol station job where the cop was shot - well, that's the case I am on. Might be quite interesting, I'll get the inside story, and it will be a lot juicier than, for example, a boring fraud case anyway. To be honest, I am really looking forward to it.' Brian Hunter is to later eat these words.

As he's driving to pick up his two children from nursery, he relishes the fact that he will miss a few days of work. But then realises that it is bitter sweet, as he will probably not then be able to see Sandra. About twenty minutes later, he returns with the kids in tow and parks in the driveway. The kids quickly jump out of the car in a rush to see Mum to show her the plasticine figures they have made at nursery. Brian turns to lock his car with the remote when he is approached by a stranger who immediately hands him a letter and says: 'I strongly recommend that you choose to read this before speaking to your wife.' Almost instantly, the man vanishes before he has the opportunity to speak with him. Upon opening the letter and reading its content, a cold chill runs right through his body.

> *Hi Brian*
>
> *We are aware that you have been chosen to be on the jury for the trial against Archibald Watson.*
>
> *You've been found out! We know that for quite some time you've been having a dirty little affair with Sandra Baxter from your work. Our proposal to you is very simple. Use your influence with the jury to ensure that Mr Watson is not found guilty.*
>
> *If he is convicted, then both your wife and Sandra's husband will be hearing all about your sordid little fling.*
>
> *We are very serious about this - beware!*
>
> *B*

Brian feels physically sick and chooses to sit in the car for a few moments in order to regain his composure before going indoors.

'Who is this person, signing himself off as B?'

'How can they possibly know about Sandra?'

'How do they know I am on the jury?'

He tries with great difficulty to compose himself before going indoors. Thankfully, when he does, Penny is entirely occupied with their two very hyper children and he can be alone with his thoughts for a few moments, but what a lonely place that is.

In the meantime, Davy Ross (aka The Badger) is quite pleased with his work and is tickled by his decision to sign off as 'B'. He is blatantly enjoying this nickname that Devlin has assigned to him. One down, one to go!

Davy is beginning to feel like some kind of 'master of retribution' as he drives to the house of his next unsuspecting target. Such power Devlin has bestowed upon him - and he gets paid very handsomely for it as well. Life is pretty good, he thinks to himself. Also, why should he feel sorry for either of these victims, after all, they have brought it upon themselves by their actions? He is merely assisting in them in getting their comeuppance. Yes, he is doing philanthropic work of a kind - he almost convinces himself that he is some kind of modern-day Robin Hood.

He then arrives at the door of Alice Murray. His recent research or "burrowing" has revealed that she lives alone. He thinks to himself that there is something immensely powerful about knowing that you have information about another person that can upset their whole world. He revels in that thought for a moment, before ringing the bell. There are yelps from a small dog before the door is opened.

'Alice Murray?'

'Yes, how can I help you?'

'I have a letter for you, a very important one, I suggest you take it extremely seriously.'

Before she is able to question him, he immediately turns on his heels. In the meantime, she is left standing in the doorway, letter in hand, bearing a mystified expression. Intrigued, she then goes into her lounge to sit on the sofa to read it. In retrospect, this is probably a wise decision, as otherwise her feet might well have collapsed beneath her.

Hi Alice

We are aware that you have been chosen to be on the jury for the trial against Archibald Watson.

We are also aware that you were guilty of embezzlement from your previous employers and that you deliberately concealed this from your current employers by producing a false reference. Our proposal to you is a very simple one. Use your influence to ensure that Mr Watson is not found guilty.

If he is convicted, then your current employer will be immediately advised of your criminal past, you will lose your employment and will be subjected to criminal proceedings.

You do not want to test us - we are very serious.

B

Not surprisingly, Alice Murray is totally shattered. The bottom has dropped out of her world. The recent elation she experienced from having been promoted has been erased in just a few strokes of a pen or a keyboard. There is absolutely no way that she can have her past "fall from grace" exposed. At all costs, she has to do what is asked of her. The stakes are too high to do otherwise. Her personal make-up is such that self-interest trumps all. In her thoughts, she does not even consider the morality of her decision. Nor does she consider that her actions could very well result in the cold-blooded killer of a policeman being absolved of any retribution.

But from the point of view of the Badger, it was a job well done. He has played to his undoubted strengths, namely an unparalleled ability to dig dirt. He can now look forward to a good payday, indeed an exceptional one in the event of Archie Watson not being convicted.

CHAPTER 65

09 January 2024
(Day two of the trial)

The first day of the trial was pretty much taken up by administrative functions and pre-trial requirements, including the lengthy jury selection process, direction of the jury by the judge and the production of exhibit lists. This conveniently leads to the giving of evidence on day two.

Being a high-profile case, both the public and press benches are crammed full. There is most definitely a feeling of tension in the air, as evidenced by a lot of nervous chatter, particularly among those with a vested interest. Sitting together on the front row of the public benches are Sid and Nancy Watson together with their son, Billy. Next to them is Meg, who is anxiously biting her nails and tapping her feet. Significantly, a few seats behind them, is Jimmy, who remains in enforced exile - with the exception of the occasional, covert visit from Nancy to see her grandchild. The Watson family have dressed up for the occasion. The males in the family are all 'suited and booted' while Nancy and Meg are wearing even more bling than usual. Perhaps they imagine that if they appear respectable, the jurors might be inclined to the view that a Watson family member could not possibly be capable of committing such a heinous crime!

Susan Yardley had contemplated attending the trial, but ultimately decided against it. She felt that she could not possibly bear being in the same room as the person who callously took the life of the man whom she loved, the father of her two young, innocent children.

The first person to give evidence is Marjorie Simpson, who was the more senior person on duty at the petrol station on 03 June 2023. It is abundantly clear that she has respect for the sanctity of the court. Slightly old-fashioned in her appearance, she has elected to wear her "Sunday best" for the occasion. From her very appearance and demeanour, one can just tell that she will be a very trustworthy and dependable witness. Defence advocate Charles Melvin immediately takes a mental note that he should try to discredit this witness at his peril. Her manner when taking the solemn oath further enhances her integrity. Yes, the prosecution appears to be off to a very solid start.

Marjorie Simpson speaks very clearly and succinctly, answering all questions put to her by Henry Worthington in a very straightforward and concise manner. She speaks of her years of service within the petrol station. She also confirms that this was the one and only time she had been subjected to a robbery, or rather an attempted robbery. Despite her very assured delivery, she makes mention of how the whole episode has shattered her self-confidence and that she is currently officially on sick leave. She even alludes to the fact that she might not ever have the confidence to return to work there, especially since her retirement is on the horizon.

She speaks of being on duty on the night in question along with her young assistant, Gary Conway. It had been a relatively quiet evening, not at all unusual for a Sunday. She tells of how she was behind the counter while Gary was in the shop area filling shelves when the man wearing a balaclava and carrying a shotgun burst into the premises. She recalls that it was approaching closing time, so probably between 10:30pm and 10:45pm. She then very systematically and slowly describes the events as they unfolded, culminating with the shooting of PC Yardley and the subsequent hasty retreat by the masked robber.

During the course of her evidence, she is invited to identify the sawn-off shotgun. When it is admitted in evidence as exhibit number one, you could actually hear the groaning of the chairs as the jurors leaned forward to secure a slightly better view. In a strange way, the physical presence of the actual weapon used in the shooting somehow seemed to make everything so much more real, almost tangible.

Also identified by witness number one is the Aldi shopping bag that was chosen to take away the loot, and this was introduced into evidence as exhibit number two.

'And I don't suppose that you would be able to identify the assailant, given that I understand that he was wearing a balaclava throughout this terrible ordeal?'

'No'

'But what can you tell me about his overall appearance, height, build, stature etc..?'

'He was quite tall, probably approaching six feet, not skinny and not fat, somewhere in between. I'm sorry, but that is about all I can say.'

'My Lady, if I may ask the accused to stand for a moment?'

Lady Fotheringham indicates her consent and asks Archie Watson to stand, which he duly does.

At that very instant, Henry Worthington has a worrying flashback to many, many years ago when he was in one of his earliest law classes at University. His lecturer, a former court practitioner gave his students some advice that has remained with him over quite a considerable number of years. He said: 'When questioning a witness, never ever ask a question if you do not know what the response is going to be. Henry Worthington chooses to ignore this advice and roll the dice.

'Miss Simpson, may I ask you to have a look at the gentleman now standing in the dock between the two police officers? Could you please tell me if this man's height and build is similar to that of the man who carried out the attempted robbery at your place of work?'

'I suppose so,' she replies.

'I have no further questions of this witness, My Lady,' very keen to end his examination-in-chief on a high note.

'Any cross-examination of this witness?' Asks Lady Fotheringham.

Having consulted his instructing solicitor, Charles Melvin, they are both in agreement that there is nothing to be gained by questioning this witness at any length for two reasons. Firstly, being such a believable witness, they would be wary of trying to question her credibility. This might risk alienating one or two of the jurors, who would simply view her as being a nice, older lady giving her evidence in a very honest and straightforward manner. Secondly, it is not at all in dispute between the parties that an attempted robbery and a fatal killing took place that evening. The only question for debate is around the identity of the perpetrator.

However, the last question addressed to the witness by the prosecution went to the very heart of the question of identity and could not possibly be allowed to go unaddressed.

'Thank you, My Lady. Yes, I do have a couple of questions of this witness, but I will be brief.'

'Miss Simpson, is it fair to say, based on your last response to my Learned Friend, that in fact I could have been that man in the balaclava?'

This question prompts a mild outburst of laughter in the public benches. Quite cleverly, Charles Melvin does not give her an opportunity to answer, by instantly taking the opportunity to influence the response she is about to provide.

'After all, I am not that far off six foot, at five foot, ten inches. OK, while nobody would refer to me as being skinny, I would also like to think that nobody would call me fat! So, I suppose, technically speaking, I could be balaclava man, could I not?'

'I suppose so, yes.'

'Miss Simpson, just one final point, if I may, one that has not been covered by My Learned Friend. I would like you to think very carefully and picture the assailant holding the shotgun. Could you please tell me whether he was left-handed or right-handed? She thought for a moment or two before responding.

'Left-handed, yes I think so.'

'Thank you very much for your time, Miss Simpson. I have no more questions, but please remain on the stand for a moment in case my Learned Friend wishes to re-examine.

'No re-examination, My Lady,' said Henry Worthington. He has already disregarded his lecturer's advice once. He has no desire to push his luck any further.

Witness number two for the prosecution is young Gary Conway. He seems extremely nervous and apprehensive. Although, to be fair, this is probably the very first time he has ever been in a courtroom.

The vast majority of his evidence is merely in corroboration of what the court had already heard from witness number one. He does not have a great deal of new information to add to the proceedings, mostly because he was lying face down for most of the time. There is just one point where his evidence could be deemed to be in any way useful to the prosecution, and that relates to the question of the boots that the perpetrator was wearing at the time of the offence. And it is no coincidence that the prosecutor chooses this as his very last question, wishing to leave the answer hanging in the air for the benefit of the jury.

'And did you notice anything at all distinctive about the robber's attire?'

'Yes, he was wearing a pair of Doc Marten boots.'

How do you know that? What was distinctive about them?

'They have trademark yellow stitching around the base of the boot. I know because I've got a pair.'

'My Lady, I would like to lodge in evidence exhibit number three,' as he walks over to the evidence table to lift up a pair of Doc Marten boots.

'Mr Conway, would you please tell the court if these boots could have been the pair worn by the robber?'

'Yes, they look the same.'

My Lady, I have no further questions of this witness.'

Lady Fotheringham then nods to Charles Melvin, indicating that he is now at liberty to cross-examine.

'Good morning, Mr Conway, I will now be asking you a couple of questions on behalf of the defence. The witness braces himself, and his face reddens as if he has something to hide, which is not, in fact, the case. He is like a fish out of water, not at all comfortable being in the spotlight. He so wishes he was back at university, sitting in a lecture theatre - more his comfort zone. His uneasiness increases as Charles Melvin goes silent for a moment. He then very slowly strolls over towards the exhibit table, lifts up the Doc Marten boots and then strolls back towards him.

'Would you agree with me that Doc Marten boots are very common?'

'Not really, I don't believe so.' Just as soon as these words tripped out of the mouth of the witness, he wished that he had simply agreed, in order to secure a less bumpy ride.

'Come, come Mr Conway. In the petrol station that evening, there were only two males present, and both have a pair. Are you honestly trying to suggest to the court that this was some kind of remarkable coincidence?'

'I suppose so,' responds the witness, what little confidence he has draining from him almost visibly.

'Would it surprise you to know that, on average, each year Doc Marten sells no less than fourteen million pairs of boots similar to these? Would it also surprise you to know that there are actually 34 dedicated Doc Marten outlets in the UK, and this number does not include the vast number of general retail shoe outlets having agency sale agreements?'

At this point, Henry Worthington, for the prosecution, jumps to his feet.

'Objection, My Lady. These are questions, the answers to which cannot be considered to be within the knowledge of this witness, he is not a shoe retailer.'

'Objection sustained,' says The Honourable Lady Fotheringham, before continuing:

'Mr Melvin, I must ask you to desist from this line of questioning.'

'Yes, My Lady. I have just one more question on this general point, the answer to which is within the knowledge of this witness.

'Alright, Mr Melvin, but let me caution you, tread very cautiously.'

'Mr Conway, I assume that you are aware that there is a dedicated Doc Marten store in the centre of Glasgow?'

'Yes, I am aware of that.'

'Ok, Mr Conway, I am now going to revert to the question I posed at the beginning of my cross-examination. On the basis of what you have just heard, would you agree with me that Doc Marten boots are very common?'

'Yes, I suppose so,' the witness answered, his face now the colour of a beetroot.

'I have no further questions of Mr Conway, My Lady.' Charles Melvin then sits down, satisfied that he has taken this witness on his intended journey, and he arrived at his intended destination, albeit it took a little while to get there.

The witness thinks his ordeal is over and, in his eagerness, to remove himself from the spotlight moves to leave the witness box.

'Just one moment Mr Conway, the prosecution have a right of re-examination.' Said Lady Fotheringham. The witness somewhat reluctantly steps back into the witness box.

'Thank you, My Lady, I will be extremely brief.'

'Mr Conway, My Learned Friend has very cleverly tried to bamboozle us with sales figures, which were obviously based on worldwide sales...'

'Mr Worthington, I assume there is a question coming at the end of this?'

'Yes, My Lady. Mr Conway, I appreciate that you are not some kind of aficionado or expert when it comes to the subject of Doc Marten Boots?'

The witness, quite rightly, viewed this as a rhetorical question and elected not to answer.

'However, to the best of your knowledge, are there several styles of Doc Marten boots? They do not all look the same as the pair we see in the courtroom today.

'Yes, I believe so.'

'Thanks Mr Conway.'

It is then music to his ears as he is told that he may leave the witness box.

Lady Fotheringham then decides that this is an appropriate juncture at which to adjourn proceedings. She then releases the jury from their duties for the day, and warns them that under no circumstances have they to discuss the case with any third party.

CHAPTER 66

The Jury Room

By the end of day two of the trial, the jurors are beginning to become acquainted. It is starting to be obvious which members are strong, dominant characters and which are less so - the leaders and the followers.

Of course, for two within their midst, the result of the trial is absolutely crucial, and they are hanging on to every single utterance in court as if their life depended upon it. If only Brian Hunter and Alice Murray were aware that they had a common goal and were fighting the same fight, then they could perhaps collaborate. Obviously, it is far too early for anyone to decide as to which way the trial is going, but for these two, every little strike made by the Defence Counsel appeared to be crucial. Basically, they are extremely grateful for any scraps that might come their way.

At the outset, the jurors were told that they would be required to appoint a foreperson, and this subject was discussed within the jury on their very first day. It was raised by a certain Amir Bajwa. Amir is an extremely successful and quite wealthy individual, being the sole owner of a large, well-known Cash and Carry business just south of Glasgow city centre. In his mid-fifties and wearing a brown suit and shoes, he is quite short with a slight paunch, indicative of someone who enjoys the good life. It becomes clear very early that he falls into the 'leader' category, perhaps derived from managing a substantial workforce in his business. He is not at all shy about putting himself forward as a potential foreperson.

No sooner has he done so when a woman, dressed in smart business attire and probably in her mid-forties, also decides to throw her hat in the ring. It transpires that Michelle Cairns is an HR Manager within a fashion business. She is extremely articulate and exudes a quiet confidence that cannot fail to impress.

In the meantime, coincidentally, the two "victims" on the jury are thinking along the same lines. While neither of them would ordinarily choose to put themselves forward for the position, they independently decide that it would probably place them in the strongest possible position in which to be able to influence their fellow jurors.

Brian Hunter is the first to grasp the nettle, and a tad reluctantly, raises his arm in the air. He then provides some background as to his family status, and his employment history, and why he feels he would be an ideal candidate to be the foreperson. Then there were three!

Alice Murray is, generally speaking, a fairly confident individual. However with the sword of Damocles hanging over her head, her self-assurance has been draining slowly, day by day. The irony is not lost on her; here she is, essentially an unconvicted criminal putting herself forward for a role where she could be largely responsible for determining someone else's guilt or otherwise. If only the other jurors were aware that she is a fraud. Nevertheless, she forces herself to fight her corner and issues her own statement as to why her fellow jurors should elect her as their foreperson.

Amir Bajwa takes it upon himself to organise the vote, when suddenly the hand of Leroy Washington is raised. Leroy is a self-employed graphic artist with a very endearing smile and engaging personality. He has a studio in the west end of Glasgow with some five or six employees.

'I would also like to put my name forward. OK, I am just a hardworking guy who has built up my small business from nothing. My life very much revolves around my family. To be honest, I am just an ordinary family guy with no agendas who appreciates the difference between right and wrong.' Although he spoke very quietly and calmly, it was clear to see that his words seemed to resonate with his fellow jurors.

'Alright everyone,' says Amir Bajwa, almost as if he has already been appointed to the position. (It flashes through Brian Hunter's head that perhaps Amir's blatant over-confidence might just work against him when it comes to the vote.)

'It appears that we now have five candidates. We have Michelle, Brian, Alice, Leroy and myself, Amir. It is now time for us to vote and it is perhaps best that this is done by way of a secret ballot. He duly cuts up fifteen pieces of paper, all of approximately the same size. For the avoidance of doubt, it is quite in order that jurors may vote for themselves. Please can each of you write the name of the person you would like to be foreperson on your slip of paper, fold it up and place it in this empty water jug. This is duly done and then Amir conducts the draw. Thus far he is clearly very happy to be taking the lead role, however permanent or otherwise that might be. Then, with a level of ceremony not entirely merited by the occasion, he lifts out each slip of paper one by one, pausing before announcing the name, presumably for dramatic effect.

- Amir
- Brian
- Michelle
- Amir
- Alice

- Leroy
- Brian
- Leroy
- Michelle
- Brian
- Michelle
- Brian
- Leroy
- Alice
- Michelle

Then, with somewhat less enthusiasm than before, Amir announces that the result of the vote is a tie between Michelle and Brian. A further vote is then required between these two. This duly takes place and, while a very close result, Michelle is ultimately elected over Brian by eight votes to seven.

Brian is understandably quite gutted that he is not going to have that position of influence that he had hoped for. However, he is gracious enough to concede that Michelle would have been his choice as foreperson had he not been able to vote for himself. We will never know how Alice actually chose to vote, but it would be somewhat ironic if she had not in fact voted for her co-conspirator, Brian, given that he lost by just the one vote.

Amir then officially announces, somewhat unenthusiastically, that their foreperson is to be Michelle Cairns.

CHAPTER 67

10 January 2024
(Day three of the trial - morning session)

The next witness for the prosecution is John Barber, the taxi driver. As with the petrol station staff, the defence team are not looking to contest the fact that John Barber picked up a passenger close to where the offences took place. After some discussion between Devlin Delaney and his Counsel, they decide that it is not in their best interests to try to dispute the fact that the man he picked up was, in fact, the person responsible for the attempted robbery and murder of PC Yardley. In essence, all the evidence points towards this being so. Rather, once again, the only area where they are at odds with the prosecution relates solely to the question of the identity of the person responsible.

John Barber's evidence is pretty much as anticipated and is very much in line with his initial precognition. He speaks to the fact that it was quite an unusual and slightly remote spot for him to pick up a fare, that he noticed his passenger's clothes were dirty and also that he was breathless and somewhat agitated. Once again, the prosecution asks of the witness if the height and build of his passenger was similar to that of the accused. Once the jury hears evidence regarding the concealed shotgun, there is little doubt that they will join up the dots.

The driver further confirms there was no conversation between them during the twenty-minute journey. He then points out on the map the exact location where he dropped off his passenger. His evidence is very short and to the point.

Charles Melvin then rises to his feet to very briefly cross-examine the witness.

'Mr Barber, we have heard your evidence to the effect that you dropped your passenger at the junction of Greenland Road and Maitland Road in Lenzie. Am I correct in saying that he did not ask you to take him to a specific address?'

'That is correct.'

'Also, I believe that the place where you dropped him off is very close to Lenzie Station - is that the case?'

'Well, yes.'

So, for all you know, your mystery passenger might well have been going to the station?'

Melvin is merely looking for a simple one-word answer and does not at all relish the response he receives.

'Very unlikely, why would he not just....'

'Mr Barber,' Melvin said in a firm tone, just managing to cut him off mid-sentence.

'It is not for you to ask the questions in this court. Indeed, that is my role.

'Mr Barber, tell me please, in one word, is it possible that the person you dropped off that evening was going to catch a train at Lenzie Station?'

'Yes, possible'

Before concluding his cross-examination, Charles Melvin once again introduced a little charade whereby it was suggested that he, himself, was actually balaclava man - with identical results as before. In all the circumstances, the prosecution were prepared to allow the defence this very minor concession.

Lady Fotheringham then asks Mr Worthington if he would like to re-examine this witness.

'Yes, My Lady.'

'Mr Barber, being a taxi driver, I assume that you are well acquainted with the area where you dropped off your passenger?'

'Yes, Sir.'

'From the point where you dropped off your passenger, how long would it take to walk at a normal pace to Lenzie Station?'

'I would say five or six minutes.'

'And just for the benefit of any jurors who might not be familiar with that area, are there any obstructions or barriers that would prevent you from dropping off your passenger exactly at the station entrance?'

'None at all.'

'One final point, if I may? I assume that you also know Maitland Drive?'

'Yes, Sir.'

'And am I correct in saying that it is quite a short road?'

'Yes.'

'And how long would it take if one were to walk from the drop-off point to a house on Maitland Drive?

'I would say about a minute or two.'

'Mr Barber, thank you so much, you have been very helpful.'

Advantage the prosecution!

Of course, the jurors have no idea of the significance of the last question, but all will be revealed when police evidence is presented.

CHAPTER 68

10 January 2024
(Day three of the trial - afternoon session)

Lady Fotheringham determined that when John Barber had finished his evidence, it would be a convenient time to stop for lunch, a little earlier than usual. The afternoon has been set aside for the police witnesses to take the stand.

The first officer to give evidence is one of the first two to arrive upon the crime scene, namely PC William Hardy. He speaks to them responding to an emergency call from Marjorie Simpson regarding an attempted robbery and shooting at a petrol station. He and PC Yusuf Khan were in the general vicinity of the crime when the call came through and were in attendance at the scene within seven or eight minutes.

'When we reached the crime scene, the ambulance service had also just arrived. We observed that an officer had been shot in the chest, and he was bleeding heavily. We now know this to be a PC Adam Yardley, but he was not known to either my partner or myself, being based at a different station. It was immediately clear that his injury was of a very serious nature. He received urgent medical assistance at the scene and was then conveyed as a matter of urgency to the Royal Infirmary Hospital by ambulance.

There were two employees present at the petrol station, Marjorie Simpson and Gary Conway. While both were clearly in a state of severe shock, they were thankfully unhurt. We were advised that the robber was wearing a balaclava and, therefore, neither party would be in a position to provide positive identification. In the company of PC Yusuf Khan, we interviewed both employees separately, and in no respect did their accounts conflict with one another. They were both found to be very credible witnesses. We took possession of an Aldi shopping bag, which the robber was having filled with cash, at the point where PC Yardley entered the shop.'

'My Lady, if I may show this witness exhibit number two?'

The witness then identifies the bag as being the one that was used in the robbery, or at least identical to it.

There was nothing really contentious in the evidence provided by this witness, and Henry Worthington announced that he had no further questions.

Charles Melvin is then given the opportunity to cross-examine.

'Constable Hardy, I will be very brief. Do you recall asking the witness Marjorie Simpson if the robber was right or left-handed?'

'I do, yes. She said that he was left-handed.'

'Thank you, Constable Hardy, I have no further questions.'

PC Hardy then stood down and PC Yusuf Khan then took the stand. His evidence was almost identical to that of his colleague. In fact, it seemed more than likely that they had been comparing notes in the witness room, which was not an uncommon practice.

'My Lady, the Crown would now like to call to the stand PC John Stanton.

Constable Stanton, thanks for attending today. I understand that you are employed by Police Scotland in the specific capacity as a dog handler, is that correct?'

'Yes, sir.'

'And how long have you been employed in this role?'

'Approximately twelve years.'

'And I understand that your canine partner is a spaniel, who goes under the very apt name of Snout?'

There are some chuckles from the public benches, who seem to appreciate this fleeting moment of light humour.

'Yes, that is correct, sir. He is my tracking dog.'

'Please cast your mind back to the evening of the third of June 2023 and tell us what your specific role was following the incident.'

'I was tasked with taking Snout to the petrol station to attempt to detect a scent from a carrier bag allegedly carried by the perpetrator. Having successfully picked up the scent, it then led him, and me, to the nearby woods. He then stopped rather abruptly at a slight clearing and started digging. Very quickly, he uncovered a sawn-off shotgun, which was buried not far below the surface. This was bagged and passed to our forensic team to be processed.'

'My Lady, if I may show this witness exhibit one?'

'You may.'

'Constable Stanton, and is this the shotgun that Snout kindly discovered for us?'

'Yes, it is.'

'And was Snout able to follow the scent beyond this clearing?'

'No, we tried, but had no success.'

Finally, My Lady, if I may, I would like to show the witness the map, which has been identified as exhibit number four.' (There is a nod of approval from Lady Fotheringham.)

'Constable Stanton, I would ask you to look at exhibit number four, which I understand to be a map of the area in question. (The map is now projected onto a large screen.) I would ask you to look carefully at this map. As you will see, it shows the petrol station relative to the adjacent woods. As best you can, I would ask you to show the court where Snout unearthed the shotgun.'

'Approximately here,' responds PC Stanton.

The jurors are all keenly studying the map. Henry Worthington continues.

'For the benefit of the record, let it be known that the witness is indicating a spot virtually halfway, between the petrol station and the spot where the taxi driver said that he picked up his passenger.

'Thank you, PC Stanton, and please pass our best wishes to Snout.'

'I do not wish to cross-examine this witness, My Lady.'

'The Crown now calls Doctor Janice Stevens. Doctor Stevens is a long-legged, willowy-type figure who gives the impression of gliding, rather than walking into the courtroom. Aged, probably in her early fifties, she is dressed in a long, floaty, green and white dress and green ankle boots accompanied by what most people would consider to be an excess of jewellery. It would be fair to say that this witness is just a fraction bohemian in appearance. She also seems quite assured, without appearing over-confident. Perhaps this has something to do with her enjoying such an excellent reputation in her specialist field, that being pathology.

Henry Worthington asks her to list her qualifications for the jury - and they are not in short supply. He then continues.

'For the benefit of the jurors and for the avoidance of any doubt, let me just confirm in the very simplest of terms that the job of a pathologist is to examine bodies after their death to try to determine what has caused the death.'

Then turning towards the witness:

'Doctor Stevens, on 19 June 2023 did you examine the body of Adam Yardley?'

'Yes, I did.'

'And could you please share your findings with the court?'

'The body was that of a white male, known to be aged 35. He was a fit-looking man of slender build. Apart from the injury sustained on the evening of the shooting, he appeared to be otherwise in very good health. As regards to toxicology, there was no evidence, having checked for alcohol, heroin, marijuana and amphetamines. In simple layman's terms, the now deceased was not under the influence of any drink or drugs which might have impaired his judgement.'

Doctor Stevens then spoke in some detail as to how Adam Yardley had ultimately died due to a gunshot to the chest fired at relatively close range. As far as the defence case was concerned, this evidence was totally non-contentious and thus, there was to be no cross-examination of this witness.

Shortly afterwards, Lady Fotheringham called a halt to court proceedings for the day.

CHAPTER 69

11 January 2024
(Day four of the trial)

Day four of the trial gets underway, as the Crown calls their next witness, the head of the Major Incident Team (MIT), Detective Chief Inspector, Karen Orr.

'DCI Orr, I believe that you headed up the Major Incident Team that was looking into the attempted robbery and murder of PC Adam Yardley?'

'Yes, that is correct. And I was assisted by Detective Sergeant Alan Smyth.'

'DCI Orr, we have heard evidence in this court that you recovered a sawn-off shotgun buried not terribly far from the scene of the crime. Is that correct?'

'Yes.'

'And was this passed to your forensic team for testing?'

'Yes, it was.'

'And what were the findings?'

'It was confirmed that this was, in fact, the weapon that was used to kill PC Yardley. Also, there was a fingerprint match with the now accused, Archibald Watson.'

(The revelation of this most damming piece of evidence causes a murmuring in the public benches.)

'And was it on this basis that you opted to charge the now defendant with attempted robbery and the murder of PC Yardley?'

'It was on the basis of this, coupled with other threads of evidence, which pointed towards his guilt.'

'Would you like to elaborate, DCI Orr?'

'Firstly, we have every reason to believe the passenger in John Barber's taxi was the person who committed the offences. We believe that person to be Archibald Watson, and after the offence, he took the taxi to his father's house.'

DCI Orr then went on to provide evidence relating to the black balaclava found upon searching the defendant's house. She also spoke to the description of the perpetrator as provided by both Marjorie Simpson and the taxi driver, John Barber. In addition she referred to the Doc Martens (exhibit number 3), recovered from the house of the now accused.

DCI Orr was an extremely competent witness, and one very experienced in delivering evidence in cases such as this. Charles Melvin prefers to pick his battles, however, there is one aspect of her evidence he is most certainly not going to allow to pass without comment.

'DCI Orr, you made mention of the fact that fingerprints matching the now accused were discovered on the weapon. Is that correct?

'Yes, that is correct.'

'Presumably, you have absolutely no idea when those fingerprints were placed on the weapon?'

'No, not for certain.'

'DCI Orr, unless you are gifted with extrasensory perception, then surely the answer to my last question should simply be a straight 'no'. Is that not correct?'

'Perhaps,' replies DCI Orr, determined not to concede the point entirely.

Then Charles Melvin throws in a quite unexpected grenade into proceedings.

'DCI Orr, were there any other fingerprints found on the murder weapon?'

Being a seasoned campaigner, she disguises her surprise at this last question and answers quite calmly.

'Yes, one other set.'

'And who did this other set belong to?'

'A certain Douglas Smith, generally known as Dougie Smith.'

'And why is this Dougie Smith also not a suspect in this case?'

'Because he was eliminated from our enquiries at a quite early stage.'

'And where is this mysterious Dougie Smith now?'

'He is currently in HM Prison Barlinnie on remand.'

'Although currently incarcerated, was he at liberty at the time of the murder of Adam Yardley?'

'Yes.'

'On what charge has he been remanded?' asks Melvin, aware that although his witness has maintained her composure throughout, he does have her very much on the back foot.

'On what charge?'

'I believe it was robbery.'

There were some gasps from the public benches and some jurors edged forward in their seats.

'Pardon?' says Melvin, who had heard her response perfectly well, but wished her to repeat her answer for maximum effect.

'I said that it was robbery.'

Melvin hesitated again, enjoying the moment.

'DCI Orr, my sources tell me it was actually armed robbery, is that not so?'

'It could be.'

'Come, come, DCI Orr, you can do better than that. Surely you would have done your homework before coming to give evidence in such an important case where a man's freedom is at stake? Or was it a case of you had a suspect and then chose to dismiss any evidence pointing elsewhere?

My Lady, I have no other questions of this witness.' Upon saying this, Melvin immediately sits down, discouraging DCI Orr from responding. Rather, he prefers to close his cross-examination with his very last question still ringing in the ears of the jurors.

Henry Worthington is not particularly wishing to encourage any more conversation about Dougie Smith. However he has few options to try to recover the situation. Accordingly, he elects for a very brief re-examination.

'DCI Orr, judging your senior ranking, may I assume that you are a veteran of many criminal cases?'

'Yes, that is so.'

Indeed, you will have been involved in investigating many very serious crimes, such as this?'

'Correct.'

'May I assume that you would have considered the evidence very carefully before eliminating Dougie Smith from your enquiries in relation to this case?'

'Absolutely, Dougie Smith provided us with an alibi, which checked out.'

'Thank you for your time here today, DCI Orr,' says Worthington only too keen to draw a line under this most recent line of questioning.

The defence team had intended leading specialist evidence to prove that the now accused is in fact right-handed. However, this matter is not disputed by the prosecution, thereby precluding the need for evidence being led to this effect. Lady Fotheringham will refer to this matter when addressing the jury at the end of the trial.

At this point, Melvin shares a brief word with his instructing solicitor before addressing the court:

'My Lady, after due consideration, I can advise that the defence does not wish to lead any evidence in this case.'

'Thank you, Mr Melvin. In that case, I propose that we now cease proceedings for today. This will provide some time for both parties to prepare for their final submissions to the jury. We will resume at 10.00 tomorrow morning.'

'Court Rise,' announces the Clerk of Court and with a swish of her gown, Lady Fotheringham exits stage left.

CHAPTER 70

11 January 2024

Just as soon as the court concludes its business for the day, Charles Melvin and Devlin Delaney decide to go down to the holding cells to have a word with Archie Watson before he is taken back to HM Prison Barlinnie.

The three of them are crammed into a small, bare, airless cell, and Melvin immediately takes the lead.

'Well, you will obviously be wondering how we feel the trial has been going. It has not been easy, the prosecution do not require a great deal more when they already have your fingerprints on the murder weapon. We are also not in a

BRENDAN MAGUIRE

position to provide an alibi for you for the night in question. I am not going to sugar-coat this, we are fighting an uphill battle.

It was never an option for you to take the stand in this trial. If you were to do so, the prosecution would be in their element, they would tear you apart. Rather, we hope to expose and highlight some inconsistencies in the prosecution case. Most significantly, there is the witness, Marjorie Simpson, speaking to the fact that the assailant was left-handed. Also in your favour is the evidence relating to the other set of fingerprints on the murder weapon. (Very significantly, neither Melvin nor Delaney mentions the fact that Davy Ross, The Beaver, had done some homework on Dougie Smith, whose fingerprints were also found on the weapon. He discovered, unfortunately, that he too, is right-handed.)

The intention is that in my address to the jury I put the spotlight on these inconsistencies with a view to putting sufficient doubt in their minds that they move to acquit. It will, however, be a tall order.'

The jurors have been dismissed for the evening. It is probably fair to say that thirteen out of the fifteen have savoured the experience, many of them welcoming a change of environment and some, a temporary escape from their usual mundane daily routines. But not so for jurors numbers five and thirteen. For these two, it is a living hell. Each strand of incriminatory evidence being like a dagger to the heart.

Brian Hunter, juror number five, is terrified that his wife is going to be told about his illicit affair. If so, what will happen next, will she leave him? Will he lose his kids or be restricted to only being able to see them every week or two? Or perhaps she would forgive him, and they could start

235

afresh? Since he received the letter, he has not been in touch with Sandra Baxter, from his workplace. She has tried to call him on a couple of occasions, but he has not picked up. He is in no doubt that he would gladly give up his illicit relationship if it meant he could preserve his family unit. Interestingly. however, in his own mind he does not necessarily commit to sacrificing his extra-marital affair, should the accused be found not guilty.

Equally, Alice Murray, juror number thirteen, is totally living on her nerves. Her whole life is up in the air. Over and above the attractive salary she now commands, she totally enjoys her new job, especially in light of her recent promotion. It has also been so comforting for her to know that her employers have identified her talents and level of commitment. Why is it that sometimes, in order to really appreciate something, we possess, we have to be in danger of losing it?

Both Alice Murray and Brian Hunter have so much to lose, but not nearly as much as Archie Watson, with whom their interests are, somewhat ironically, aligned. As are the interests of Devlin Delaney, who would be very much a beneficiary if Archie Watson were to be found not guilty. Also falling into this category would be Davy Ross, who would be very handsomely rewarded for all his successful digging.

Matt Goldstein has missed very little of the trial thus far. One or two of his colleagues have questioned his inordinate degree of interest in the case. He has just tried to explain it away by virtue of it being a policeman who has been killed and the case being so high profile with a massive public interest. If only they knew! Matt looks a shadow of his former self and some of his colleagues are still questioning privately whether he has any serious health problems. His insomnia issues have continued and when he does manage to sleep, he is still plagued with nightmares, usually involving incarceration and retribution.

Ironically, the lives of so many could be markedly enriched should fate look kindly upon Archibald Watson.

CHAPTER 71

12 January 2024
(Day five of the trial - morning session)

'Court, please rise.'

Lady Fotheringham duly appears and takes her place on the bench.

'Good morning to all. Now, we have heard from the defence team that the accused, Archibald Watson, will not be giving evidence in this case. Jurors, this is perfectly normal and acceptable, and no inference should be taken as a result of this decision. At the end of the day, the onus is on the prosecution to prove the case against the accused.

So, Ladies and Gentlemen, lest you are not familiar with court procedure, Senior Advocate Henry Worthington will now make his final submissions to you on behalf of the prosecution. Thereafter, Charles Melvin will do the same on behalf of Mr Watson. Following that, I will then address you before you are invited to commence your deliberations.

Mr Worthington, the floor is yours.'

'Thank you, My Lady. Ladies and Gentlemen of the jury, as you have just heard, it is now for me to state the case for the prosecution. I will be very brief because, relative to the vast majority of cases I have been involved with, this one is extremely straightforward with minimal facts or evidence for you to consider.

As you are aware, the defence has elected not to provide any evidence in this case, as they are fully entitled to do. So basically, we have not heard any testimony from them suggesting that anyone other than the man sitting in the dock here was responsible for these terrible crimes. Nor have we been provided with any alibi on behalf of the accused which could absolve him from suspicion.

Ladies and Gentlemen, I would submit to you that the case against Archibald Watson is nothing short of overwhelming. Of course, the most damaging element is the existence of the fingerprints of the accused on the murder weapon. Well, they say every picture tells a story! Then, the police find a black balaclava in his house, similar to the one used in the attempted robbery. And then there is the evidence regarding the Doc Marten boots that the defence team would have you believe is a complete coincidence.

Ladies and Gentlemen, how many clear signposts do we need to establish that Archibald Watson is guilty of the crimes as charged? Each of these strands of evidence on their own is quite damming, but when woven together, they create a tapestry, a tapestry of guilt.

The defence team has tried to make some mileage from the fact that the accused is right-handed, a fact that is not disputed by us. Ladies and Gentlemen, let me address this point head-on. You have all heard the evidence of our first witness, Marjorie Simpson. I don't believe that there is a single person in this courtroom who would doubt that this woman was a totally honest, forthright and credible witness, one who came here to do her civil duty and to tell the truth, the whole truth. Honest, she most certainly is, but infallible, she is not. Given the general weight of the evidence against Archibald Watson, I would suggest to you that Marjorie Simpson was simply mistaken. Her memory has been playing tricks with her, not at all uncommon for someone approaching the age of retirement. In support of my theory, and most significantly, when specifically asked as to whether he was left-handed, she responds:

'Yes, I think so.'

'Ladies and Gentlemen, the important word there is "think". I would suggest that the very word itself implies an element of doubt. And talking of doubt, I have little doubt that the prosecution will try to blow this little piece of evidence out of proportion. I would caution you to attach the level of importance to it that it actually deserves. Please keep in mind Marjorie Simpson's age and the fact that she was in a position of unfathomable stress at the time of the attempted robbery. Who could blame her in the circumstances if she has made an error? When you add to this her response "Yes, I think so", I am sure you will give this matter exactly the weight it deserves.'

'Adam Yardley was an off-duty serving policeman whose only mistake was being in the wrong place at the wrong time. Susan Yardley has been denied a husband, the man she loved, and her two young children have lost their beloved dad all because of the cowardly and vicious actions of one man, Archibald Watson. So, I would ask each and every juror to carefully consider the points I have raised and return unanimous verdicts of guilty on all charges. You owe it to the court and also to the family of the late Adam Yardley. I thank you all once again for your time and have every confidence that you will arrive at the right decision.'

Matt Goldstein is sitting in the back row of the public benches, once again wishing to keep as low a profile as possible. Listening to the compelling arguments from Senior Counsel has further deepened his mood. He now feels quite positive that a conviction will follow on and that Archie Watson will probably not be the only one going to prison.

Lady Fotheringham then invites Charles Melvin to address the jury on behalf of the defence:

'Thank you, My Lady, I too intend being brief in my address.' He then remains silent for a couple of minutes for some dramatic effect, and then in a very slow but determined and confident fashion, walks over towards the jury and leans on the railing in front of the first row of jurors.

'Ladies and Gentlemen, the prosecution would normally assimilate various strands of evidence and with a fair wind this might ultimately lead them to the guilty party. However, I would respectfully suggest that in this instance they have decided in advance who they believe to be the guilty party and then built a narrative to support this - a narrative built of straw.

I am not saying that my client is an angel, not at all. He has done a number of things in his past that he himself is not proud of, but that does not make him a killer - far from it. Yes, there is a fingerprint match, but there is also a match for a certain Dougie Smith. Perhaps he is the killer? How robust was his alibi, and was it thoroughly checked out? We do not know the answers to these questions. It does appear to me that the police were already convinced that they had their man. For whatever reason, Dougie Smith was not produced as a Crown witness, which, of course, is their entitlement. However, had he been here, then I could of course have fully tested the strength of his alibi.

There has been mention made of the balaclava discovered during the house search of my client's house. However, Ladies and Gentlemen, please note that there has not been one shred of evidence linking it to the armed robbery.

The prosecution was also clutching at straws when attempting to place the accused at the scene of the crime simply because he was wearing Doc Marten boots. These are just two examples of trying to get the narrative to fit their desired result.

In addition, of course, there is the taxi journey and the evidence provided by Mr Barber, the driver. It very conveniently suits their version of events to suggest that not only was my client the passenger, but that he was going to his parent's house. So, what the prosecution would have us believe is that Archie Watson was involved in an armed robbery, he shoots a policeman and then, instead of going home, opts to pay his parents a little social visit. A highly unlikely course of events, would you not think?

Finally, we have clear unequivocal evidence from Marjorie Simpson that the shooter was left-handed. Why would she be mistaken regarding that? The prosecution wants it both ways. On the one hand, they wish you to accept her evidence, keeping in mind that she is a Crown witness. On the other hand, they would like you to totally ignore the one piece of her evidence that directly supports the defence case. And for the avoidance of any doubt, please remember that the prosecution has formally accepted that Mr Archibald Watson is, in fact, right-handed.

Ladies and Gentlemen of the jury, the bottom line is that there is no real evidence placing my client at the crime scene. Do you not think if he had been at the petrol station, there would be some evidence to this effect, either DNA or otherwise?

Is there any single one of you on this jury who can say with any strong degree of conviction that Archie Watson was there that particular night? As My Lady will shortly direct you, if you do harbour even a reasonable doubt about my client's guilt then you must acquit him. Even if you suppose that he might be guilty, would you really wish to have somebody locked up for the rest of their natural life, based on supposition? I think not!

I thank you all for your kind attention and would ask each and every one of you to return a verdict of not guilty on all charges.'

'Ladies and Gentlemen, thank you for sitting so patiently through the evidence in this case and also to the closing arguments of Counsel for the Crown and the defence. It is now my task as the presiding judge to address you to ensure that you are fully aware of the most important role that you play in this process. You are, in effect, the most important people in this courtroom.

The judge and the jury have two quite distinct functions in a jury trial. I am the arbiter of the law, and so any directions in the law given by me, you are obliged to accept and apply to the case. In contrast, you, the jury, are the arbiter of the facts and have sole discretion in this area.

Let me first advise you of the concept of burden of proof. The prosecution must prove its case against the accused. The accused is innocent until proven guilty. It is not for him to prove he is innocent but for the prosecution to establish guilt. In this particular case the defence have chosen not to place the accused in the witness box. They are completely entitled to make such a decision, and no inference should be taken from this. This is entirely his right.

As well as the burden of proof I would like to address you on the standard of proof. To prove that an accused is guilty, the prosecution must prove its case beyond reasonable doubt, often referred to as the jury being "satisfied so that they are sure" of the accused's guilt. This is not to be interpreted as a whimsical or fanciful doubt, but a reasonable one. This is the standard of proof. If, after hearing the evidence, you are less than sure of the accused's guilt, then he is entitled to be acquitted, namely, found not guilty. This means that even if the jury thought the accused was probably guilty, but were not sure of their guilt, the verdict should not be one of guilty.

Let me now revert to the particular facts of this case, which are relatively straightforward. There is absolutely no doubt that on the evening in question, an attempted armed robbery took place, and a police officer was shot and subsequently died as a result.

There is one specific point that I would like to touch upon. You will all recall the evidence from the Crown's first witness relating to the assailant being left-handed. Let me reconfirm to you that in order to save the court time and to save unnecessary inconvenience to any witness or witnesses, it was agreed between Mr Worthington for the prosecution and Mr Devlin for the defence, that the accused in this case is, in fact, right-handed. For the clear avoidance of any doubt, this matter is not up for dispute.

Unlike many court trials, you might see on television where an accused can be found to be guilty or not guilty. We have a third option, the verdict of 'not proven' which is only available within the Scottish legal system. The legal implications of a not proven verdict are exactly the same as a not guilty verdict - the accused is acquitted and is innocent in the eyes of the law. There is no statutory, case law or generally accepted definition of the not proven verdict, nor of the difference between the not guilty and not proven verdicts. Indeed, the Appeal Court has actually instructed us judges not to attempt to describe the difference to jurors! In essence, a not proven verdict is returned when the jurors believe the case has not been proven beyond reasonable doubt.'

'Members of the jury, I am now going to send you out to begin your deliberations. A man's freedom is at stake, so please take just as long as you feel is necessary. Any conviction will be on the basis of a majority verdict, with eight jurors required to decide that the accused is guilty. Should fewer than eight of you declare a guilty verdict, the accused will be acquitted. So a hung jury is not a possibility.

Ladies and Gentlemen of the jury, I now discharge you to carry out your deliberations. I thank you all for your kind attention - just one final cautionary note. Please remember not to discuss any aspects of this case with anyone other than your fellow jurors, including your family members. Good luck with your deliberations.'

CHAPTER 72

12 January 2024
(Day five of the trial - afternoon session)

The jury duly retire to the jury room to commence their deliberations. No sooner have they sat down than Amir Bajwa voices his opinion.

'Well, I don't believe this will take us too long as it is perfectly obvious that he is guilty as sin.'

Shattered to hear this early pronouncement, Alice Murray places an early stake in the ground.

'I think our intended role is to discuss the merits or otherwise of the prosecution case and come to a balanced decision. In any event, I had understood that our spokesperson, Michelle, was to manage our deliberations.' It becomes immediately obvious from his facial expression that Amir is not accustomed to being put in his place - and certainly not by a woman!

At this early stage in proceedings, Brian Hunter thinks he might just have an ally in the jury room. If only he knew!

Michelle then enters the conversation in a very dignified, reserved, but assured manner, choosing to completely ignore the recent exchange.

'In order to invite some frank discussion around the table, would anyone like to tell us their own view of the evidence?

Strategically, Brian feels he should not pass up this opportunity to try to influence some of the jurors.

'I see things quite differently to Amir.' He lied. 'While I accept that the evidence does not look good for the accused, I am not absolutely convinced of his guilt. It is perfectly obvious to me, and I am sure to most of us that the accused is involved in a life of crime. Indeed, any doubt on that front was removed, given that his fingerprints are on the murder weapon. However, that does not mean he was at the petrol station or that he pulled the trigger. Surely it is also concerning that there were also other prints on the weapon, and the prosecution seemed to play it down?'

Then, in an attempt to appear to be favouring a more balanced or neutral perspective, he continues:

'I think it quite possible that Archie Watson is guilty, but I don't want to be responsible for him being locked up for life if I am not absolutely sure. I mean, had he actually been spotted at the petrol station, things would be quite different.'

Upon hearing this, Amir raised his eyebrows and allows himself an audible sigh, making his views on what he has just heard perfectly clear, without having to say a word.

By contrast, Brian's unwitting tag-team partner, Alice, spots an early opportunity to voice her view and decides to take full advantage.

'I tend to agree with Brian. I do think the accused might well be guilty, but don't think the evidence is conclusive. We have been told by the judge that if we have a reasonable doubt then we shouldn't convict. Well, I am telling you that I fall into that camp.'

Then Leroy, who had remained silent thus far, decides to join the discussion:

'I must say that I left the courtroom convinced he was guilty, but all this talk about reasonable doubt and having listened to both Alice and Brian, now I am not so sure. I mean,

I don't think I could live with myself, if I were to send someone to prison for life, if I had the slightest doubt about their innocence.'

Amir, then instantly responds:

'Yes, but could you live with yourself if you were to find him not guilty and then he went out and murdered someone else.'

There were then a few moments of silence as these last comments hit home.

'Does anyone else wish to express their views?' Prompts Michelle in an attempt to stimulate more debate.

A youngish man, probably in his late twenties, dressed in a very smart business suit, was in little doubt about how he interpreted the evidence.

'I one hundred per cent agree with Amir. I have absolutely no doubt that he is guilty. Apart from the fingerprints, there are the other bits and pieces of evidence that all point in his direction. Also, if you were in his position, wouldn't you want to give evidence to try to clear your name?'

Almost immediately, another older female juror stated that she agreed. She went on to say that if it had been her, and she were innocent, she would most definitely want to let the court hear her side of the story.

Upon hearing this, Michelle once again chooses to intervene.

'One word of caution, if I may? As I understand the situation, having listened to the judge, the fact that the accused did not provide evidence should in no way influence or cloud our views as to his innocence or otherwise. Apparently, he is not obliged to say anything as the burden to prove guilt lies entirely upon the prosecution. For all we know, the defence solicitor could have plenty of reasons for not wanting him to give evidence. Inwardly, both Alice and Brian feel a debt of gratitude to Michelle.

The day is now drawing to a close and it is quite clear that no consensus is to be reached in the short term, so it is universally agreed that proceedings should be held over for another day. For Brian and Alice, the anguish continues. As for Matt, well, he has been enduring extreme anguish for quite some considerable time, but one way or another, it is now reaching an end.

CHAPTER 73

13 January 2024
(Day six of the trial)

The following morning there is a palpable sense of expectation around Glasgow High Court. The "word on the street" is that the jury in the case would not be out for very long. This view is most probably in anticipation of an early guilty verdict. In any event, nobody wants to stray very far from the court, just in case.

The main hub is the court canteen. The benefit of this location is that an announcement will be made there as to when the jury is about to return. In one corner are the Watson family, now out in force. Jimmy is sitting on his own in the opposite corner - some wounds are very slow to heal.

In another area of the canteen is a sizeable number from Police Scotland, including those who gave evidence during the trial. Not surprisingly, when one of their own loses his or her life, it intensifies that sense of belonging and strengthens the already strong bond that exists among them. Suffice to say that they can barely look in the direction of the family of the accused, whom they consider to be nothing but scum. It is a potentially volatile situation as tensions run high, and it would only take one out-of-place remark from either faction to spark off an ugly scene. Of course, the courts are no strangers to such circumstances, and there is very visible security in place, keeping a close eye on this potential powder keg situation.

Elsewhere in the canteen, sitting at a table on his own, is someone else who has a very vested interest in proceedings. Not attracting any attention to himself, he goes unnoticed as he quietly sips his coffee, alone with his thoughts. For The Observer, the verdict will have a truly massive impact on his life, one way or another.

Susan Yardley could not bear to sit through the trial. She is still enduring unimaginable pain at the very tragic and sudden loss of her young husband. The wound is still far too raw. She is, however, kept fully up to date with proceedings by her older brother who has been sitting through the trial in its entirety. Each evening, he would provide his sister with a progress report. Susan has never had a vindictive bone in her body, but then again, she has never been in such a state of utter desolation. So, perhaps it should come as no surprise that she has taken some perverse delight in hearing how the evidence has been stacking up against Archie Watson. She only harbours ill will for this man - the man who she feels sure is responsible for decimating her family unit and destroying their future. With this in mind, perhaps it is not a total surprise that she has chosen to be present for the delivery of the verdict. However, she does not wish to be in close proximity to the Watson family, whom she has labelled as "vermin". Rather, she is found nursing a coffee in the Court Cafe, located a convenient few hundred yards from the High Court. She sits there impatiently while awaiting a call from her brother to say the jury is about to return their verdict.

In the meantime, it is now late morning, and the jury is still discussing the relative merits of the prosecution case. While there is a clear consensus in favour of convicting, there is still a certain ebbing and flowing, very much to Amir's chagrin.

By contrast, Brian is trying to steer the jurors in his direction while at the same time wishing to appear at all times to be taking a moderate rather than radical stance.

'Overall, I must admit that there does seem to be a general consensus that Archie Watson is most likely guilty. I think we would all tend to agree. But is "most likely" sufficient when there is so much at stake for the accused? Also, is "most likely" actually our own layman's way of saying that there is a reasonable doubt?'

Just when Brian and Alice are thinking and hoping that his argument is actually gaining some traction, they are dealt a severe body blow. A quite mature, very well-groomed lady who had kept her Counsel since their deliberations commenced, decided to make her contribution:

'Forgive me for being blunt. However, I have been sitting here listening attentively to all that has been said. To be honest, and with the greatest of respect, I simply cannot comprehend how totally misguided some of my fellow jurors appear to be. It is so absolutely, blatantly obvious that this man is guilty. One must appreciate that in any criminal trial, it is probably impossible to say 100% that an accused person is guilty - unless you have the benefit of seeing the offence committed live on video. But this case is as close to 100% as you are ever likely to get. I am sorry, but I really do believe that some people on this jury truly need to take a reality check.'

There is silence for a moment or two as the jurors take stock before Michelle tactfully proposes that it might be an appropriate juncture to stop for lunch.

CHAPTER 74

13 January 2024
(The Verdict)

It is approaching late afternoon, and to the surprise of the majority, the jury deliberations are still ongoing. Nerves are jangling, fingernails are being bitten, and caffeine is on overload as the anticipation levels increase.

Suddenly, just when it is feared that proceedings are going to extend into yet another day, there is a scurry of activity amongst the media who are covering the trial - a true tell-tale sign that something is in the offing. There follows a buzz of excited conversation throughout the High Court building while the TV crews jostle for a prime position. In the event of a not guilty verdict, they will be looking to capture Archie Watson celebrating, perhaps even providing him with a cheap bottle of fizz to enhance the image. However, should the decision go the other way, they will be just as happy to capture the anguish on the faces of his closest relations. For them it is very much a win/win situation.

The public areas are immediately populated, with eager beavers rushing in to try to secure a prime vantage point. Nobody will have noticed Susan Yardley slipping into the back row along with her ever-supportive brother. She is so very keen to see justice done but nevertheless is not deluded enough to imagine that such closure is likely to relieve the pain which she endures each and every day of her life.

The Watson family, excluding Jimmy, are all seated in the very front row, having reserved their places by having earlier placed various garments across the seats - towels on sun loungers come to mind. And, being such an intimidating bunch, nobody would dare to move them.

Once everybody else is in situ, the jurors are invited back into the packed courtroom, all looking fairly frazzled after hours of heated deliberations. The clerk of court has to call for quiet on two separate occasions, and eventually, there is an expectant hush. At this point, Lady Fotheringham takes centre stage,

'I absolutely appreciate that this is a highly charged atmosphere, and feelings and emotions are running very high. However, the court will not tolerate any outbursts when the verdicts are delivered. Anyone ignoring this warning will be deemed to be in contempt of court and will be dealt with very harshly. I hope you all take this on board.'

The accused, who has remained pretty expressionless throughout the trial, is then asked to stand in anticipation of the verdicts being delivered.

'Members of the jury, would your foreperson please stand?'

Michelle Cairns instantly rises to her feet.

'Has the jury reached verdicts on which you are all agreed?'

'No,' responds Michelle in a loud and clear voice. At this point, the tension in the air moves up a notch or two, and Meg Watson, Archie's wife, becomes extremely light-headed before falling forward. Lady Fotheringham asks a court official to come to her aid and, a half glass of water later, proceedings continue.

'Has the jury reached verdicts upon which a majority of eight are agreed?'

'Yes, we have,' says Michelle.

On the charge of being in possession of an offensive weapon, how do you find the accused?'

'Not proven.'

(There are murmurings in the courtroom.)

'On the charge of attempted robbery, how do you find the accused?'

'Not proven.'

(There are louder murmurings in the courtroom.)

On the charge of the murder of PC Adam Yardley, how do you find the accused?

'Not proven.'

Notwithstanding the earlier warning from the judge, the court goes into complete uproar. There are shouts of both anguish and jubilation. Tears are running down the face of Meg Watson, tears of unmitigated joy. Archie Watson looks over to his family in the public benches with a look of total bemusement on his face. They respond with very hearty cheers and fist pumps in triumphant salute. In the moment, Archie even acknowledges his younger brother, Jimmy, who is smiling from ear to ear. Perhaps, just perhaps, the ice there is beginning to melt.

Devlin Delaney and Charles Melvin indulge in a warm embrace, the former, absolutely delighted in the knowledge that for him it is a payday extraordinaire. Davy Ross is also heartily celebrating his newfound wealth.

The clerk of court once again calls for order, but he can barely be heard amidst the mayhem and chaos. There is further racket from the stampeding press as they clamour in their unbridled enthusiasm to go to print, even if only digitally.

By contrast, the police officers in the gallery stare straight ahead in utter disbelief, their overwhelming feeling being one of betrayal on the part of the criminal system and the stark realisation that all their efforts have been in vain.

Susan Yardley simply sits with her head in her hands, sobbing uncontrollably. She thought at the time of Adam's death that she had reached rock bottom, but she has now discovered even new depths.

Also extremely emotional is Matt Goldstein, but for quite different reasons. If anyone from his department had spotted the tears of relief cascading down his cheeks, they might have been forgiven for thinking that he had defected to the other side. Wiping his face, through tear-filled eyes, he messages his wife:

Hi
Brilliant news – it's over!
The case wasn't proven. I cannot tell you how relieved I feel. I've to drop a couple of things off at the office on the way home, and I'll also stop off to get a bottle of champers. Why not book somewhere for dinner?
Love you xxx

Liz is over the moon to receive his message and thinks to herself "There is a God!" With a renewed spring in her step, she promptly looks out and dusts down a couple of champagne flutes that have not seen the light of day for many a long time. This calls for a true celebration.

Had juror numbers five and thirteen been aware of their respective circumstances, they would no doubt have wanted to give one another the very warmest of embraces - but then again, that might have given the game away! (Likened to the scenario where a fervent football fan is only able to secure a ticket for the opposing end of the park and is obliged to sit on his hands and be denied the sheer exhilaration of being able to celebrate his team scoring a goal.) At least Brian will be able to relive the moment with his wife, Penny. Whereas Alice's two cats would probably simply be wondering what all the fuss was about!

By contrast, when the verdict is announced, Amir Bajwa and the young, well-dressed man simply stare at one another in complete disbelief, with the former actually feeling quite angry that other jurors have not interpreted the evidence in quite the same way as him. He gives the distinct impression of a man who seems to be taking the outcome somewhat personally.

Eventually, a semblance of order is restored, and Lady Fotheringham has a few last words for the jury.

'Ladies and Gentlemen, the trial is now at an end, and I thank each and every one of you for your time and attention. You have carried out a most important role in our society and I am most grateful to you for your service. I am pleased to say that you are now released from all your obligations.'

Lady Fotheringham concludes by also thanking both the prosecution and defence legal teams for their professionalism before formally advising Archie Watson that he is now a free man. At this point, she takes her leave and retreats to chambers.

CHAPTER 75

13 January 2024

Liz Goldstein has been very much on a high since hearing the fantastic news. In anticipation of their all too infrequent "date night", she has already showered, washed her hair and has chosen to wear her new red dress. Well, not exactly "new", as it was purchased some months previously before the very dark cloud appeared over their heads. It has been hanging, somewhat neglected, in a wardrobe since it was first purchased. She then applies make-up, another rare occurrence but symbolic of her new-found zest for life. Not wishing Matt to be undone, she also lays out his favourite blue suit. In addition, at very short notice, she has managed to arrange a sleepover for Daisy. (In his excitement, Matt seems to have overlooked this crucial detail!) She has already booked a table at a new local Italian restaurant, just a short drive away. Given that they will be indulging in bubbles before leaving and they enjoy wine with dinner, they will not be driving. The table has been booked for 7:30pm, so she books a taxi for 7:15pm. She still has a little time to kill and so decides a little cleansing of the soul might not go amiss. So she elects to ceremoniously burn each and every one of the blackmail letters they had received and truly embraces the ritual.

It is 6:45pm, and Matt is not yet home. Liz is beginning to become a little concerned as she has tried to call his mobile, but no reply. She considers that he has perhaps left his car at the office and decided to go to a nearby bar he has been known to frequent, where, sometimes quite conveniently, there is no mobile reception. At first, she feels a little disappointed at this prospect and then, just as quickly, her heart softens. After all, he has been through so much of late, one cannot really blame him for wanting to let off a little bit of steam after the trial.

CHAPTER 76

13 January 2024

Jean and Myra have been working together for Clyde Office Cleaners for about six years, and they make a formidable team. Appreciated by their employer for being very fast, fastidious and reliable cleaners, they are also known to enjoy a laugh or two along the way. They are considered to be completely trustworthy, which is absolutely crucial given that they are custodians of keys for many of their clients as well as having access codes for their security alarms.

It is a Friday evening, and their weekend will soon be kicking off as they had just one last office clean on their weekly schedule. They have this Friday evening ritual whereby they always pop by a local bar for one glass of wine before going home to their husbands. As Jean enters the digits on the alarm keypad, Myra is sharing a joke with her at the expense of her husband and they both laugh heartily.

Somewhat unusually, it transpires that the alarm had not been set. Upon entering the office, Myra is in mid-sentence, saying that someone must be working late. Suddenly, they are both totally awestruck and open-mouthed, horrified and shocked at the sight before them. A man is hanging from the mezzanine floor, his body fully suspended, a belt around his neck. He is so very obviously dead, but the gruesome and grotesque image is made all the more chilling as his body continues to sway back and forth, almost rhythmically. This movement has musical accompaniment in the shape of an eerie squeaking sound. Myra and Jean recoil and then exit the office before calling the emergency services.

Two police officers arrive approximately ten minutes later and are met by Myra and Jean at the entrance to the office block. Both are still in a state of abject shock. They experience numbness and also a feeling of complete detachment, not unusual in such circumstances. Another couple of police officers arrive on the scene, and statements are taken from them both before one of the officers kindly provides them with a lift home.

The original two officers cut the body down and examine the scene while awaiting the arrival of medical and forensic teams. From a driving licence contained in his wallet, they determine that his name is Matthew Goldstein and, as one of the private offices has a plaque bearing his name, they correctly deduce that he has, or rather had, a position of some seniority within the prosecution service.

His office desk is almost entirely clear, save for an envelope. On the envelope, in handwritten block capitals, it simply reads:

MR MATTHEW GOLDSTEIN (STRICTLY PRIVATE)

The envelope is empty, but lying adjacent to it is a folded letter.

Hi mATT
Yes I alSo kNow wHeRe yoU wOrK - YoU caNNot esCApe!
I jUSt WanTEd tO tHAnK yOU mOst sINcERelY.
YOu DiD veRy weLL.
sO muCh sO tHat I hAvE aNoThEr little rEQueST!
I nOW wAnT £100k iN CaSh. YoU haVE two dAYs.

The Observer

Over the ensuing couple of days, the forensic team has been sieving through potential evidence obtained from Matt Goldstein's office and also his house. In addition to the apparent blackmail letter, other circumstantial factors have clearly indicated that it was a genuine suicide and no third parties are being pursued in relation to the death.

Officers are very keen to know if Liz Goldstein has any knowledge of the blackmail situation, but she is currently too distraught to be interviewed. In these special circumstances, they are prepared to bide their time.

Liz is consumed with grief, her only consolation being the enduring love she has for Daisy. Her mind has been working overtime since she heard from the police about the alleged blackmail letter from "The Observer". Had she succeeded in feigning complete astonishment at the thought of her husband being blackmailed? And if so, will she be able to continue to have them fooled?

She considers her position. On the one hand, she could come clean and cooperate, and then the police might, with her input, be able to catch the blackmailer - but her husband's name would be besmirched. The alternative is to keep up the pretence. She decides that while neither option holds much attraction, she is going to protect the reputation of her late husband and Daisy's late father and deny, deny, deny!

The death of Matt Goldstein has now become public and has been covered by social media. While reports do not say specifically that it was death by suicide, one can easily read between the lines. The Observer is absolutely devastated.

CHAPTER 77

Some months earlier

In recent times, Paul Alexander's life has been almost literally in the gutter, his dependency upon drugs taking centre stage and being the most influential factor. He has also been in and out of prison with increasing regularity. As his drug habit has increased, so too has the cost of trying to feed it. To meet this cost, he has been relying more and more upon illegal money lending operations, which in turn has created other problems for him, problems of an extremely dangerous kind.

However, life was to change for Paul, but it was to get worse before it would get better due to his accumulation of debts. It actually reached the stage where he literally owed thousands of pounds to a moneylender. Also, as he had missed scheduled repayments, the amount outstanding had been increasing daily by prohibitive amounts. He has been on a very slippery slope.

Paul was aware that a guy he knows from the local pub, who goes by the name of Harry, had gone down a similar road with these moneylenders a couple of weeks earlier. His severely mutilated body was soon discovered floating in the River Clyde - a salutary and quite public lesson for any potential offender. This placed Paul in panic mode, being now only too aware of the levels of violence that can be dispensed by these money lenders. He even considered deliberately going to prison as a means of escape. However, on further reflection, he was aware that the family running the moneylending racket also had contacts inside. All he could do was run and hide.

Being in fear for one's very existence tends to concentrate the mind. And Paul had somewhat of a lightbulb moment. This threat made him appreciate just how much he actually wanted to live, to really live - a life not dependent upon substances. He suddenly realised that he would give anything for a plain old, simple, or ordinary life, like one of his brothers. He had never had an epiphany before in his wretched, so this was a truly unique turn of events. From that very moment forth, he turned his back on drink and drugs. After having abstained for a few weeks while being on the run, he became a little more relaxed and complacent, perhaps even careless. He gradually took to the streets once again and came out of hiding. This was to prove to be a big mistake!

One evening, while walking along a quiet side street, he was suddenly grabbed from behind by a couple of "heavies", a bag was thrown over his head, and he was then bundled with considerable force into the back of a transit van. After a journey of about fifteen to twenty minutes, he was led, still hooded, into what he later discovered to be a deserted warehouse before being unceremoniously bundled onto a chair. Paul had seen enough gangster movies to know what was coming next. His plight seemed all the worse because his body and mind were no longer numbed by drugs as per normal. He was riddled with fear and dread as he anticipated what they might have in store for him.

After what seemed like an eternity, but in reality, was probably only a few minutes, the mask was very roughly pulled off his head. He struggled to see, given the contrast of the ultra-bright, overhanging strip lights. As his eyes gradually adjusted, he was faced with Billy Watson, the very sight of whom would put fear into the heart of many a man. He was aware that the Watson family was in the moneylending business, indeed behind many a criminal enterprise within the Glasgow area. His life was at risk, and desperate situations called for desperate measures. He made a personal pledge to the Lord that he would abstain from drugs forevermore in return for some timely divine intervention. If only he could have spoken to his brother, Darren. He could perhaps have persuaded him to lend to him one final time on the basis that he had finally turned a corner and started afresh. But then again, Darren, even if he had that amount of money, would just have thought it to be yet another false dawn, having broken so many promises in the past.

At this point, Billy Watson was simply staring at him, not having said a word, perhaps contemplating what particular form of sadistic torture to administer. In any event, the silence was making Paul feel even more terrified. And then, Billy pulled out what appeared to be a large bread knife with clear and obvious intent. Billy's two minders then held Paul down on the chair as Billy approached. At that point, Paul urinated uncontrollably. He was simply paralysed with fear. Billy eventually spoke:

'Well, you've been fuckin' warned and given every chance. But you've chosen to disrespect the Watson family and if others hear of that, they will think the Watson family have gone soft. We can't have that, now, can we? But you haven't listened and since you never listen there is absolutely no point in you having any ears is there?'

At that very moment, just when his first ear was about to be sliced off, inspiration came to him, from the very deepest depths of his consciousness. Perhaps, after all, it was the divine intervention that he had been pleading for a short time earlier. Just when he was teetering on the very edge of the precipice, he was thrown a lifeline.

'Stop for fuck's sake!' he shouts. 'I can help you. I can honestly help you. Stop just for two fuckin' minutes to listen to what I have to say. Honestly, for fuck's sake, trust me on this.'

Paul pleads with Billy.

Slightly intrigued and with nothing to lose by listening to him:

"OK, I'm curious, but this had better be good. You've two minutes,' responds Billy.

'Your brother Archie, the murder charge. I can get him off. Please, please believe me.'

'And how the fuck can you do that?'

'I know things. I have inside info on a real top dog in the fiscal service who will do absolutely fuckin' anything to keep me quiet.' (Yes, his brain had been pretty scrambled for a long time now. But somehow, he had never ever forgotten the conversation with his brother Darren, about the night a man was killed in a hit and run. Nor had he ever forgotten the fairly distinctive name of Matthew Goldstein. He had actually seen him being interviewed on television a few months ago, and it had reminded him.)

'Honestly, if your brother does not get off the charge then you can do anything you want to me. How could I possibly make up a story like this?'

Paul is beginning to think he is perhaps making headway, as he can see that Billy's now at least weighing up his suggestion.

'I suppose you'll say fuckin' anything to save your bloody skin.'

At that point, he moves away and makes a call, which is obviously to his dad, Sid. He then returns a few moments later.

'You are one very lucky man, but your body will be found in the River Clyde feeding the fishes, if my brother is convicted. We will come after you and your family and you will all wish you had never been born.'

He was then once again hooded and bundled back into the van before being unceremoniously dumped at the side of the road in the city centre. Paul Alexander knew just how fortunate he had been and planned to take full advantage. He intended to use this experience as an additional springboard for a new life, one free of drink and drugs. But right now, he is on a mission. He has some serious detective work to do as well as some letter writing.

Thanks, Lord!

EPILOGUE

One Year Later

One year on, and Police investigations have still not uncovered the identity of "The Observer". In their defence, their efforts have not been assisted by the fact that Liz Goldstein, in a brief moment of euphoria, had destroyed all his previous letters.

In the prosecution case against Archibald Watson, the accused was surely blessed with good fortune. Who would have thought that an event occurring almost sixteen years earlier would have impacted positively upon the result of his trial? However, one year later, he has still not learned any lessons. Once again, he is incarcerated following a conviction on yet another charge of robbery. On this occasion, no amount of legal jiggery-pokery or connivance on the part of Devlin Delaney is likely to keep him at large. Moving forward, for Archie Watson, it seems likely that the doors to Barlinnie Prison will be of the revolving variety.

By contrast, Andy Wilson (aka Handy Andy) has still never seen the inside of a prison and is not likely to. Police Scotland, while in absolutely no doubt about his involvement in the robbery, were never able to collate sufficient evidence to justify a prosecution against him. Young Andy had tried stepping up the criminal ladder only to discover that he was scared of heights. His ten scarred fingers are a testament to his failed attempt. However, one year on and having truly learned his lesson, Andy has turned his back completely on his life of crime. In fact, he has now settled down with a partner and has managed to secure permanent full-time employment.

Paul Alexander was never a slave to his conscience. Rather, he was a man who has always looked after number one, with total disregard for any resultant collateral damage. And yet, he is another who has turned a corner. Having pulled himself together he has managed to remain drugs and drink free. In addition, he has joined Gamblers Anonymous, thereby relieving himself of yet another addiction. He is now in regular, secure employment, working full-time in a warehouse close to where he rents a small flat. While none of this has been easy, he now has aspirations and is no longer constantly looking over his shoulder.

One may be totally justified in feeling unmitigated disdain towards Paul Alexander. Nevertheless, however grudgingly, one might just feel the slightest shred of admiration for the man's fortitude in having managed to turn his miserable life around.

Paul's brother, Darren, is the one and only person who has stood by him through thick and thin. He is appreciative of his brother's herculean efforts to stay clean, and as a result, has welcomed him back into the fold. Having said that, he remains blissfully unaware of his brother's involvement in blackmail. The two of them now enjoy a normal, healthy, brotherly relationship, and Darren is so very relieved that Paul is now a transformed character. This is manifested in very simple, seemingly innocuous ways. For example, Paul now gratuitously meets up with Darren for a coffee, just for the sheer hell of it and not for any ulterior financial motive.

Paul's older brothers, Brian and Bobby, have also offered him an olive branch. While it will take a very long time for these wounds to completely heal, if at all, at least there is now some communication back and forth. Bobby and his partner, Simon, did eventually circumnavigate the tortuous adoption process, and for the fruits of their endeavours, they now have a gorgeous baby boy, Cameron. There is even some talk of Uncle Paul being invited to his first birthday party. Now, that represents progress!

The Watson family, while having spared Paul's life, still demands to have their debt repaid. Their concession only extended so far. But they were so grateful to have Archie back in their midst, that they showed a scrap of compassion by not applying their usual, exorbitant interest rates. Darren, in recognition of Paul having changed his ways, has settled all of Paul's dues and for once in his life he is debt-free, a platform upon which he is now able to build.

Not surprisingly, the Watson family remain an ongoing gravy train for Devlin Delaney. He has recently purchased an eye-catching, white, badass Range Rover Sport complete with black alloys, funded largely by the mammoth fee received from Archie's last trial. And to complete the desired look, he has purchased a cherished number plate, 123 DD. This peacock of the legal profession is now in full plumage!

One thing Devlin Delaney can be credited with is incredible staying power. Whilst sailing very close to the wind, he remains a constant while people around him fall like skittles. Devlin is one of the world's eternal survivors, and his business continues to thrive. He remains the solicitor of choice for those wishing to engage someone prepared to bend the rules. However, Mother Nature is catching up with him, and retirement is on the not-too-distant horizon. With this in mind, he is currently looking to purchase a villa in the Costa del Sol, where he has visions of spending long lazy days in the sun in the company of some like-minded people.

DCI Orr, while a seasoned campaigner, has never quite been able to get over the jury's decision to allow Archie

Watson his liberty. She had made a promise to herself that she would ensure he paid the price for his heinous crime. After the trial was over, she was quite forthright and even vociferous in her condemnation of the jury. She now consoles herself that she has a further bite at this particular cherry, as he is currently once again on remand awaiting trial.

Tea Leaf is currently at liberty, but if history is anything to go by, this will not last long. He remains an easy-going, hapless and largely inept criminal. Perhaps not surprisingly, he does not bear any grudge for his failure to receive any financial reward for supplying key inside information on the abortive petrol station job.

The turf war between the Watson and Byrne families still exists and might well yet transcend a few generations. Nonetheless, for a myriad of reasons, there is no longer the same intensity. While it has never been actually voiced or acknowledged, this could be in part due to the union of Jimmy and Cara and their thriving little family unit; Cara is now expecting a second baby. A divide had been crossed. It is also perhaps quite significant that the attack by the Byrne family on Jimmy Watson was never avenged. Indeed, nor is the Byrne family any longer on full alert, fearful of reprisals. Without the words having actually been uttered, perhaps, just perhaps, this is tantamount to a vague line having been drawn in the sand.

Susan Yardley, not surprisingly, is really struggling to cope with the death of her young husband. It was not as if he had a longstanding, progressive illness, and she could gradually become accustomed to the inevitable. Rather, Susan was sadly denied the luxury of having time to come to terms with what fate had in store. For Susan, it was the suddenness that made it all so desperately unbearable. One minute she was preparing dinner for Adam, and the next, she had police officers at her door to say that he had been shot - unimaginable cruelty.

Susan has drifted through the last twelve months as if in a trance. Even now, she still often wakes up of a morning, wondering if it has all just been a bad dream or nightmare. One glance at the adjacent empty pillow and her question is sadly answered.

Yes, she has some days that are slightly better than others. On such days she forces herself to look to the ceiling rather than the floor. On such occasions she sometimes considers that in a year or two she might dip her toe into the shark-infested waters of online dating. After all, she does not want to live the rest of her life without a partner. Nor does she believe that Adam would have wanted her to. However, when her mind does drift in this direction, she is always pulled back as if restrained by an enormous, invisible elastic band. And it always returns her to the same place in her mind, that place where she feels she is in some way betraying Adam's memory. Susan does not realise it now, as her situation is still very raw, but such feelings of betrayal will inevitably evaporate with time.

In the meantime, Susan fortunately still has moments of joy. That is when in the company of her two little boys whom she loves with her every breathing moment.

Liz Goldstein has maintained a vow of silence and has remained true to her husband's memory. She has never acknowledged to the police that she was aware her husband was being blackmailed. That secret will go with her to the grave. Her way of coping with her grief is to fully immerse herself in her daughter Daisy and everything about her. She is almost scared to let her out of her sight. If she could wrap up her up in cotton wool, she would most probably do so. Daisy in turn is still besotted by Goldie, who has now outgrown the puppy stage. In some ways, Goldie is a substitute for the little brother or sister perhaps denied them by the actions of Archie Watson. Since her husband's death, Liz has been receiving grief counselling on a weekly basis.

Juror Brian Hunter had faithfully promised his Lord that he would change his philandering ways if he were not exposed. He has failed to be true to his word. Almost immediately after returning to his place of work following the trial, he resumed his affair with Sandra Baxter. His wife, Penny, still remains oblivious to his extra-marital activity.

Alice Murray is another who was mightily relieved by the outcome of the trial. She can now once again enjoy her promoted post at work without feeling that the rug might be pulled from under her feet at any moment. Her two feline companions are also well and remain totally unaware of the stresses their loving owner has endured in recent times.

And as for our canine friend, Snout, well he is still sniffing his way to the top!

The End

A NOTE FROM THE AUTHOR

I would like to say a huge thank you for choosing to read *One Sad Day*. I really hope you enjoyed it. If so, I would be most grateful if you would provide a review on Amazon.

Also, I love hearing from readers! So, if you have any thoughts or comments you would like to share with me, please do not hesitate to contact me on

brendanmaguire5@gmail.com.

Finally, if you would like to read another legal crime story that I have written, why not order a copy on Amazon of *Whatever it Takes*?

Printed in Great Britain
by Amazon

61165285R00163